'Infused with the lush and terrible beauty of the Trinidadian landscape, *When We Were Birds* weaves dreams and apparitions, religion and myth, into a story of love in its many manifestations'
Barbara Jenkins

'Exceptional. The originality of its premise, the power and beauty of its prose, the depth of its explorations of what it means to love and be loved'
Jacob Ross

'Ayanna Lloyd Banwo is one of those rare voices you come across once in a long while – strong, confident and necessary. She reminds us what we should expect from great writing'
Helon Habila

'It's a knockout, and Ayanna Lloyd Banwo is a star. I want to read everything she writes'
Niven Govinden

'A love story, a ghost story and a coming-of-age story, all masterfully woven into one. I loved it'
Claire Adam

'*When We Were Birds* has a similar power and depth to *This One Sky Day* . . . A love story between two outsiders but also a love letter to language itself. I cannot wait to read what Ayanna writes next'
Anna Ellory

WHEN WE WERE BIRDS

WHEN WE WERE BIRDS

Ayanna Lloyd Banwo

HAMISH HAMILTON
an imprint of
PENGUIN BOOKS

HAMISH HAMILTON

UK | USA | Canada | Ireland | Australia
India | New Zealand | South Africa

Hamish Hamilton is part of the Penguin Random House group of companies
whose addresses can be found at global.penguinrandomhouse.com.

First published 2022
001

Lines from 'Bird-Man/Bird-Woman' on p. ix reproduced by kind permission of Olive Senior.

Set in 12.6/15.4 pt Fournier MT Std
Typeset by Jouve (UK), Milton Keynes
Printed and bound in Great Britain by Clays Ltd, Elcograf S.p.A.

The authorized representative in the EEA is Penguin Random House Ireland,
Morrison Chambers, 32 Nassau Street, Dublin D02 YH68

A CIP catalogue record for this book is available from the British Library

HARDBACK ISBN: 978–0–241–50279–2
TRADE PAPERBACK ISBN: 978–0–241–50280–8

www.greenpenguin.co.uk

To my parents, Gale and Ronnie.
Dead, but not asleep.

AUTHOR'S NOTE

The island of Trinidad is real. The geography, characters and places in this novel are fiction.

Come. The first lesson: how to fold your wings
into a heartbeat.

– from 'Bird-Man/Bird-Woman' in
Over the Roofs of the World by Olive Senior

CORBEAU

Morne Marie, Trinidad. Yesterday

I

Yejide

'First thing you have to remember,' Granny Catherine hold her granddaughter, Yejide, close on her lap, 'is that there was a time before time.' She press the first layer of tobacco down into her ebony pipe. The flame from her silver lighter make a small blaze in the cavern of the bowl and the pipe settle between her lips. 'Before we come to live in this house, before the settlement in the valley, before the quarries, when the forest was so thick that no man could cross it, Morne Marie was the home only of animals. But not like animals we see now, oh no!' Catherine open her eyes wide and the blue smoke curl out of her nostrils. 'The ocelots was big like tigers, the deer run so fast that no man could catch them even if he dare enter the forest to hunt them, and the little green parrots that sing at dusk was as big as the blood-red ibis that live in the swamplands. The animals could talk to each other, just like I talking now, and they build a mighty city in the forest. But this city was nothing like Port Angeles. It had no buildings, no boundaries, no gates, and the animals live together without territory to guard and borders to mind.

'But one day a warrior wander into the forest. He see that it full of animals to hunt and fruit to eat. When he look at the trees he only see the houses he could build, and when he look at the land he only see what he could take. The animals try to talk to him and tell him that there was so much more there than what he could see, but he did not know their language and so could not understand them.

'That warrior bring more warriors and with the warriors come builders and with the builders come farmers and with the farmers come priests. With the priests come governors and with the governors come death.'

'But the animals fight them, right?' Yejide squirm on her granny lap. Nothing she love more than this full-cupboard feeling: the sweet smell of tobacco, the even rhythm of the rocking chair, the green hills and her granny face brimming with story. She think of the sharp teeth of the ocelots and the tight grip of the macajuel that could suffocate a man in its coils; no way any human with just two legs, very small teeth and no poison at all could ever defeat the wild animals of the forest.

Catherine look at her and puff on her pipe. 'Who telling the story, you or me?'

Yejide grin and quiet down again.

'The animals had always live in peace, but they know then that it was time for war. The battle rage bloody and terrible. The quarry you see there' – Catherine point out the window to the deep, brown crater on the hillside – 'was where the animals make a stand in a battle so fierce that it leave scars on the mountain.

'All that killing cut the forest deep. Wounded, it went into mourning and that bring the longest dry season ever on Morne Marie. The rivers hide in the earth and the trees wilt and die away. The ocelots shrink small like house cats, the howler monkeys get timid, and the deer and manicou and lappe, who had live in peace before, start to look at each other and see food. The warriors suffer too, for no one, man nor animal, could survive when nature decide to withhold its bounty.

'Then one day when all were weary, and it look like the war would claim not only the fighters but the whole forest, a great storm set up in the hills. Fat, grey clouds empty out into the green and the men and animals rejoice to see the rivers rise again, and the forest drink deep of the rain. Thunder and lightning pelt down for three days and three nights. But remember I tell you, this was a time before time, when a tree could reach full-grown in a day and a boy could reach manhood in a night, so this storm was longer and fiercer than any of the animals had ever see before. The earth slide down the hillsides and crash into the valley below. Trees older than any animal could remember lose their hold on the earth and topple over. The rivers burst their banks and rush over the land. Rejoicing turn again to sorrow. It come like the whole forest turn on them and demand its share of the lives who defile its sacred places with war.

'Now, the green parrots, the ones who cackle and sing and chatter, just like you' – Catherine pinch Yejide lips together to stop her from giggling – 'well, they were wiser than any of the animals give them credit for. The parrots watch the rain and watch the hills and watch the rivers and watch the dead pile high. They gather together in the branches of the last sacred silk cotton tree and hold a council. At the council's end, the parrot battalion split and divide in two. One half fly to the east and the other half fly to the west.

'The parrots that went west get small and become the little green birds we see today, those that sing and fly toward the setting of the sun. But those that went east toward the sunrise mute their green feathers to black and curve their beaks into sharp hooks. Their bodies get fat and their wingspan stretch so wide they darken the land below them as they fly. They release one last great song that make all the animals and men tremble, then grow grey hoods around their heads and necks that silence their throats forever.

'You know what they turn into, Yejide?' Catherine stare out the window, smile and puff on her pipe.

'Corbeaux!' Yejide cry out. She love getting the right answer. No matter how many times she hear the story, knowing the answer always make her feel grown up and very important.

Catherine nod and pull deep from the pipe. 'When the change was complete, they feel their bellies get hungry for flesh. They spread their wings wide and circle the land slow, searching out the dead. And with their new long, curved beaks and talons sharp like caiman teeth, they tear into the flesh of the animals who was once their friends and the men who was once their enemies. When they done, they take to the silk cotton tree again, leaving nothing but bone.

'The living look on in horror to see the devouring of the dead. They don't understand how the birds they once knew could do something so terrible. But the chattering parrots they knew were gone. They turn into something else entirely now. When they shed their green and change their form, they take on a sacred duty – to stand at the border between the living and the dead. So they wait for the dying and watch over the carcasses and consume the flesh. And no one but the corbeaux know that inside their bodies the souls of the dead transform and release.'

Catherine lift Yejide off her lap and put her to stand on the wooden floor in her white patent-leather church shoes. 'Right. Story done. Now make sure and put those shoes away. And your nice dress. Hang it on the back of the chair in my room. Don't let me come and find that you just leave it anyhow.'

But Yejide know the ritual well. 'Story not done, Granny. What happen next?'

Catherine look down at her granddaughter. Just now she would be too tall for little-girl dresses, too grown to sit on her lap. But not yet – she reach her hand out and Yejide run back into her arms. Not yet.

6

'Well, when the sun rise on the fourth morning of the great storm, when all the corbeaux stomach full and everyone weary with pain and grief, the rain stop. No more flood. Balance come back to the forest. But after they get saved, nobody like to think of who rescue them. In this way people and animals are the same. Everyone begin to fear the corbeaux. So, they fly away to live at the edges of the forest of Morne Marie. They alone know the world changing and it would have work for them in the cities of men to come. And so, like in all the stories that change the world, over time everyone forget that the ending of the storm happen at the same time the corbeaux born. Everyone, of course, except the corbeaux—' She bend close to whisper in Yejide ear. '*We* remember.'

OATHBREAKER

Port Angeles, Trinidad. Today

2

Darwin

The beat-up white Bedford slow down and pull off the road, orange indicator flashing. Darwin nod at the driver, an old man with a newsboy cap low on his forehead. The girl in the passenger seat don't even look up, her eyes down in her cell phone.

'Port Angeles?'

The old man nod to the cargo tray in the back. Darwin scramble up before the man change his mind, and tap the metal panel to let him know that he inside. They head down the highway, the fields brown from the dry spell and bush fires passing in a blur.

He push a big crocus bag full of what feel like potato or dasheen or some kinda provision to one side, a heavy curl-up rope to the other, and settle himself in between two ridges on the floor of the cargo tray so he don't tip over when the truck hit a pothole. Then he lean back on the tailgate and look up at the sky. That hour the day was usually still clean and pink, but Sahara dust was bad this rounds. Make the pink hazy and the clouds look like bundle-up dirty clothes.

Sky like this make him feel a way. Easy to feel hopeful when the sky clear, the air have some leftover rain in it and the hills green and lush. Make a man feel like he know where he going, and what he about. Like things would work out even if he not sure what coming next. But this kinda dirty-clothes sky make him feel like the place could blow up any minute.

Breathing in dust and ash and smoke like is a war zone you living in.

But even in a dusty time, sometimes a man does catch some luck. Like a drop into town from an old man in a pickup. People don't stop for nobody at this hour just so, sun not up good yet. When he was young, was easy to hitch a ride anywhere. Always somebody heading down to the coast or into the city. Easy to join a group of boys from up Dalia Street going anywhere, no shoes, no shirt, laughing. Don't even have to be friends. But these days different. And he is not no little boy again.

He shift so his back rest in the middle of the tailgate and the old man could see him clear in the rear-view mirror. He can't blame him, the way things going these days, but when he feel the driver eyes on him he stare right back, hard. It feel good when the man look away first. What he think Darwin going to do? Jump out, hang on to the moving truck, scramble through the window and cut his throat? He might be plenty things, but he eh no bandit and he eh no killer.

Smoke rise from the brown fields in the distance. He try to remember when last it rain. The hot-sun pause in the rainy season usually welcome, give the earth a chance to dry out little bit, but Petit Carême come early this year and that, plus the bush fires, turn the heat up like a furnace. He study the provision in the crocus bag, and wonder if the old man is a farmer, carrying produce to the market. Must be have it extra hard this year. He would have like to ask him, maybe chat on the way, talk about the city that he going for the first time. Up ahead abandoned cranes come up from the land like fingers, and an overpass stop in mid-air like a road to nowhere in the sky. Since the big construction companies close up shop and the government stop work on the highway project halfway between Mount Perish and the lowlands to the south, wasn't much work anywhere anymore except the city.

Last week, when he had reach the front of the line in the government employment office in Wharton, he couldn't believe his good fortune. He know bout men who wait for hours and before the line move even halfway the boss lady inside say everything they have for the day done give out, come back tomorrow. So, when the clerk hand him a form from the pile on her desk for him to sign his name, he say a prayer of thanks because Jah know.

MRS JAMESON – SENIOR CLERK. She had make her own cardboard name card for her desk. She was the only one really working too. Some other men was in a corner, dress shirtsleeves roll up, knocking a game of All Fours on two desks push together. One of the men was shuffling the cards like an expert, a wicked grin on his face like he just know he going to win everybody money. A lady next to them was arguing with somebody on her cell phone.

'What kinda work it is, Mrs Jameson?' Darwin look at the form she hand him.

'When you hungry and somebody give you food, you does ask what kind?' She push her glasses up on her face and keep sorting her files.

'I mean, what Fidelis is, exactly?'

'You don't know Fidelis? Is the big cemetery in Port Angeles. On St Brigitte Avenue.'

'A cemetery? With dead people?'

'You know another kinda cemetery?'

'What kinda work it have to do in a cemetery?'

'They need another gravedigger.'

Darwin swear every hair on his body had raise up same time. 'You don't have anything else?'

13

'Look, give me back my paper and go.' She reach out her hand for the form. 'When you desperate enough you go find yourself here again.'

Like if it had anywhere else to go. By the time people reach that office looking for work, any work, it mean they done stand up in every other line, sign every other list, and this was the last stop. The second he leave, there would be somebody else just like him, or a woman with a baby, a lady with handbag that had see better days, a man with good shoes who only just fall on hard times, out there in the hot sun to take his place. The line was already long all the way down the street and around the corner.

'Emmanuel Darwin?' She read out his name.

'Yes. But just Darwin, ma'am.'

She push her glasses up again and look at him properly for the first time – his full beard, the tam covering his locks, down to his battered boots. Her eyes soften a bit. 'Listen, Darwin, if it had something else I would give you, but this is what I have right now. You could come back but . . .' She look behind him at the line.

So, he sign the form. Six weeks' work to start, and if he get on okay, they might keep him. Feel like signing his life away. But this world had a way of doing you things like that. And maybe this is what it mean to be a man. Doing the things you never think you would have to do, making a hard choice when the only thing in front you is hard choices.

He feel eyes on him in the rear-view mirror again. But this time it was the girl. He didn't get to look at her good when he get in the truck but in the better light he could see she wasn't no girl at all; maybe his age or a year or two younger. She keep looking from her phone to the old man and then to Darwin in the mirror, half-smiling at him with her eyes like she don't want the old man to see.

He wonder if, like him, she was just getting a ride into the city. Maybe the old man was her father, her uncle. Look too old to be her man but you never really know with how the times was hard. Maybe if they get off the same time he could talk to her. He try to see whether she was in office clothes, just something to gauge what kinda girl she was. Then he think about Marcia and the last time he see her, the whole new life she must be have now. He watch the lipstick on the girl mouth, the long hair that look expensive, and then he think about the next to nothing he have in his pockets. He look away. Too much trouble. Probably just like the idea of dealing with a Rastaman to piss off Daddy.

It hit him like a cuff all over again that the man Mrs Jameson see a few days ago and the man the girl see in the rear-view mirror today wasn't the same. He not sure what anybody see when they look at him now. What a way life could change in a week. Like bush fire.

He run his hands over his shorn hair, his head feeling like it belong to somebody else. Six in the morning was still six in the morning even in dry season; he not used to the cool air on his almost bare head, the back of his neck, his ears. At least his mother had make sure he leave her house with a whole coconut bake, still warm and smelling of her hands. She didn't wake up to watch him go, but she leave the bake on the counter for him where he could see it. That had to mean something, that she make breakfast for him, even if her face say he wasn't her son no more. He feel the weight of it in his rucksack and hope that, no matter where he end up, when his mother say her prayers his name was still in her mouth.

They switch lanes on the overpass and join the bulk of the traffic heading toward the city. He look up at the sky, lighter now that the sun was higher, but still kinda cloudy, hazy, and he see black specks circling. Corbeaux. Better than any signpost.

He watch the birds circling slow. His mother, Janaya, used to say that once you see so much corbeaux, you know you nearly reach Port Angeles. Is not like they ever do anybody anything but is something about the silent way they does circle, and how sometimes you could see a whole set of them just sitting in a line on a telephone wire, watching. Once you see corbeaux you know is dead they there for. And in the city, dead don't bound to be a stray dog or a manicou or old meat that restaurant throw out in the drain. Could be a woman head that the police never find even after they find the rest of her body; could be a man floating, fat and swell up with water in the harbour; could be a child in a crocus bag that nobody know there till they see the corbeaux flying.

When he was a small he used to ask Janaya how come they never went in town to go cinema or concert like everybody else. She give the same answer that she give when he ask about his father, if he was still in Port Angeles: 'Is only dead in the city, Emmanuel. Rasta don't deal with the dead.'

Traffic slow to a stop as they reach the main intersection and Darwin could see the big concrete arches of the Port Angeles transit station. The driver pull up at the traffic light and before babylon could come out from nowhere, blue lights flickering, to give the old man a ticket for carrying him in the tray, Darwin bang the side again, 'I go take it here, uncle!' and jump out.

He cross the road to where a long line of people was hustling into the station, everybody face set up, walking fast-fast like fire ants. Some heading up long stairways, others down corridors and the rest pouring through the gates into the city centre. He turn back for a second to look for the truck and the girl inside it, but the traffic light had done change and she gone.

He feel his foot brush something on the ground. Look down and see it was a man asleep on fold-out cardboard boxes, the crowds walking around him. He hitch his backpack up on his shoulder. Probably better that he didn't try anything with the girl. Better so. He walk through the tall concrete arches and melt into the city.

3

The line of people outside the fast-food place at the city gates long like judgement. It start at the counter and stretch all outside on the pavement. The place smell like piss and old cooking oil but people still stand up waiting for fried chicken like if they don't know morning was time for tea and bake, time to settle yourself with something good that smell like home before you have to face all the people who come out in the day with wickedness.

Darwin try to get his bearings and figure out which way would take him into the old city. A set of cars park up on the taxi stand with drivers fighting for passengers so they could leave first with a full trip. A bright red car, drop low, zoom past, skip everybody else and pick up two women on the go instead of parking and waiting their turn. They speed off in the direction of the harbour and the other drivers cuss them as they pass. The newspapers say that whole area, where the cruise ships come in and businessmen and politicians sip drinks while looking out toward the sea, going to be the new and improved Port Angeles. He sure nobody bother to ask old Port Angeles how it feel about that.

Darwin ignore the taxi stand and keep walking. They wasn't getting his hard-earned dollars so early in the morning. It wasn't far and, if he was lucky, he could eat the bake before work start in the yard.

Town wasn't nothing like he imagine. Big city suppose to have plenty tall buildings and shiny stores and restaurants with fancy-looking people sitting outside. Maybe that is the

Port Angeles in the harbour, but here the city flat and hunch close, everybody living one on top the other.

He pass fruit vendors selling yellow bananas, Julie mangoes, juicy papaw and red watermelon split in half right up against fish vendors weighing carite, snapper and kingfish on shiny scales; corner shops block up with wrought-iron burglar-proofing and customers calling out for what they want, sticking their hands in through the bars to collect goods from the shopkeeper; street preachers dress up in long white robes waving Bibles and crying hell and damnation on all city dwellers; boys hustling loose cigarettes, dinner mints and chewing gum from old glass Crix jars with vagrants sprawl out next to them, hoping somebody give them a little change before they go; two men selling pirate CDs on opposite sides of the road – 'To God Be the Glory' on one side and a heavy dance-hall bass booming out on the next – square off like a sound clash; women in high heels and skirt suits rushing to work while young fellas try to get their attention as they pass; schoolchildren walking slow like if they planning to miss the school bus or break buisse so they never reach at all; couples walking and holding hands, man whispering in he woman ear, woman giggling; and everything cover down in a blanket of blaring car horns from the nearly standstill traffic crawling down the road.

A Bobo Shanti bredrin pass pushing a green cart, Ites Green and Gold flags blowing in the breeze, sweet smell of honey-roasted nuts following him. Darwin hail him but the Ras barely see him at all. He keep moving, slow and solemn, and his eyes pass over Darwin like he was just another stranger.

As he follow the street signs the crowds thin and the city quiet down. He turn a corner and, just so, the road open out into gold: a big park with tall poui trees spread wide, yellow-gold flowers scatter over the grass, an old fountain with green mermaids covered in birdshit, dancing around in mid-air and fish spouting nothing where water used to be. Governor Square. Crumbling like everything else in the city that have anything to do with Queen, King or Governor.

In the middle of the square he pass an empty pedestal with nothing but half of one leg, broken off at the thigh. Rusty metal sign at the base but the name fade away. One of them statue from the old days that people tear down when the Doctor used to preach to the people, talking about revolution. Now, was only blackbirds sitting on the pedestal, the steps, and the Governor one foot. He remember hearing about the Doctor in school when he was small. His face was on the back of all the copybooks. Darwin used to think that he woulda like to be around in them days when the people was on fire and planning how to make Port Angeles a different place, how to make the whole country a different place.

The trees make him feel good, though, spread like big golden umbrellas. He figure some of them must be older than the whole city. He like the idea that something was still standing from before the rotting benches, the crowded pavements, the quarrelling taxi drivers, the governors and revolutionaries, the very road he trod. It good to know that some things does still live long and stay beautiful no matter what going on around them.

He turn one more corner and see the street sign for St Brigitte Avenue and the tall stone walls of what must be Fidelis Cemetery. The soft cool that come with the early morning gone and the first beads of sweat start to run down his temples. He take out a kerchief from his pocket and wipe his forehead, startled for a second not to feel the thickness of his dread, just short tufts of hair, ragged from the blunt scissors.

The wall so long he can't see the end of it. He stick to the pavement on the opposite side of the cemetery and over the wall he see what look like pitched roofs, stone arches, bushy palms and the green spread of samaan trees.

He never went in a dead yard before, never see inside. It make sense to have people in the world who work this was – people working in hospital, morgue, cemetery – but he never thought he would be one of them. Even in his village, when them children used to cut through the little cemetery on their way to the shop, he would cross the road and make sure to stay away. He wasn't frighten. Is not like he believe in dem ting – ghosts and demons. He know a dead man can't jump up out a grave and do him nothing, but even he know the dead is for the dead and the living is for the living.

He reach the intersection where St Brigitte Avenue split into two, check the street signs again: right was Queen Isabella Street, St Brigitte continue left. He turn left and, the longer he walk, the stone wall smooth out a little bit, like if somebody fill in the jagged places with new cement. Further along he see rusted plaques, white wax from burn-out candles on the pavement, and empty rum bottles in the drain.

A tall, black wrought-iron gate yawn open in front of him, the bars thick and straight except for where they curve to form the date 1806 at the top. That was it. Like if the gate, the wall and the date was enough and if you can't tell where you is from that, then you have no business there. Darwin look around the street. After the crowds, the square, the traffic, St Brigitte was quiet.

Now he not sure what to do. Maybe if he just stand outside and wait for a while one of the workers would bend the corner and they could walk in same time. To walk in just so feel like going in somebody house when they didn't invite you.

He peek inside. The gate open into a long driveway leading to a concrete building. Two men lean up on the side and three more sit down on the front steps, comfortable like they born there. An old man with a neat, grey beard and bowlegs lean up on the wall smoking a cigarette, and a next one, tall and wiry but slouch down till he was the same height as the greybeard, stand up next to him drinking from a Styrofoam cup.

One by one they turn to look at him. He feel like a little boy who get catch peeking at something he wasn't supposed to. One last look around at the quiet street, the high walls, the arch above his head, and he walk through the wrought-iron gate into Fidelis Cemetery.

4

'Greetings.' Darwin nod to everyone. Nobody answer. Worse, they done have on work overalls and dusty boots. He still in his one good pants and shirt. Mrs Jameson didn't tell him if to come in the work clothes or if to change when he reach. He didn't like the idea of walking through the city in overalls for everybody to know where he working.

'I looking for Errol.'

'For what?' The man with the Styrofoam cup look at him.

Darwin dig in his bag for the letter from Mrs Jameson and hand it to him. 'Mrs Jameson from the regional corporation send me. I supposed to start working here.'

The man don't even look at the letter and the boys on the steps face hard. 'So why you stand up outside and peeping? You waiting for a invitation?'

Darwin feel sweat running down his forehead but no way he was going to reach into his pocket for his kerchief to wipe it. 'Well, I didn't know—'

'Somebody tell you is office work you come here to do or what?' The man take a sip from his cup and look Darwin up and down, taking in the khaki pants, shirt and old but clean shoes.

'I have overalls in my bag, I just didn't know if we was doing a interview—'

'A interview?' One of the boys on the steps laugh out loud. 'Allyuh hear that?' He look at the man next to him. 'Jamesy, you do any interview when you come here?'

Jamesy answer is a screw face that make Darwin feel

like he is the one sitting on the steps and Jamesy looking down at him.

'McIntosh,' the same man continue, 'you had résumé and ting when you come?' McIntosh just steups and take another sip from the cup.

Darwin try again. 'Listen, just show me where to find Mr Errol and let me—'

'Is shame, the boy shame, Cardo,' Jamesy laugh. 'Eh want them woman in town to know he does dig grave for a living.'

'I not shame, I just didn't know if—'

'If is pretty-boy work you want' – the old man who standing next to McIntosh, silent and watching, peel himself away from the side of the building and start walking toward Darwin – 'you could go by Mrs Jameson and tell her put you back on the list.' The bowlegs should have make him limp a little, but they don't affect him at all. Man walk like a gun-slinger in a old Western movie. 'You could wait till they hiring in them government office with air-condition and office chair and woman to make tea for you in the morning.' He keep walking, stepping slow till he close enough for Darwin to see his eyes, one full black, the other milky and dim like a river stone. 'You could wait and wait and stand up in a next line and a next one, while the last bit of money in your pocket run out and your belly start to eat itself from the inside and you can't do nothing but watch yuh woman turn whore to buy flour and dem boy on the block keep gun in yuh mother house and she can't say nothing. Hmm? How that sound?'

Darwin feel blood rush up in his head. He eh come this far for no old man to disrespect him like he is a little boy. The rest of men watching him, waiting to see his next move, and it take everything in him not to grab the old man by his throat, or walk out Fidelis and never look back. But he think of his mother house at the end of Dalia Street, the water that only come two days a week, the medication for her hands that hurt when the rain set up, the arthritis so bad.

He push it down, hide it away. 'I need to work. I could work hard. Just show me where to find the bossman.' His voice don't even tremble. He hear a car horn in the distance, bass from a car stereo for a second, then gone. The city just outside but sound far away. McIntosh stop drinking from his cup. Jamesy and the other fellas on the steps lean forward.

Then the old man start to laugh. He laugh so loud, Darwin swear it bounce off the walls of the building. Then McIntosh join in, then Jamesy, then the other boys on the steps, and Darwin feel everyone can hear them laugh all down the street, past the long, grey walls and into the city. The old man mouth open so wide Darwin could see all his teeth, white and perfect, nothing like a half-blind old man at all.

'Relax nah boy, Darwin, we just fuckin with you.' The old man clap Darwin on the shoulder and he feel his knees nearly buckle. The bitch strong too. Everybody smiling and relax like they was all bredrin now.

'How you know my name?'

The old man grin again but this time it make the hairs stand up on the back of Darwin neck.

'I am Errol, boy. You working for me.'

He change into his overalls and still feel like a damn fool. Too clean, too new. His orange-bright like a new traffic cone, the rest of them own rusty brown or dirty khaki. He thought the uniform woulda make him feel more certain, but it just show up the difference between him and the other gravediggers. And it don't help that Errol keep watching Darwin like he trying to work out how useful he would be, what shape he could bend him into.

'Come, boy, lemme show you the place.' Errol walk him from the admin building to the end of the drive and they make a left.

First thing that come in his mind was bone. The place look like a city of bone. Everything grey stone and white marble and concrete that stretch into the distance and spread out wide. From outside, Fidelis look like maybe three blocks, but from inside it look big like the whole of Port Angeles.

Headstones stick out of wild weeds; concrete monuments that look like churches, so old that they turn black and mossy; others with fretwork like the long-time houses in parts of the old city; statues that look like dead babies with wings and mothers crying for them; and everywhere black wrought-iron, rusty red and painted white fences, crosses reaching out like rotten fingers from the ground.

Darwin feel Errol watching him, but he keep his face straight. He know that everything from here out is some kind of test and no way he going to fail it so early. He could see the samaan trees and the bearded palms better now, and some ragged red ixora hedges that need fixing up. They look like people decide to push through them rather than walk around to use the roads. Ixoras don't need too much tending – his mother grow them in her garden at home – but these need some trimming, shaping. Somehow, he find himself wanting to fix breaks in the hedge and restore the borders and he wonder whether this going to be part of the job too. They look like no one do anything to them in a long time.

Almost everything look tired and break down in the harsh light of the morning. Everything except a runner with leaves like deep purple knives spreading over the graves that had no fence to separate them. Don't even look as though anybody plant it. Just run from grave to grave like it have its own plan. He feel something soft and hot rush up in his chest as he look at the runner. Don't need nobody to look after them, these purple plants. They just decide to live.

'Fidelis old,' Errol say as they continue down the main road. 'You see the date on the gate when you come in. That mean everybody here is old planter family and people they used to own. The place build like Port Angeles, see? Like a grid. This is the main road we on here – north to south,' Errol point like police conducting traffic, 'and all the other roads go out from here, like so – east to west.'

Darwin look up and see blue and white street signs where the main road break off into lanes, some wide enough for a car to drive down, others so narrow that two men could barely walk down side by side.

'All the streets have names, all the graves have numbers. Shirley does see about the records, collect people grave paper, and tell us which plot to dig. Our job easy. Dig the graves.'

Darwin nod and look around. 'With a backhoe?'

'You seeing anywhere a digger could fit inside here?' Errol laugh. 'Like I tell you, Fidelis old. Is only shovel, fork, tarp, blood and sweat in this graveyard. When people come to bury, we dig part of the grave before – them fellas will show you – and then we do the rest while the people singing or praying whatever the hell they does do.'

'Why you don't dig all before the people come?'

'Tradition. Is how we do it here. People have their rituals and this one is ours. All kinda people does bury here so sometimes is hymns, sometimes is drums, sometimes is no funeral at all really, just a few people come to watch the burial and then they go home. Those easy.'

'How often?' Darwin ask.

'How often we have funeral? Well, it depend on the time of year or if the city decide to turn up the heat on itself.' Errol give a sideways grin, pull out two cigarettes from his pocket, light one and hand the next one to Darwin.

'Nah. I good, thanks.' Darwin shake his head.

'You don't smoke?'

'I don't smoke cigarette. I don't mind if you smoke it.'

'Hear you nah!' Errol laugh again, soft this time or maybe they was just so deep into Fidelis now that the bone yard swallow it up. 'You doh mind if I smoke. Like if what you mind mean anything inside of here.'

Darwin figure is best to not try and answer. He know Errol pushing for some reaction. He not going to get it.

Errol take a long draw on his cigarette.

'So, where you from, Darwin? Country, nah. You look like a country boy.'

'Not really.'

'Keeping secrets from me already?'

'No secret. It just don't matter where I come from.'

They turn left at the end of the main road. Sign say 21st Street. And suddenly Fidelis change. The graves on this side look like somebody plant them in rows. Clean, marble gravestones, low concrete walls to separate each plot from the other. Look like they even get a fresh coat of paint too. A whole section cover in lantana, the tiny pink and yellow flowers spring up out of fresh soil. A next set of graves wall off and pave over with concrete, small pockets built into the headstones with incense sticks sticking out, the ends burned down to the wick.

They reach a grave cover with chrysanthemums and white roses with a white marble headstone. A mangy stray dog nose down in the flowers, sniffing. Darwin heart thump. A fresh grave. The inscription say: ANTHONY GRAHAM, LOVING FATHER. NEVER FORGOTTEN. He get a flash of a man in his good suit, lying in a box, face stiff like the wood they bury him in. And he and Errol standing there, so close to it, talking like if it was nothing.

Errol notice him looking. 'Where a man from always matter. Tell you what kinda man he is, what he stand for, what he does let slide, you know what I mean?'

Darwin keep his eyes on the dog. He don't want to even look over at Errol. Something about the old man two-coloured eyes make him feel a way. Errol might look half-blind but Darwin certain that nothing don't get past him. 'I tell you already. I is a man who does work hard. Nothing else don't matter.'

The dog catch a scent. His whole body get stiff, tail sharp and pointing up in the air. He start to dig up the flowers, scattering them, burrowing into the soil.

'Go on, dog!' Errol growl at the stray. The sound echo in the quiet; the dog scamper, looking back at them as he run off. 'Don't mind them pot hound. They always here sniffing around for ends of food. Sometimes people does leave offerings and ting.'

Darwin nod and they move on. 'How come them other graves there have concrete over them?' he ask.

'Sometimes the rest of the family go away to live and no one else burying in that plot. Maybe people decide to cremate. Some people feel it is to keep somebody from interfering with their dead, you know. People superstitious like that.'

Darwin know Errol didn't forget his question about where he was from but seem like he was going to let it rest for now. At least he get one back after his misstep this morning. He peek at the old man out of the corner of his eye. All this time they talking Errol was cool, total contrast from when Darwin first walk into Fidelis. He even walk with a small limp now. Make him look harmless.

They round a bend, and again Fidelis show Darwin a different side. These graves squeeze in together with no walls, no mausoleums, no gates, no crying statues, no crosses, no marble headstones at all. Here the headstones make from plain concrete and the inscriptions paint on by hand. Tall weeds looking like feathers, ti-marie bush that close shut when his foot brush them, razor grass, and the spiky runner he see before cover whole sections in deep purple. Plenty rubbish too. Old bottle, wrappers, one side of a slipper, juice carton, things people leave behind.

'You have family, Darwin?' Errol start up again.

'Just my queen,' Darwin answer, then he think of his mother's friend Ms Enid, who was as good as a next mother to him. 'And my aunty.'

That is good. A man should always make sure his mother good and take care of his people. I hate ungratefulness, you know? Can't stand to see people who does just leave their old parents to fall by the wayside. People who don't know how to be grateful to those who help them when they couldn't help they self.'

Errol walk a little faster and Darwin find himself hustling to catch up. They back on the main road now, the admin building up ahead, and Darwin could tell the tour was nearly done.

'You go fall in nice, man. I could tell. I have a sense about people, and I feel like you going and work out alright.'

Darwin wonder what the old man see when he look at him, what his answers say. Maybe he notice him looking at the flowers. Make him forget that he was in a place for the dead, where a man like him, or a man like he used to be, eh have no business. Don't help that Errol make being in Fidelis seem like the most normal thing in the world, just like any other job.

'Look.' Errol hand him a set of keys. 'Big gate and admin building.'

'Everybody have keys?' Darwin take them from him.

'Nah. Is only one set of keys here. That is the rules. Corporation have, city police have in case of emergency, but they say they don't want too many keys with the workers. Security risk.'

Darwin look around at the old trees that need trimming, weeds, broken-down building and stone. 'What it have in here to steal?'

'Well, you know, people used to come and steal the iron from the fences and ting. You see all them cross and Hail Mary and baby angels? Marble. People used to come and steal them too. They could still do it eh but it harder to jump the wall with a big stone angel on your back.'

Errol laugh like he make the funniest joke in the world, but Darwin feel cold all down to his new boots. How long it would take? Hours? To chip away at a pedestal, to rip out a fence that sink in the ground with concrete, to break off brass, copper, anything set in stone? How a man does reach a point where he could rob a grave?

'Yuh frighten?'

Darwin feel like he on the backfoot again. 'I just want to know what to expect.' He keep his eyes on Errol.

'Don't frighten, boy.' Errol voice smooth-smooth, not like a grizzly-looking old man in work overalls at all, more like he should be in a three-piece suit in one of them high-rise building in the harbour. 'Is only the dead here.'

Errol nod at the keys in Darwin hand. 'Since you come in my yard dress up in shirt and pants like you want to work security, you get to hold the keys. Reach for six in the morning. Six thirty in the evening is last rounds. Make sure that nobody still here visiting. It wouldn't be good for somebody to get lock in here.'

'How you mean last rounds? You mean me alone in here? In the night?' Darwin coulda kick himself for the way his voice crack at the end.

Errol look straight at him, a slight smile. 'Big man like you fraid the dark?' He turn and walk away.

Darwin watch Errol go up the main street to the admin building and push through the red front doors. What he supposed to do now? Errol never say, and the rest of the crew disappear. He don't want to just wander about by himself. A different place and he would find something to clean, to straighten up, something to make himself busy doing. But, with Errol gone, Fidelis was just bones again. He don't know a place could be empty and full same time.

The sun high in the sky. Must be hours since he walk in the front gate. He run his hands through his uneven hair. He feel more tired than he should seeing as he eh do any actual work yet, but the morning take something from him. Darwin start to walk toward the admin building when Errol stick his head round the door and call out to him, 'Boy, is lunchtime. Yuh eat?'

Is only when Darwin shake his head, no, that he realize he forget all about his mother coconut bake.

5

Bellemere was close enough to the city centre that Darwin could walk there from Fidelis, but far enough that if you had a house in the nicer parts you could feel like you move up a little bit in life. In the early-evening light it had something about the too-close-together apartment buildings, shabby houses with flower gardens, men washing their cars with foamy buckets, and the kind of corner shops that never close and sell everything from slippers to cigarettes to cooking-gas tanks to bread to other things that you had to collect out of sight by the side door, that had a kinda beauty about it if you squint your eye and look at them in the right way.

Bellemere streets had a different pattern to Port Angeles proper too. The city centre was a grid that you could find your way in once you figure out the system. But Bellemere like it grow up wild. No street signs, no house numbers. It move along like a river on rough terrain, broadening out when the land flatten and then splitting into two, three, four streams and going its own way when it get rocky underfoot. Only difference is that the Bellemere streets does flow uphill instead of down, little snaking streams going up into the last bits of forest in the hills that Ms Enid say they used to call Freetown.

Her directions was good. By the time he pass the corner shop with the green shutters, the brown and white house with music blasting from inside, the townhouses that look like whoever build them try to squeeze them into too small a space, and he reach the crossroads that she tell him cut Bellemere in four, the one with the big purple house, he know he was going the right way. A group of fellas liming by the lamp post watch him make his way toward them just like Ms Enid said they would be. He not worried. He know the protocol. Walk past slow enough to hail them, let them see his face, act harmless enough but with just enough eye contact to show he not hiding nothing and not looking for nothing neither. They nod and hail him back and he feel eyes on him as he take the left and continue on as the road start to incline.

He doing that dance his whole life. The boys on Dalia Street learn to leave him alone after a while too. He was about thirteen and had now start to put on a little size when somebody in school say something about how he and his mother hair so nasty and how Janaya cyat must be nasty too. Next thing he remember he was in the principal office with his hands mash up and blood running down in his eye. Mrs Potter start to talk suspension and she look at him like she never really see him before.

When he reach home, his face swell up and his knuckles bleeding, Janaya make a soup for him, bandage him up and call him her young lion. By the next day they transfer him to another class, and no one say anything about him or his mother again. He didn't make no more friends, but it didn't have no more fight after that neither. Was enough for them to know that the Rasta youth mighta be the last one to look for a fight, but if fight find him he was good for himself.

So he eh worried about the fellas on the block. He used to making his way, keeping his head down and knowing how to be invisible when it suit him.

At the top of the hill he see the house Ms Enid describe to him. A white two-storey with a small yard in front and a red gate. 'Evening, Ms Margo!' he call out and tap the gate with the latch bar a few times.

Somebody inside pull the curtain and peek out the front window. 'Ms Enid send me, ma'am.'

The curtain drop, and in a few seconds the front door open. A short lady with curlers in her hair walk out on the gallery and peer at him over the porch railing. 'Emmanuel?'

'Yes, ma'am. Janaya son.'

Her face break open in a big smile and she beckon him in. 'Come, come.'

'Evening, ma'am.' He push the front gate, walk up the small driveway and the three steps to the gallery. 'Thanks for having me.'

'Call me Margo,' she say and grab him in a hug. 'That is only for you, though. Ma'am for everybody else. Come nuh. Rest down yuh bag.'

They walk into the living room and for a second is like he in his old house on Dalia Street. This coulda be Janaya living room. Same kind of maroon-colour couch that had seen better days, except Margo own was still cover down in plastic. Same heavy dining table with mismatched chairs. Same picture of the Doctor on the wall, but a real poster with a fancy picture frame. Below it a small round table with an open Bible.

And just like that he see his mother, how she look when he was small, sitting on the couch and turning the pages of the Bible, the cloth that always wrap her dread making a crown high on her head.

'Sit down nuh.' Margo guide him to the couch, and she take the armchair next to it. 'I cook something if you hungry. It cover down there on the stove. Nothing fancy. Some tomato choka and sada. I does like to eat light in the evenings. Plus is just me here. Is only you I have now but I expecting two more in the next few weeks. I doh cook for everybody eh, mind you. It not good to give people bad habits, especially these days. Everybody want to take advantage. I don't mean you, dear, I done talk to Enid about you and rent so don't even worry about that until you able. I come from country too, you know. Me and Mr Arnold come here when we was young, God rest his soul. People here, they see an old lady and figure they could do me anything but I good for myself. Let them only try . . .'

Darwin halfway listen to Margo but all he want is a little quiet to come to terms with the day. He sneak a look toward the beaded curtain and the kitchen behind it and study the sada she offer. He could eat something, as she mention it, but he could tell Margo anxious for company and would talk his head off if he stay.

'Come let me look at you.'

Darwin pull himself up a little bit from the seat and straighten his back for inspection.

'You look like you mother bad, boy. When she was young. You must be feeling good now, ent? With all that thing off your back? I mean, I know you was used to it but look how you handsome! Enid didn't tell me you was so handsome. When you going to cut yuh hair properly? Shave up nice. You looking like if you and the barber fall out . . .' Margo falter like she see something in his face. 'I . . . I don't mean anything by it eh, I just saying . . .'

He look around the room and try to find something to say, anything to change the conversation. The sada gone out his head, he wasn't hungry now. He just want to be alone.

The silence stretch for what feel like minutes, then Margo get up. 'Let me show you the room and where everything is. It small but I does try to keep the place nice for people.'

She guide him out the living room and down the corridor to the back.

'After you work whole day, I find people must at least come home to somewhere clean to rest they head.'

She retreat back down the corridor and Darwin close the door, drop his bag on the floor and look around. A single bed with fresh sheets, a chair in the corner, a small plastic table. He walk across the room to a narrow window and he look out onto Bellemere. The hill high enough that he could see the rooftops of the houses below like a quilt make from silver, grey and rust, with coconut, governor plum and mango trees growing out from the patchwork. A car driving slow, winding its way up the hill; a cat sitting on top a balcony opposite licking itself; a woman on her back step combing a little girl hair. He look higher up the hill and see smaller houses, each one far from the next; clearings with small farms in between; flashes of yellow cassia trees like flame. Then higher, only bush and then sky.

He wonder what Janaya doing now. Round this time, she take a break from the sewing, brew some tea and walk out on the back step to chat with Ms Enid. She probably know that he reach; he sure Margo woulda call Ms Enid and tell her. Maybe they talking about him right now.

He pull off his boots and overalls, take the rest of his clothes out his bag and hang them over the chair in the corner. Then he put his Bible on the side table and stick his fresh kush wrap up in foil paper in the back of the top drawer. His skin feel dusty and he want to take a fresh before he lie down on Margo clean sheets, but the tiredness hold him. The pillow feel strange on the back of his neck, and he don't know how to get comfortable in a strange bed in a strange lady house. He don't even know when he fall asleep.

6

It wasn't a vow so much as law – like how water does run down a mountain and not up. Like how from November the sun start to set just a little bit earlier every day and the breeze get a little chill in it. Like how no matter how hard Darwin used to stare at the mango tree in the schoolyard when he was a little boy, he could not force it to bring forth fruit outside of its due season. It had no ceremony, no words that he had to memorize and repeat in front a crowd, but it was as irrevocable as high tide.

> All the days of his vow of separation, no razor shall touch his head. Until the time is completed for which he separates himself to the Lord, he shall be holy. He shall let the locks of hair of his head grow long. All the days that he separates himself to the Lord he shall not go near a dead body. Not even for his father or for his mother, for brother or sister, if they die, shall he make himself unclean, because his separation to God is on his head. All the days of his separation he is holy to the Lord.

It had always been he and his mother Janaya living like their own island at the end of Dalia Street. There was no one else like them on the street and, other than Ms Enid next door, nobody really care. It was enough for the adults in the street to know that the boy from up the road was quiet and respectful, never bother nobody, never take up too much with the other boys. They couldn't understand why his mother didn't cut his hair and have him looking decent, but they know better than to ask Janaya her business and leave the family alone with their ways. Everybody know Janaya was the best seamstress in the area. She was reserved, almost solemn, but all they had to do was ask and she would sew their children school uniforms and, when times was hard, let them pay her when they could. Is so he and his mother lived in a community of two. Well, three, if you count Ms Enid, and he always did.

Even when Janaya hands start to twist and pain like old roots, he still see them as they looked when he was little, as she turned the pages of the Bible that she kept on her bedside table, the cloth that always wrapped her hair making a crown high atop her head. He almost never see her hair underneath it, and he used to think that her head just shaped that way, like the Nefertiti picture she had tacked onto the wall in the front room of their house. It was right next to the photo of the Doctor and the other of His Majesty and Empress Menen. Them three photos was like a trio of gods in the house when he was growing up: the Conquering Lion of Judah and his Empress; the Egyptian queen that had been the most beautiful and powerful woman in the world; and the Doctor – the Crown Prince of the Sufferers of Port Angeles, she used to call him. It was the only remnant of her life in the city, the place she grow up from small. If it wasn't for that photo, he would have thought his mother had come into being when he was born and had always been there in their house, in their yard.

All she ever say was that she turn her back on dead and consecrate herself and her new son as Nazarites – separate, promised to Jah, in the world but never of the world. She would stroke the pages of the Bible as she read the vow to him. The razor. The locks. The dead. Her voice was soft as what he imagine lambswool feel like, but when she wasn't looking he would find a place to himself and cry long, long tears to think of his mother dead, alone in her bed, and that he would have to leave the house he grow up in because it was just he and she and who would take her away? He wouldn't have nowhere to go if no one would take his mother from the house where they live, and God would smite him if he so much as peek at her, just one last time to say goodbye.

Ms Enid would gather him up as he sit crying on their back steps when she come out to do her washing and tell him not to worry. 'Your mother too damn stubborn to die,' and she would stroke his head and give him a piece of pone to eat and he would forget about the image of Janaya lying dead in the empty house.

Is all that weigh on his shoulders the last day he come home to his mother. He take off his shoes by the door and meet Janaya in the kitchen peeling green fig, steam rising from a pot on the fire. Only a few more sweet potato left in the basket on the counter. The big bag of rice reach halfway; the glass jar with black-eye peas halfway too.

'Evening.'

'Emmanuel? That is you?'

'I bring mango for you.' He pull them out from his bag and rest them on the kitchen table.

She turn to look, her voice light up. 'Starch?'

'What else I go bring?'

She laugh and stick her cheek out. He kiss her and take over peeling the green figs. 'Rest yourself, Ma.'

She leave the pot and head straight for the mangoes. He lean his back on the counter to face the kitchen door, the green fig skin peeling off easy in his hands, and watch her. She touch each mango and choose the brightest yellow with a few black spots on it – the sweetest one – wipe her hands on her skirt and sink her teeth into it. Her teeth rip off the skin bit by bit and she suck the golden flesh until the juice run down her fingers.

40

He don't know Janaya to smile too much, but starch mango always turn her into a child again, make her forget her worries a little bit. Her hands don't look twisted and painful when she eating mango, her face glowing and bright.

He finish peel the fig, then the sweet potato and the last bit of pumpkin, and put them on the boil.

'Take a next one, Ma.'

He start to chop the seasoning for the peas. Onions, garlic, parsley, some chadon beni, some chive.

'You don't want? You know I will eat all.'

'I bring them for you.'

He feel her smile even with his back turn.

The kitchen quiet for a while, just the smell of starch mango, the heat from the steam rising from the pot where the provision was boiling, the seasoning sharp in his nose, the peas soaking in a bowl of water, the low hum of the radio.

She two mangoes down now. As good a time as any. 'I get through at the office today.'

'Praise Jah!' She clap her hands and the laughter pour out of her mouth like bells. 'I tell you you will get something. Ent I tell you?' She rush over to him by the stove and hug him from behind. The top of her head barely reach the middle of his back. 'Patience, I tell you. Just patience. Blessings don't come when you decide they must come, but they does come when you need them the most.'

She move away and he hear her pull up a chair by the kitchen table and sit down. 'But why you didn't say? You stand up here so long and you eh say a word? Leave that and come and talk to me nuh.'

The second pot hot enough now. He pour a little oil, wait for the fine line of smoke to rise from it, then throw in the garlic and onion, stir it with a wooden spoon. The pot start to sizzle and little flecks of oil jump, the sweet salty smell of the onions rise up.

'I don't want the onion to burn.' He pour in the peas, stir it in good with some water.

'Alright.' She disappointed but then the excitement rise in her voice again. 'Well, what kind of work? Where it is? They start back up construction on the highway?'

He lower down the fire, cover the pot and turn around. She still smiling, her fingers reaching toward the other mangoes on the table. 'Look it have some coconut milk in the fridge, don't forget it.'

'Ma,' he take a deep breath. 'You know how things are these days, how long I looking and can't find anything. And the lady I talk to say that is all she have . . . Is in a cemetery, Ma.'

Janaya whole face change now like when rain set up sudden. The gold mango blush gone and her eyes flat and hard like slate.

'In a what?' Her voice pitch high and she push back from the table; the chair scrape and clatter down to the wooden floor. She hold on to the kitchen door to steady herself. 'Where?'

'Fidelis. The big one in Port Angeles.'

'Go back and tell them you want something else.' Her voice turn to steel.

'It have nothing else!'

'Well, you can't take it. Not in no dead yard and not in that dead city. Something else will come. You can't go in that place and mix up in them people.'

He gesture around the kitchen. 'You think I don't know how you stretch every bit of groceries I does bring home? You think I don't see that your hands can't make with the sewing machine anymore? How the orders coming in less and less?'

'I will manage! Enid make a rub for my hands and it helping, it not so bad again. I good, Emmanuel, I doing good now.'

'You think I blind?'

'Money is not everything, Emmanuel. You know what kind of man I raise you to be. You know I never ask for no help from nobody. I never bring no next man in this house for him to play like he is more man inside of here than you. You know how I rate you, and what hopes I have for you, and this is what you going and do me? Do yourself? I grow you with a clean heart. You think it have any silver and gold in this world that could make up for your soul, Emmanuel? You think anybody in that place care anything about your soul?'

He feel his whole body tense, bubbling with the thing he want to say but cannot say. The thing that always in the house with them, that they step over and around and pretend was never there. It make him want to break something, tip over the whole table, fling the pot off the stove.

'We will manage, son.' Her voice quiet, almost pleading. 'You ever starve in my house? I ever send you out in the world without your stomach full and your clothes clean? You ever want for anything once you here with me?'

'I can't spend my whole life here with you.' The words come soft but firm, before he even know he saying them.

The slap echo in the kitchen and his face sting. They stare at each other.

'Here with me eh good enough for you, Emmanuel? What it have to see over there? Dead-people bones? Police and tief and prostitute and dutty politician. You want to be out there in that life? Is glamour life you want?' He see her eyes filling up with water and all the anger leave him one time. He don't even feel the sting on his face anymore because he know that what he say hurt her more than any lash she coulda give him.

He turn around and shut off the fire under the provision. Feel her watching him while he stir the pumpkin and the

43

coconut milk in the peas, release the fragrances into the air. He lower the heat.

'Son,' her voice sound quiet now, like she spend all the rage she have in her, 'I understand. I understand what you saying, but that place. That place could swallow a man whole. Plenty woman watch they son, they daughter, they husband walk out they house looking for more, talking that same story you talking now. And never see them again. If you go to that place, if you leave this house, you not coming back.'

'You putting me out, Ma?' He can't bear to turn around. He don't want to see the answer in her eyes.

'I make you. You is mine. But if you leave this house to go and live in town, you not coming back.'

He hear her footsteps get softer as she walk down the corridor and the door to her room close. The space she leave when she gone feel like something carve out of his insides. When the food done, he take a bowl from the cupboard and put out some green fig and provision. Pour over a spoon of the fragrant stew peas, still steaming. Find the small glass bottle of kuchela from the fridge and add a little bit on the side. He sit down on the kitchen steps and eat his food alone.

The evening come fast, like it rushing him, don't want him to give in and change his mind. When he finish dinner and clean up the kitchen he know what he have to do. He not going by no barber. No stranger was going and touch his head. He find a scissors in the kitchen drawer, test the blade with his thumb. Sharp enough. He sit down by the zaboca tree in the backyard, a plastic grocery bag from under the sink at his feet, and take his tam off. His locks drop heavy on his shoulders, his back. He sit for a while with his eyes closed and let the last of the afternoon sun warm his skin, settle in his dread. He roll his neck and feel the weight of twenty-five years. He don't remember what he look like before. There must have been a before. But as long as he know himself, as long as it have a Emmanuel in the world that he know is him, he was a natty dread. A Rastaman. What it mean to not look like that anymore? What it mean to break a promise? He know one thing for sure, he not walking in that place as the man he know. To do that work, he go have to be a different kind of man. Take in front before in front take him.

Deep breath. Grab a fistful. Cut. The blade slice halfway through one lock and he have to cut again, sawing his way through. He stare at the black coils as they fall in the bag at his feet. Something catch in throat. Like walking uphill. Another fistful and the hill steeper, and it harder to breathe. He could only find his way to take some short shallow gasps and he never want to breathe deep more in his whole life. Everything in the yard look greener and the air thicker and his body like it don't belong to him anymore. With each cut is like he watching himself do it. The long ropes pile higher and higher. They overflow the bag that holding them, spread out among the zaboca leaves. They reach up his chest, his neck, and wrap themselves around his throat and he can't breathe, can't breathe, can't breathe. But is not him, not his body, not his throat, and the man sitting under the tree is somebody else, and with the last cut he finally take a deep breath in, his head shorn. His old self, floating somewhere above the tree, exhale.

Before first light he swing his feet off his new bed in Margo house, dig down in his bag for the small package he pick up on the way home last night and walk down the corridor to the bathroom, soft so he don't wake up Margo. He lock the door behind him. Tiny moths buzz around the blue fluorescent bulb hanging from the ceiling. For a second, he think he see his old self in the mirror with locks long and falling past his shoulders, down his back, his beard full, eyes flashing like lightning. But the man in the mirror don't look nothing like Emmanuel at all. He recognize some things – the sharp bones of his face, the little marks in his skin from the acne he had when he was a youth, the scar over his eyebrow where a boy once hit him with a bottle – but the tufts of hair, like a small blue halo in the half-light, his eyes that just look lost and empty, he don't know them no more.

He flick the switch on the electric shaver and the buzz travel up his arms. He start at the top of his forehead, touch it to his scalp and feel the buzz of the blades, the wool of his hair fall on his shoulders and into the basin. He cut a path through the middle of his head like a road in a cane field. His scalp look pale under the harsh bathroom light, black swirls falling on his nose, his chest, tears on his face.

When he done, his head like a dome, he pick up the new, sharp scissors and start to trim his beard. He couldn't handle the electric blades nowhere near his face. He feel like it would get away from him, become an instrument of justice and bury itself in his throat. The scissors is just him and his hands and how steady he could keep them.

Each snip get a little easier. He lift the moustache on his top lip and cut, trim his sideburns closer too. By the time he done is just short whorls of hair like soft comfort protecting his upper throat and jaw. He brush them off his head, his shoulders, the back of his neck, his face.

Even all the way in the city that she say would swallow him whole, he can still hear Janaya crying for her one son who going out naked into Babylon with no shield to protect him. Don't go, Emmanuel, she say, don't go. He slide down the bathroom door, feel the wood grain against his spine till he sitting on the damp mat, and watch the moths circle the light; the ones who fly too close burn away in the heat.

THE RIGHT AND PROPER
WAY TO DIE

7

Yejide

Is three days Yejide curl up on her bed under the mosquito net, listening to the storm outside. Three days since the wind set up and the first few fat raindrops pound the roof. Three days since her mother Petronella lie down in her bed to die.

Soon as the storm start, Yejide feel her belly begin to rise and swell with a weight that feel like a hole. She have no other way to describe it – a hollowing, a dread, slow emptying out. She hear about mothers who lose their children to early, unexpected death. They washing dishes, cleaning the house or at work in town, and the minute the child gone they feel a hole in that keening place, feel it pull taut, like the womb know the second the child leave the world. Yejide womb empty, and she have no dead children to mourn, but that is how it feel, like something in her anticipating absence. It pin her to the bed. The storm outside, the mosquito net and the half-light of dawn press down against the air above her.

She tell herself is not grief. Grief is a thing that come from love and love simple like breath. But what she feel for her mother was never simple. She don't know if she have enough room for a big, solid word like grief along with everything else that exist in her heart for Petronella.

She toss and turn in the bed, in her room at the end of the corridor, sheets wrap around her body like a shroud, and listen for a knock on the door. She think she hear footsteps on the landing, whispers on the stairs, someone stopping outside her bedroom, listening and then moving on again. Every creak of the floorboards, every shudder of the windowpane ask the same question: why her mother don't call for her? Petronella can't go before she call, but what stopping her, even now, from calling for her only daughter? Every time Yejide open the door to look, hoping that they send for her, she find the long corridor dim, yawning and empty.

It hard to know if she asleep or awake, what real and what is only dream. First day of the storm, she see her mother's twin sister, Geraldine, dead more than a year now, walk into her room wearing Petronella clothes – a long green dress with lace at the collar – a cup of tea in her hand. Yejide could almost smell the earthy turmeric root and feel the heat of the steam rising from the cup. Geraldine put the tea on the bed-side table, walk to the window and step out through the glass pane into the night air.

Second day, she thought she wake up in a bamboo patch in the middle of the forest, no storm, no vigil, just cool breeze blowing sweet and the smell of green on the wind.

Now, in the soft early-morning light of the third day, she remember the great storm, many years ago, that take Granny Catherine away. Yejide was only nine then but she remember like it was yesterday.

The rain had start after church on Sunday. The baubles around her plaits too tight and she hate the stiff, white ribbons wrap around their ends, but the first few drops of rain mean freedom. She look around for her best friend Seema so they could walk home together but Seema had already head off with her own mother, Laurence. Yejide feel a stirring of excitement. She pull off the shiny patent-leather shoes, drag the knee-high socks off and start to run up the hill for home, feeling the wet earth squish under her bare feet.

Mud splatter her white dress and she don't even know where she leave her socks. If her mother see, she would be vex with her for running barefoot in her good church clothes and losing yet another pair. Granny Catherine would pretend to make a fuss too, for Petronella's sake, but Yejide know she wouldn't really mind. Once Petronella back turned, she and Granny would giggle together and snuggle in the big wooden rocking chair in the front room.

She run up the drive out of the rain and tiptoe through the side door of the kitchen. In a house as sprawling and bustling as theirs, with everyone coming and going, with big people always doing big-people things – some who live there and some who just passing through – and Petronella and Geraldine lock away in their secret world that no one else could enter, Yejide know she could slip in unnoticed. But that day was different. She didn't even need to sneak in; the house was in uproar. A woman she don't know rush past her from the laundry room, through the kitchen into the drawing room with a pile of fresh sheets in her hand. Peter, who always pull her plaits and say, 'How the princess going today?', walk past her and head upstairs with his arms full of black sage bush like if she invisible. Laurence was there too with a whole set of people that Yejide never see before. Even Seema creep past her up the stairs, trying to balance a cup of tea, her eyes full of confusion. The kettle screech in the kitchen; no one care enough to take it off the heat. She could not find Granny Catherine anywhere.

The storm reach its height and daytime turn to night before Peter find her, still wearing her damp church dress, sitting in Granny Catherine chair. His eyes flick from her to the living-room door, down at his feet and back to her face.

'How the princess going today?'

But the words sound wrong. Like they hiding things. Peter love Petronella for as long as Yejide could remember; he was not her father but was as good as. She never see him look nervous before.

'What happen, Peter? Where Granny?'

Peter shift from one foot to the other. Keep looking around to see if anyone else there, like he not sure if it is his place to say anything to her.

'The storm come for your granny. She going.'

'Going where?'

'Where she must.'

She should have known better, but she ask anyway. 'Where Mummy?'

Peter look down at her with a half-smile that she recognize even then.

'Your mother doing what she must too. She waiting for her mother to call for her.'

'Granny Catherine going to call for me too? I want to see her.'

Peter shake his head. 'Only person Catherine calling is her daughter.' He take her hand. 'Come. Let's find somebody to get you out these clothes.'

She move to the window seat and watch the rain. It come down in grey sheets, the wind snatch and snap branches, crashing them into the windowpanes, and the Lengua River roar through the settlement below, full to bursting, threatening to spill itself into the valley. When you live in the hills, close to the sky where the clouds gather first and press down, you learn to read the rain. Granny used to tell her that they come from the storm and the storm come from them. Make her think that every time it rained it was because they had willed it. She would run out into the garden and raise her arms high, she and Seema dancing like rain was a gift for them alone because they had been good or because they had been especially bad and gotten away with it. It take years for her to realize that all storms not the same.

When Geraldine die last year and the whole of Port Angeles flood away, the house brace, thinking it was Petronella time. But the way the raindrops crash on the galvanize roof and thunder peal out was nothing compare to the way Petronella bawl to find her twin sitting in her chair, crochet needle in her hand, red thread piled around her lap, fingers still. Peter make the sign of the cross, grateful not to lose Petronella, but none of them coulda prepare for the grief to come. Geraldine funeral was small and quick; she always said she didn't want no fuss. But even with the repast done, Geraldine clothes pack away, the requisite time pass for respect till they could open the shop again and the shroud of mourning start to lift from the house – Petronella was still on pause. Yejide couldn't remember when last Petronella sit at her desk with the ledgers, when last the workers see her in the shop, and with no Geraldine to tether her to here while the heart of her take wing and fly elsewhere, all Petronella was prepared to do was move from one chair to the next. In the morning was the rocking chair on the porch, her sister's matching rocker empty beside her; in the evening was the velvet armchair with Geraldine crochet on the headrest; and once the sun set it was the garden bench where she and her sister used to ask questions of the stars. Then, when the moon high and the dark thick and deep, she walk up the stairs to her bed without saying a word.

And is so the time pass till the pattern so set that Yejide don't have to look to know where her mother is. Just once she try to reach her in that place, not long before the storm come back. She find Petronella on the porch, taking in the last of the sun. Yejide fill the black kettle, put it on the stove and turn the burner on high. Two cups with the flower pattern, the good ones for company. Not like they does really have as much company again. Since Petronella start to play musical chairs whoever here is more family than company, and those who used to pass through all the time from since Granny Catherine days don't come so much anymore; Petronella grief drown them out.

Yejide root around in the bottom cupboard and find the jar of dried lemongrass. The smell fill the kitchen, the orange and blue flame flare beneath the kettle and the light from the window filter through the white curtains.

All of them well know that mourning is not a thing that have an end – is not a rope – but every day they carry the hope that today might be the day that Petronella shake herself up and start back living. Every now and again Yejide catch a whisper between Peter and Mr Homer. She know they worried – bout the business and bout the other kind of work that they can't see – now that Petronella hiding away inside herself.

When the kettle start to scream she hear it call for Geraldine like it miss her. And she know is not the steam but Petronella outside, her grief loud like a kettle on the boil. Yejide feel like her hands might be good bread hands like her granny say, but her shoulders too slim to carry the whole house, the whole family, her mother whole grief. She know she should, but she don't miss Geraldine one bit.

She sweeten the lemongrass tea with honey and put the cups on the doily coasters, a linen napkin on the tray. She had to try. Maybe, with Geraldine gone, her mother would look upon her face and see something in it to find favour with. At least she could start with tea. Tray in both hands, walking slow so the steaming liquid don't spill and stain the linen, Yejide walk out the front door and bend the corner. Petronella sitting in her chair, back straight like a board, and next to her was Geraldine, dead, but there, plain as day. Yejide feel her hands tremble but she catch herself before the tea spill.

The twins move in unison like always, elbows and shoulders moving up and down, fingers pulling long lines of deep crimson crochet thread from the same skein between them. The bedspread that they start making a year ago flow from Petronella fingers, onto her lap and down into the basket at the side of the chair. But nothing spill from Geraldine fingers. There was just the motion of the needle, her shoulders, her elbows, the basket beside her chair empty.

Resentment flare in Yejide but she breathe deep and push it down in her toes. She pretend she don't see Geraldine. 'I bring tea for you, Mummy.' She set the tray on the small folding table beside her mother's chair. Petronella don't answer, her fingers picking at the thread, the gold needle flashing. She wind the red thread around it, pull it through the loop, the pattern growing more and more intricate.

Yejide bring a smaller chair from further down the porch and sit next to her mother. 'I went down by the store today. Things in okay shape. Shelly pregnant again so we will have to find someone else at the cashier soon but she good for the next few months.'

There was no other sound than the breeze and the buzz of the tiny hummingbirds darting around the plastic feeders that hang from the veranda.

'Your tea will get cold if you don't drink it. I put extra honey in it for you.'

The two women, one dead and one alive, keep their eyes on the thread as if she not even there.

'Mummy, you can't keep going like this. You have to talk to me. I trying but I don't know what to do. I not ready.'

She can't make no sense of the store's ledgers on Petronella desk since she insist on keeping all the records by hand, and the suppliers still had a way of watching her like they was just waiting for her to make a mistake. And there were other things Petronella was supposed to be teaching her too, things more important than accounts for the shop and how to manage the shipments, who to bribe in customs.

The steam had stop rising from the cup. It would get cold soon. She reach for the tray, hoping it would spur her mother to action, but Petronella hand flick out fast like a humming-bird and block her hand, brush it away. She put the crochet down on her lap and drag the folding table with the two cups of tea closer to her and Geraldine. Yejide out of the circle again. She fight tears. Geraldine reach for her tea.

8

This time Yejide not wrong. It wasn't a trick of the ear or the storm. Footsteps shuffle outside the door. Before she could get up, Seema walk softly into her room, close the door behind her and sit on the empty bed.

'You didn't eat anything.' Seema look at the trail of ants that come from the window, across the floor, up the bedside table and into the bowl of soup that Yejide left untouched.

'Not hungry.' Yejide shake her head.

'Hungry have nothing to do with it. You have to eat.'

'You eat?' She doubt whether anyone in the house remember.

'Whether I eat or not is my business.' A half-smile tug the corners of Seema mouth. 'You forget, Jide, that I am not you.'

It was the thing that had always hung between them – the thinnest of lace curtains, almost transparent, yet unmistakably there.

Seema eyes look tired, brow furrowed. The last year wasn't easy on her, on them. Since they small they inseparable. The word 'family' had nothing to do with biology in the house on Morne Marie. Kin was better, and Seema people had live in the house as long as Yejide's. But Seema was more than her sister, more than her friend, so they never think too much about what coming for them, so far in the future that it seem impossible. They know some time in that distant never-coming future it would be different. But is one thing to know that Yejide must eventually take Petronella place as the matriarch of the house, is another to watch it happen slow, day by day, when her mother still here, doing her best to fade herself away before time.

'Anyway,' Seema continue, 'you don't know what going to happen when Ms Pet gone. I figure is best you face it with some food inside you. Stop wasting my good soup.'

Yejide climb down from window seat and sit next to Seema. Lace Seema fingers through her own. 'Stop trying to feed me all the time. Let me feed you sometimes nuh.'

Seema laugh. 'The way you cook? To poison all of us inside here?'

'I not that bad.'

'You worse!'

Yejide frown, bite her lip. 'You could teach me, you know.'

'Jide, I like cooking. I good at it. Everybody in this house have a role. I good at mine.'

They both pretend not to hear the edge in her voice.

Yejide lift Seema hands and kiss them, one then the other. They tiny and delicate-looking, nothing like Yejide's, but coarse like hers from planting in the garden and running the shop and loading the crates and doing all the other things needed for living in a house as old as this, with all the people that depend on her family. She feel a warmth in her chest, in spite of everything.

'Want to trade?'

Seema reach out and stroke her cheek. 'Not for all the money in Port Angeles.' Her eyes start to twinkle again. 'Besides, Port Angeles don't have as much money as it used to. If I had to get the shittiest destiny in the world, it shouldn't come cheap.'

And they both laugh harder than they had in days, drowning out the storm, and the branches on the window, and the flapping sheet of roof galvanize that threaten to blow away in the wind. For one moment they was just girls again.

'Come.' Seema shoo Yejide off the bed and gather the mosquito netting. 'Gimme these sheets, clear up a little bit. Will make you feel better.' She tuck it out of the way behind the bedhead and then pull off the sheets. Yejide start picking up clothes from the armchair, the floor. It feel good to be useful, helping Seema clear away the detritus of the last three days. She open the top drawer on the bedside table, shake a green mosquito coil and tiny silver stand out of a box, stick the prong into the centre of the coil to hold it upright. She light a match and touch the flame to the end of the coil and place it in a small saucer in a corner, out of the way. The smoke curl upward and its acrid smell fill the room.

She brush the white dead-moth dust from the keepsakes on the bureau with her hand. A pocket watch that belong to Maman, her great-great-great-grandmother. A dark blue, fleur-de-lis enamel pill box belong to Babygirl, her great-great-grandmother. The heavy gold bangle was from Deborah – Babygirl daughter and Yejide great-grandmother. And finally, her favourite, her Granny Catherine ebony pipe. Catherine was the only one she know in the flesh and she stroke her pipe like something precious. Soon something of her mother's would be there. Her silver cigarette case? Her jewellery box? And then one day there would be something of her own to be added, like another bead on a rosary. But she had no daughter. Who would be there to select it?

'Seema?'

'Hmm?' She was pulling a clean fitted sheet onto the corners of the mattress.

'Remember when we used to talk about running away?'

Seema smile. 'Get an apartment in town, smoke cigarettes and drink red wine whole day.'

'The one time we try it, we realize we didn't know where to go after we reach the main road.'

'And Mummy find us by the junction on her way home from the market and carry us back up the hill.'

'She never tell on us.'

'Cut my tail, though,' Seema grumble.

Yejide remember it happier. She and Seema heading out into the world, no idea where they was going and no intention of coming back.

'I still feel to do that sometimes, to run away from here, go somewhere else. Sometimes it feel like the only thing we do in this house is die and pass death down the line. You ever think about it like that? Nobody does ever tell you about what to do when we living but everybody know what supposed to happen when we dying.'

Seema pause. The quiet settle. 'Don't worry.' She smooth the top sheet on the bed. 'She will call and you will be alright.'

Yejide wipe her dusty hands on her leg. 'Right.' She almost taste the resentment on her tongue.

'She don't have a choice. Ms Pet know – even if she like to pretend not to – that this is about more than just you and she.'

'Ms Pet didn't give a damn about what she was supposed to do when it come to me for all this time. Why you so sure she have damns to give now?'

Seema smile and take her hand as if to say enough now and draw Yejide back to the bed. She lie down and watch Seema unravel the mosquito netting and drape it over her. Through the gauze Seema look like a ghost. She lift the net, crawl in beside Yejide and cover them both. The warmth of her body pressing against Yejide's make her forget her worries a little bit, just lie there listening to the rain and Seema soft voice.

'You know what I remember from standing on the junction, running away, no idea where to go? The feeling that nobody down there knew where to go either. That they was all just as lost. Most people out there, people down the hill, people in the city, all of them fraid dying. Fraid it every day. Is like a black curtain that block out everything they think they know. They don't know that death is a blessing, a balancing. That it have women living on this hill who whole life is about making sure that death don't have to be a thing to fear, that somebody here to make sure that is nothing more than a good, long sleep. To be able to do that, to be part of that, is a blessing too.' She glance over and stroke Yejide cheek. 'But you not dying, Jide. Not today . . .'

A little light filter through the curtains as the sun rise. It bathe the room in a cool blue. Yejide curl her body around Seema's and tuck her head into the space between her shoulder and chin. She smell like clove.

Seema hands stroke her hair, her shoulders, trace down her back, her hip, lower.

Yejide press into Seema, then feel her body let go and drift. She push the resentment down and lock it away.

Yejide spend her whole childhood searching Petronella face for signs of her own. She never find any. Her face round and soft, her hands wide and calloused. But Petronella and Geraldine thin and spare, like the maker really had just enough for one woman and last minute decide to try and make two. With twins, it common for one to be the sun and the other to be the moon, but with Petronella and Geraldine – one didn't make sense without the other. Petronella never stop moving, like if she fill up with a kind of energy that hum in her bloodstream and make it impossible for her to stay still – rifling through piles of papers and neat black ledger books, swishing her long skirts busy-busy as she head out the front door to manage the store in town. Geraldine was always in her wake, quiet and still except for fingers that was agile like spiders when she crocheted. Whatever bond there was supposed to be between Yejide and her mother skip a generation. No accounting for twins.

But Yejide had Seema. They was like two manicou, Peter used to say, always sneaking out the house, always listening to big people from corners, always running in the bush, have a way they move quiet-quiet so nobody even realize they there. Even when she get older and Peter shake his head and bouf them for sneaking away, 'Is time you start to act like you have some sense, Princess. Why you don't come with me to the shop?' But from the time his back turn she and Seema would speed out the house and disappear into the green. Her mother already ignore her enough at home. Yejide don't need to go in the shop for her to do it there too.

She only know her mother through moments meant for someone else – glimpses through a half-open door, a snatch of conversation she wasn't supposed to hear. She put each of the moments into boxes. Sometimes she open them, spread out their contents to take inventory.

A small light-blue box that smell like loneliness. She was nine. The first few months after Granny Catherine gone. She and Seema playing in the corridor outside. Petronella brown legs hanging off the side of her big bed, her toes barely touching the floor. Faint sobs drifting out the crack of the door. Peter murmuring soothing sounds.

A round rose-gold box, the same colour as one of Petronella fancy dresses that Yejide would sneak into her room and try on when she wasn't looking. She was eleven. Petronella sitting at her bureau, Peter bareback behind her, his hands on her shoulders, stroking her neck. Petronella spraying a tiny bottle of something that smell sweet on the inside of her wrists, putting deep red lipstick on her mouth. Her face beautiful and grave in the mirror.

Forest-green box. Wide, with a false bottom. Space enough to hold this from when she was thirteen: Petronella and Geraldine in Geraldine room on opposite end of the corridor laughing quiet and whispering to each other; Geraldine sitting at an identical bureau, Petronella fingers oiling her sister scalp, the whole room smelling like rosemary.

Another, black. A tiny sickle, padlocked and humming with the knowledge that her mother did not belong to her. She was fifteen. Petronella sitting silent, her body taut, almost vibrating, straining with the energy it take to keep herself still, her eyes staring at a point in mid-air, and Geraldine next to her crocheting, like if not for her hands making chains and loops and stitches Petronella would lift off and fly up into the air, leaving her daughter with no mother at all.

Purple box, heavy like an unanswered question. Sixteen. Their voices identical. She can't tell who talking until she peek around the corner and see Petronella and Geraldine arguing. 'You have to teach her.'

'I don't have to do shit except stay alive.'

Geraldine mumbling but she can't hear.

'. . . and when it don't need me anymore? Expect me to just dead like all I good for is this?'

Footsteps on the landing coming closer toward her. Yejide

back away, press her body tight into a nook just out of sight, until she can't hear them.

The cobalt box pulse and change shade depending on when she open it. She was seventeen. Old Year's Night. Moon heavy. Fireworks lighting up the sky from Port Angeles in the distance, villagers bussing bamboo in the valley. The whole night bright and full of energy and she and Seema sneak out past the gathering in the living room – Petronella and Geraldine sipping port, Laurence playing guitar, Peter and the rest of men cooking black-eye peas in the kitchen to bring them luck and good business for the year to come. None of them even notice when she and Seema slip out the front door and take off across the yard, stolen cigarettes and Granny Catherine lighter in her pocket. She remember the wind on her face as they run through the bush, the smell of carbide burning in her nostrils. A low whistle lead them to the clearing and the boys' eyes light up to see them. They couldn't believe their luck – them girls from up the hill give them the time of day, and on Old Year's too! They would have a story to tell for months with this one.

The red one with thick curly hair pull out the rum bottle from his back pocket and grab Seema hand. She tip her head back and he pour the brown liquid down her throat and they collapse on the soft clearing, laughing and melt into the shadows. The next one skin shine like midnight and he look at Yejide like he never see anything like her a day in his life. His eyes make her shy, but she shake it off and pull out a stolen cigarette and light it, pout her lips like she see Petronella do, wonder what his hands would feel like on the back of her neck. She exhale slow and pass the cigarette to him. He take it from her and, when he done, grind it into the ground. They kiss and it taste like smoke and rum. He fumble with her dress. His

64

lips firm and the bark of the tree up at her back rough. He kiss his way down her collarbone and a giggle make her look up, over his shoulder. Halfway in shadow, Seema breasts bare, her hand gripping the hair of the boy on his knees in front of her. Yejide stifle a giggle of her own as a tongue curl round her nipple. She and Seema hold each other's gaze, the boys none the wiser. This moment was theirs, and theirs alone, while the bamboo keep bussing, lighting up the hill.

Hours later the hill quiet, the edges of the sky turning pink, they run back to the house, tipsy from the rum and drunk on their own power. When they reach close, they muffle their giggles and out-of-breath laughter so nobody can't hear them. They tiptoe up the drive, up the few steps to the wooden porch, and hope nobody awake so early downstairs to hear the creak of the floorboards. Yejide feel alive. She wasn't thinking about her mother and why she don't like her and what she ever do wrong and nothing about any old legacy that nobody ever really bother to explain to her. Her spirit flying so high, she almost miss it. If she didn't take one last look at the sky she woulda never see the faint orange light through the window on the landing upstairs, the outline of a woman standing there looking out. The lamp flick off quick; she know she not drunk enough to imagine it. The thought fill her up and make her feel warm: her mother stay up to see her home.

When she and Seema finally make their way back downstairs, late for New Year's breakfast, Petronella, Geraldine, Peter, Mr Homer and Laurence was already finishing up at the table. Petronella drinking lime-bud tea and Yejide reach over and take a float from the tray in front her mother and smile at her a little bit. She want her to know that she see her, but Petronella don't look up, just continue reading the newspapers.

She coulda kick herself. She imagine it after all. The euphoria of Old Year's, the boys, Seema, actually make her think her mother care whether she come home or not. She reach for the coffee pot, feel the disappointment settle in her, let it quieten down. And then she feel eyes on her. Geraldine gazing at her silent like always, but this time a faint smile on her lips.

9

Seema calling her name and shaking her awake. 'Mom say is almost time, Jide. Let's go.'

The room blaze with daylight, the storm raging like somebody get it vex. Yejide follow Seema up the short flight of stairs from her room, down a winding corridor filled with pictures of every kind: large oil paintings, charcoal sketches, formal framed portraits and candid photographs in black and white.

Was Seema who call it the Walking Gallery when they was little girls, and the name stick. On blissful days when all the adults busy doing something or other, they would play along the dark corridor, recite the stories they had been told about the women in them, and make up their own versions.

Through pictures they could trace the house over the years. In one, it was a large estate house with wooden jalousie windows and a wraparound porch and a back kitchen with smaller buildings off in the background. Men and women in broadbrim hats stand in the grounds, cutlass in hand, piles of cocoa from the plantation at their feet. In another, she could make out the same house but with a floor added, propped up by the original levels below. It look as if at any minute it would collapse. In another, an annex appear that don't match the original building at all — too square, neat, with modern, rectangular glass-pane windows. The wraparound extend round the addition but the cocoa houses where they used to dry the beans gone. No more men and women with cutlass; now, ladies with umbrellas posing on the wide porch steps.

Granny Catherine used to say that her mother, Deborah, always swear that one day this ramshackle monster of a house bound to fall down around their ears, but that never happen yet. It just grow and grow to accommodate the needs of each generation. Yejide and Seema and everyone who live in that house could trace their line to someone in that picture; if they squint hard enough could recognize features in their faces as their own.

As they hurry down the corridor, Yejide see the seam in the wall where they cross from a newer part of the house, where her bedroom was, to the older part where Petronella lay. The shift from concrete to wood split time in two. They go up another half-staircase that end in a landing outside of Petronella room and they stop. Pairs of shoes pile up outside; no one would lose the key to their brain and go in Petronella room with shoes on. Yejide feel the walls start to rattle, hear the wind howl, branches crash outside and the galvanize roof flap like the storm centre all its energy here. If she make it out of this, if she survive whatever was supposed to happen to her, she would have to see about getting a new one.

Seema and Yejide take off their shoes and add them to the line. For a moment they both stand at the entrance. What if her mother change her mind and don't want to see her? She imagine Petronella flinging the sheets off her body, leaping from the bed and shrieking, her death whites floating behind her in the wind. Seema give Yejide hand one last squeeze and leave her to enter at her own pace. Yejide take a deep breath, cross the threshold and walk into her mother's bedroom.

The windows open wide to let in the storm, the room littered with slick green leaves from the surrounding forest and everything damp with rain, from the scarred, wooden floorboards to the cedar bedhead etch with their name – St

Bernard. The acrid smell of burnt sage bush fill her lungs. Rainflies buzz around the room. The ones dead or too weak to fly settle in clusters on the wet windowsills and the white sheets like spots of black ash. Dr Arthur stand by the bed, pour Alcolado onto a cloth and dab it on Petronella temples. Seema join those at the bed and tuck the sheets closer around Petronella too-thin frame, Mr Homer wipe down the side-board with a now-sodden cloth, only to see it wet again within seconds as the rain blow in, and Agatha and Angie who live downstairs faces wet with either tears or rain, Yejide can't tell. And Peter, dear Peter.

Yejide stay as near to the door as she could manage, avoiding the open space at her mother's bedside. One by one everyone look up at her quick and return to attending to Petronella. Peter step careful, so he don't slip on the rain-slicked leaves as he move back and forth to empty the buckets around the room collecting the leaks from the old roof. She stop him, touch his forearm. 'Anything yet?'

'Not yet, Princess. I would have come running down the corridor to find you myself.' Peter face look like Seema's – worried, lined, like he holding something in him so tight that if he let it go he might drop the bucket and jump out into the night like Geraldine.

She feel a twinge of guilt. She should have check up on him, ask how he was going. So busy studying herself in her room. Bad enough to fall in love with anybody at all, but to love a woman who heart split in two, the other part residing in the body of a dead woman. She wonder if Peter ration his own heart, loving just enough so he have something left for himself when Petronella up and leave, just so when the storm decide it was time. If there was anyone else in the wide world who know what it felt like to always be second in the life of the person they loved, anyone who know the ache of loving Petronella, it was Peter.

He put the bucket down, place his hands on her shoulders and turn her to him. 'Listen, Princess, is a long time I here with your mother. Don't worry. Soon. Storm nearly reaching its peak.' He kiss her softly on her cheek, pick up the bucket and walk down the corridor. Yejide look after him – strong, brown arms, wiry with years of work, back straight and sure – and for a minute his strength and vitality despite his age seem obscene next to her mother, his woman, lying in the bed, a lump amid white, rain-soaked sheets. Peter in their lives, steady as a tree, for years but even he can do nothing now but wait.

She feel suddenly tired. This was how it was for them – death and dying and living all at once, this relentless cycle. And just like that she see the truth plain. All this waiting have no point. Her mother would not speak to her; she would carry the secrets to her grave and be reunited with her sister, which was all she ever really wanted.

Yejide suppose she can't grudge her mother that, even after everything. Is not an easy thing to carry, even she can see that, and perhaps a woman have the right to say enough is enough and die on her own terms. Maybe this would be it. They could end it now and she could be free. Nothing passed on. Nothing tying her to the women who came before.

Yejide glad she didn't look too hard at the bed, didn't break the code and look at her mother face before she call her. She would remember her mother as she was in life – cold and distant, yes, but also a woman who whisper to her sister in corners as they arrange the deep red ginger lilies from the garden. She would remember them making tea together, each stirring the other's cup and knowing just how much sugar and milk the other liked, finishing at almost the same moment.

She would not remember Petronella alone in the rocking chair. She would not remember her in this bed with the storm raging around her. After all these years, perhaps it was time that the dead learn how to stay dead, how to take care of themselves without the St Bernard women to keep them company.

She turn away and step back across the threshold to the corridor, just a single step, and she feel a pull, low and deep inside her, like somebody sink a hook into her belly and yank from behind. The same hollow keening place fill up and spill over. The pain of it make her stumble and she hold on to the doorframe to catch herself.

'Daughter.' Her mother voice cut into her, strong as ever. She turn around expecting to see relief on the faces of everyone in the room, that Petronella was miraculously well and had spoken at last. She raise her eyes to her mother face and almost fall over with shock. Petronella age about twenty years in the last three days. Her smooth cheeks lined with folds, her mouth shut up in a frown, her lips downturned like her face heavy and her mouth can't hold it up no more. The fine moles that had dotted her face look larger and more plentiful now. And her skin have a grey, ashy undertone. But no one else seem to hear her voice. Agatha still weeping, Mr Homer still wiping the windowsill, the rainflies still buzzing and no Peter. Even Seema remain at the bedside, her gaze on Petronella old-lady face.

Yejide swear she starting to hear things. She need sleep, can't remember when last she eat. She will go downstairs and find some of the soup that she sure Seema leave keeping warm on the stove.

But as she turn to walk away, the pull worsen. The wind

pause, the slightest break in the rain, and her mother voice again, twisting her insides.

'You really think it would be that easy?'

She hear Agatha voice droning the rosary, the sound of wings flapping and then nothing.

10

Darwin

Darwin walk up the wooden staircase to the top floor of the admin building in Fidelis and knock on the door.

'Come!' a woman voice call out.

He push open the door and walk into an office that look like it about as old as Fidelis – overflowing filing cabinets and rusty chairs with the inside fluff coming through the outside, wooden floorboards and dingy walls. Mrs Shirley buzzing around, her white hair a little bit purple. Darwin smile to himself. A sweet old lady. Only thing missing was the rollers and hairnet.

But when she turn around, he realize her hair had nothing to do with her age at all. Finger waves neat against the hairline, silvery lilac curls tight against her head. She had on a pressed skirt suit and her nails was bright red. He see a little spot where she darn a hole in her jacket, but the work was neat. If he didn't grow with a seamstress all his life, he woulda never notice.

'Morning, Mrs Shirley—' She raise a hand and cut him off and she whirl from the files on the desk to the cabinet and start to dig up in them, her lips moving but no sound coming out.

He wander over to the small window and look out on the cemetery, waiting for her to finish. From above he see the layout of Fidelis clear – the main roads line with tall palm trees make a giant cross in the centre. A big sprawling tree with branches spreading wide stand in each corner, and the perimeter is a thick grey stone wall. Inside, everything is white and stone and moss and weeds. From above, the mausoleums look like small houses – some with pitched roofs, some flat like galvanize, some concrete with stalks growing out the cracks. He see McIntosh and Jamesy sitting on a culvert, sharing a cigarette on the main road, a car driving down one of the narrower streets, wilted flowers on low piles of dirt. He even see Errol stand up just inside the big gate talking to a man he never see before. He look closer. Maybe is another worker come to join the crew. The man pull a envelope out his jacket and hand it to Errol. The foreman don't look at it, just nod and stick it in his pocket too. Then the man walk out the gate onto St Brigitte Avenue, get into the backseat of a fancy car, peel off round the corner and disappear into the city.

Outside the cemetery walls look like a different world. Cars in traffic, glass-front stores with people going in and out, the tall steel towers of the electricity company in the distance, smoke puffing from the stacks into the sky. And although he not high enough to see much further, he imagine the rest of the city look like the same grid expanding outward – from slate-grey headstones and crying-baby-angel statues, to shops and cars and vendors and booths and bars that open already and bars that never close, to people that sleeping rough on the pavement, others looking for a fix to get them through the day. Port Angeles seem even bigger now than he imagine it before, a place that not only wide but have all kinda layers and hidden corners and subterranean levels that you could only find if you know where to look.

He imagine the city spreading bigger and bigger until it reach the foothills where the wide roads melt into narrow lanes and winding paths that the government never pave yet, until it disappear into surrounding mountains. If the city not big enough to hide you, the forest will take you just as well. How much times he read in the papers that somebody disappear walking between they office and they car a block away? Or a mother turn from a child for a second, look back and child gone? A woman get in the wrong taxi and never reach home? 'That place could swallow a man whole, Emmanuel,' Janaya say. He could see it.

'Right.' Mrs Shirley was ready for him. 'You is the new boy?'

'Yes, ma'am. Darwin. Errol send me for the information for the burial today.'

'How you only now come up to see me?' She frown at him.

'Sorry, Mrs Shirley—'

'Just, Shirley, dear.'

'Sorry. Shirley.' He didn't know he was supposed to come and see her. Errol didn't say nothing about that.

'How long you come?'

'Last week.'

'Humph. Okay. Lemme take a look at you.'

She watch him up and down, her eyes sharp. 'You eh looking too worse for the wear yet. How you managing?'

'It okay. Errol say things slow for now. They mainly have me doing some cleaning, picking up rubbish. I getting to know the place.'

'Right. Well, first thing lemme tell you. Them fellas will have you think that is them running things here, but you see these?' She hold up a file with flimsy pieces of paper sticking out all over. One of them float down to the floor. 'A cemetery is just fertilizer for the trees without these.' She stick the file in the magic expanding cabinet, take a next file out, as tattered as the last, and push the cabinet halfway shut.

'Everybody who bury here have a file. They have nobody

down there,' she point out the window, 'that not in here. And this is just what we have on site. They have a whole set of other records in the archives. Anything you want to know about Port Angeles, who live here, die here, who had money and who had none, who in the family plan for the future and who have to scramble last minute to figure out grave business because they never think about dying in they life – all here in these files.'

'Everybody who ever die in this city bury here?'

'Don't be stupid. This is not the only cemetery. And cemetery eh the only place people bury either, if you know what I mean. But, is the biggest so.' She shrug.

Something flutter like a tiny echo in Darwin chest.

'Right! Look the file here.' She pull out a brown Manila folder. 'Mrs Emily Julius. Husband, Beresford Julius. He come a few days ago with the grave paper, poor soul. I had to make a cup of tea for the man, fuss he look like a strong breeze could blow him away. It hard when they have no children, eh, and is only them. When one die the next one don't know what to do with theyself.

'Seeing here on the death certificate that she was eighty-five. That is a good age! She bat a good innings, live a long life, and no one could ask for much more than that. The Father going to call us all home one day and all we could do is make sure we right in His sight when the number call, amen?' She look up at him when a beat pass and he hasn't responded. He nod in agreement.

'Right. 12th Street, plot 45. Best to dig this one nine feet deep. The way the husband look this morning he going to follow not too long after.' She scribble something on a piece of paper and hand it to him. 'Plot 45. Nine feet. Don't forget. Look, I write it down for you. Just in case.'

But Darwin still trying to wrap his mind around it all. A whole story, a whole death just there in black and white, on tattered bits of paper. He take the scrap from Shirley hand and shake his head. 'Is something else, eh? This one room have people whole life in it – but just files, just paper. Something that anybody could just come and read. I never imagine a place like this.'

'What? You want me lose my work? Not at all. Nobody can't come and dig up in these files but me. And it have other places too, other clerks in other record offices. Any person want to see them would have to make a request.'

'Right. Okay.'

'You want to find out something?'

'I just thinking about what you say. What the grave papers do to make the cemetery real . . .'

Shirley study him and lean back on the rickety office chair. 'You know what a grave is, Darwin? Is the only piece of real estate most people own in they whole life. Each one have a deed like a house, like any other piece of land. When people bring in this,' she pull out a yellowing piece of paper from the file and flap it at him, 'it let me know that the plot belong to their people and so they could bury somebody in it. It does pass down in families, see? So, each grave have a story. Could have four, five, eight people bury there one on top the other over the years.'

Darwin swallow hard. In his mind he see bodies and bodies lying one on top the other like in a slave ship. Rotting bodies, best suits crumbling into nothing, one setta bones mix up in another setta bones. Every step he take in this place he walking on dead people.

Shirley wasn't done. He feel like she spend time rehearsing this speech, and she want him to hear all of it, make sure he understand. 'Why you think we don't just bury people anyhow? Why people bother with headstone and decoration and flowers? Is to remember. Grave is home, grave is lineage. Grave is to know where your people is, even if you can't see them anymore.'

She lift up a few files and shake them at him. 'Every person, they family, where they bury, how deep, where they come from, what version of God they feel waiting for them all in here. This room,' she flick her hand and gesture to the cabinets, the shelves, the piles on her desk, 'is the real heartbeat of Fidelis. Don't forget that, no matter what them fellas outside will tell you.'

'Right.' He nod at her, his head spinning.

'Go on. Errol waiting for that paper.'

The boys stand around the plot where they going to dig the grave — Jamesy and Mikey on one side, Ricardo on the next.

The day still young and the dew make the tall grass wet and cold but the only thing in Darwin mind was the old lady, Emily Julius — how a whole life could fit in a hole in the ground.

Jamesy take out a spray-paint bottle from his back pocket, step one foot on the plot and start to shake the bottle, clack-clacking the little ball that stir the paint. 'So, I tell her, big-man ting, is time to cut the boy hair. She can't have no son of mine walking about looking like he is a little girl . . .'

Jamesy watch the plot as he talk. He walk around it, size it up. 'I mean, was alright when he was a baby, but he going primary school jus now,' he spray the paint on the ground, one long line on the left, short one to the top, long line to the right, no ruler, no tools, just his eyes and feet to measure the space, 'but she say she family from Venezuela nah, so she have this ting about sorf hair and she like how the boy hair curly-curly.'

'Bout Venezuela.' Cardo steups. 'Is up in the cocoa she from. I hear bout she sister an dem.'

'That is what you get for going behind red woman, eh?' Mikey laugh.

Jamesy steups and keep marking out the plot. 'You know I doh run down no woman. Is she who come looking for me!'

Darwin put his foot up on the overturn wheelbarrow next to him. He try to look like if it was the most normal thing in the world, to stand on the solid ground and watch it turn into a grave. He half-wish he could join in, say something funny and make them all laugh, slap him on the shoulder. But he can't say a word. All he hear in his head is the broken vow. *All the days that he separates himself to the Lord he shall not go near a dead body.*

'I don't see no problem,' Errol grumble. 'Cut the boy hair and breed yuh wife again. Give she a daughter to study. Matter fix.'

'Doh worry boy, Jamesy,' Mikey jump in. 'If you eh able I could help you.' Everybody laugh out into the morning.

Darwin try to laugh too but is like a ball stick in his throat. He break his vow, make his choice, but standing there on top somebody else bones, waiting for the work to start, make him feel like any second Fidelis would swallow him whole.

He think about the woman who they was going to bury. He don't even know her, but he keep studying how just a few days before she must be was reading papers, drinking tea on her gallery or baking bread for her husband, the same sad old man Mrs Shirley tell him come to see about the grave paper for her funeral. Darwin glad he didn't see him; woulda make the whole thing too real. But thinking about Mrs Julius alive and doing alive things help him keep himself together. He don't look at the plot.

Cardo come to stand next to Darwin. 'Don't worry, man. He only looking like he eh taking on what he doing, but Jamesy is a boss. He could measure ting in his head exact. Just how wide and just how deep. He have a sense about them tings.'

They watch Jamesy dig along the white lines. When he done, Cardo stick his shovel in the ground at the head of the grave and use his boot to push it deep. Then he pull it out full and empty the soil on the side, on top the neighbouring plot. Jamesy move to dig in the centre and Mikey at the foot.

Errol don't dig at all but stand to the top of the wall, watching. Darwin can't see how three big man could fit on one grave. It get bigger for them, or maybe they doing it so long is like a dance and they know how to make space, so each man don't tangle with the other. Sometimes one shovel hit the next one and the sound when they clash make Darwin cold all down to his boots, but it don't bother the rest of them at all and they just keep digging.

The pile of dirt get higher. Darwin hold on tight to the handles of the wheelbarrow. He know his turn coming, that he have to take his own shovel and dig into the dirt piling on top of the next grave, load it onto the barrow and carry it off to the side so it don't slide back into the hole, but he can't move, and the air that was only a little cool just before start to feel like it cutting into him. His hands feel like stone. He hope that them fellas so busy digging that they don't see him just standing there like a fool. He sure any second now somebody go see how it taking everything in him to stay put, see his lips moving, muttering, *Yea, though I walk through the valley of the shadow of death, I will fear no evil: for thou art with me; thy rod and thy staff they comfort me.*

He stay on the outskirts. The red-brown dirt dry from days of no rain pile higher and higher and Jamesy knee-deep in the hole. Darwin try his best to look somewhere else, anywhere, but the pile start to slip, Jah it start to slip back in the hole. He watch it, helpless.

'Darwin boy, yuh sleeping!' Errol shout at him. Darwin wheel the barrow closer to the edge of the mound, grip the shovel and stick it in the pile of loose earth. He bend his back into it and fill the shovel with the red dirt and empty it into the barrow.

One, then another and another, and he hear Errol grunt like he satisfy to see how they working. Then is a rhythm set up between him and the crew, a relay – one shovel hit earth and a man scrape and empty it on the side, another man shovel hit earth and he too empty it on the side – and then Darwin dig into the pile, a softer crunch and the small stones and the dry earth settle in the barrow. Cardo, then Jamesy, then Mikey and now him, shovelling the dirt and filling the barrow, and the sound of the steel on the dirt and the shovels clanging against each other and his shovel hitting the iron of the barrow and is all sound and muffled sound till the barrow full. He rest down the shovel and wheel the barrow just a few feet away. Them feet save him, and he could breathe again, just a little bit. *Thou preparest a table before me in the presence of mine enemies: thou anointest my head with oil; my cup runneth over* . . . until he empty the barrow and go back to refill it. Once, twice, three times, four.

Jamesy in the hole, up to his thighs, up to his chest, and Darwin try not to look at him, his body disappearing with each movement of the shovel, each deepening of the pit. He try not to look, he try, but like the hole just keep pulling him and he can't help it: the more Jamesy disappear into the earth, the more the pit pull Darwin and he have to look.

And then down in the hole he see his mother, Janaya, lie down in the dirt watching him, watching him dig a grave, watching him prepare the way for a woman who had bat a good innings and who husband needed tea from a stranger to brace himself, to keep putting one foot in front of the other. And her face was like if ants start to eat it away, her locks long, thick and digging into the earth, her mouth full of black beetles trying to live in the back of her throat. But it was her eyes that nearly kill him. Her eyes still open, still perfect, still clear, watching him and crying till she cry so much that her tears fill the hole and drown the grave.

The hole get deeper and the mound get taller and Darwin realize that everybody quiet. Nothing but the sound of big men breathing and shovel scraping dirt and iron clanging on iron. And just so is like he see all the men for the first time, like he see all down to the parts of them that nobody else don't even know there. No matter how much they joke and laugh and act like this work was nothing, even them fellas know a grave, when it there just open in front of you. He hold the last of the psalm tight for himself and for them too. *Surely goodness and mercy shall follow me all the days of my life: and I will dwell in the house of the Lord forever.*

II

A old-model Corolla drive through the big iron gate and park up on the wide main street. Then a next car reach and a next one until is about ten or so people, face serious, heading toward Mrs Julius grave. Is mostly men – one younger woman look like she is the wife of one of them and a next older lady who walk with a cane – but mostly men. Some look like around McIntosh age, fifties, some forties. Some young like Darwin. He wonder if some was father and son. He find himself looking at their faces, how they shape, the eyes, the way they walk, how they shoulders set. Then the black hearse with LONG WALK FUNERAL HOME in gold on the side drive in and Errol tell the crew is time to go back.

As soon as Darwin reach the graveside he could tell which one was Mr Julius. He look just like Shirley describe him with the grey suit wrinkle like if he barely manage to dig it out and put it on last minute. He stand up right at the edge of the grave, shoes almost bury in the dirt. A next old man keep trying to pull him back – 'You too close, Beresford, you going to fall' – but Mr Julius shake him off. He look like, between living and falling into the grave with his wife, he figure he would take his chances.

Darwin never went a funeral before, but he assume it woulda be plenty crying, some kind of priest, people singing hymns. Every time he pass one in the village, was always a priest in long robes praying and somebody bawling and making a big production, so some friend or family would have to hold them up and carry them away or rub them down with some Alcolado or bay rum to keep them cool and in they right mind. But this funeral quiet. A man in a white suit say a little something and Errol and McIntosh dig a few shovels even though the grave near-empty. Then two men wheel the shiny mahogany coffin out the hearse, stand it up on a metal rack next to the grave and open it so Mr Julius could look inside one last time. Darwin turn away. He can't take that one, can't take watching the old man look in the coffin. Mr Julius make a sound like the end of a fight when you get so much blows that it eh even make sense to bawl anymore.

McIntosh look at the man standing next to Mr Julius, the one who was trying to stop him falling in the grave, and he nod at McIntosh – yes, go ahead. The next man who come with the hearse close the coffin and the boys lower it into the hole. When the first shovel of dirt hit the casket, Mr Julius stumble and they have to brace him. Darwin wish he have somebody to steady him too. The last time he use a shovel to transplant flowers in his mother's yard, the sound of the dirt filling the clay pot had hope in it. When he put earth into a pot and pack it and water it and cover it down with his hands, it was the beginning of something good. But it have no beginnings in the sound of old red dirt hitting a coffin.

They fill back the hole like something chasing them. Darwin body feel like it on fire. He wasn't no stranger to work, but gravedigging have a heaviness that take something from his spirit. All the while he keep watching Mr Julius. Each time the dirt hit the coffin something dim in the old man face and his shoulders hunch a little more. Each return with the barrow make Darwin feel more lost and he don't know how he could do this again, day after day, month after month, year after year, how he could be the person that take a man wife from him for the last time, the person that throw dirt on the only thing he have left to love in the world.

When they finish, the mourners dress it up with yellow-gold marigolds and white lilies. Mr Julius just stand there looking at his hands. McIntosh touch Darwin on his shoulder. 'Time to go, boy.' And they walk away, leaving the people with their dead.

No one say much until they reach the admin building. Errol pull out a bottle from under the steps, crack it and pour a little bit onto the concrete. Then he pass it around to each of the men. McIntosh take a long drink then pass it to Jamesy. Darwin hang back out of the circle and look toward the main street. One of the men get in a car with the lady who needed help to walk, then drive off and another man walk out of the gate. He wonder about Mr Julius, if he have anyone to stay with him. He wonder what go happen when he reach home to an empty house.

'You work good today, Darwin,' Errol call out.

'I tell you I could work hard.' Darwin make a point to stand straight so Errol can't see how much the day really take out of him.

'Ent fellas?' Errol look around at the crew. 'The youth man handle himself good today?'

The men grunt and agree. McIntosh clap Darwin on his shoulder. Cardo take the bottle from Jamesy, point it at Darwin like a salute, then drink too.

'See? I does have a sense about these things.' Errol smiling at him. 'I know I was giving you trouble first but I feel good about it now. You alright, man, you could handle yourself.'

Darwin feel his muscles ease a little bit. 'Thanks, boss.' The heaviness in the air when they was digging gone and

Darwin feel like finally pass one of the tests he failing since he walk into Fidelis.

Errol reach down into his pocket, 'Here,' and hand Darwin money in some rolled-up bills.

'What this for?' Darwin already collect his pay at the regional corporation office. Errol is the boss, yes. But he a different kind of boss, not the invisible one who sign the cheques.

'Somebody give you money and you ask where it come from? You eh easy.' Errol laugh at him, mouth open wide, and Darwin could see every one of his too-white teeth.

Darwin take the bills from Errol hand and stuff them into his pocket. Errol give cash to the other men and everybody take it like is a normal thing. But when Cardo hand the bottle to Darwin, he hesitate.

'Is rum, boy, not poison.' Cardo turn up his face at Darwin like he always know something had to be wrong with him. 'You don't smoke and you don't drink either? You is a monk ah wha?' He shake his head and pass the bottle to Errol instead.

Darwin don't answer. He never taste alcohol in his whole life, but he don't want to break the vibes growing between them.

'Listen, boy, this is not a vice ting.' Errol shake the bottle at Darwin. 'You can't do this work and not share something with the dead. That is ting to get yourself in trouble.' He press the bottle into Darwin hands. 'Is an exchange, is a trade. Here.'

He take it. The liquid clear like water, but it smell like the medicine Ms Enid use to clean cuts and scrapes. He put the bottle to his mouth and tip his head back. It burn like fire and he only drink little bit before handing it over. His throat hurt but when the bottle come back again, the circle of men open for him. And just like that, he is one of them.

12

By the time the boys gone Darwin could only sit on the admin building steps and watch the ground spin. No wonder them fellas does only drink this after. Puncheon was the devil. It wasn't a high like when he sit in the backyard and smoke with his mother. When they pass a chalice between them, his heart feel full and he could see abundance everywhere.

Herb make him feel like planting, watering the flowers in the garden or running his hands over the leaves to check for bugs or blight. It make his mother rock back and hum soft and ease the pain in her fingers and it make him feel like he could pull green from the earth anywhere he trod. But the rum make him feel heavy and slow, like he might sink into the ground if he stand up long enough.

He sit on the steps and lean against the door, head bad. Was the only comfortable position he could find. But maybe it was worth it, just a small thing to make sure that the fellas don't give him such a hard time. And anyway, he have money now. Is not plenty money but more than he had in his pocket before. Between last week pay and the extra that Errol give him, he already have something to send back to his mother. He wonder if she would take it. True, she leave the bake for him, but money he earn from dealing with the dead was a different thing. Ms Enid would have to talk some sense into her. Nothing honourable in being hungry.

The door open behind him and nearly send him tumbling down the steps. He look up and see is Mrs Shirley smiling at him.

'Darwin, you still here?' She shake her head like she catch him doing some little-boy foolishness.

He stand up to let her pass and then sit back down on the steps again quick. 'Yes, ma'am. Just closing up.'

'You alright, son?' She push her glasses up on her face.

Darwin nod but don't trust himself to speak. The shift from sitting to standing to sitting again make him feel like he was trying to walk through water.

'Don't worry,' she tell him. 'It will get easier.' She dig around in her handbag and pull out her car keys. 'You just wait until you have to bury a child. Those tiny coffins. You think this was hard? Even after all these years sometimes I does need to take a sick day after those.'

Darwin breathe deep and try not to let the picture of a baby-size coffin form in his mind.

'Anyway,' she turn to go, 'see you tomorrow.'

He lean back on the door and watch her walk away.

'And Darwin,' she call over her shoulder, 'next time when they pass the rum, just pretend to drink it. Don't let them boys tie you up!'

Was the best idea he hear all day.

When the afternoon bustle outside turn to evening sounds and his head stop spinning, he force himself to make the rounds before locking up. Errol now start to trust him, and he don't want to think what he would say if Darwin start slacking off already.

He make his way along the spine of the cemetery, looking down each street. Where he have a clear view he could tell easy that no one lurking, but where a big mausoleum or structure block the path he had to walk all the way to make sure he don't miss anyone. His head still spinning but the walk doing him good. With each step he feel a little more steady and the air feel less thick now that the heat start to leave the day and fewer cars outside blowing exhaust fumes. But drunk is drunk so he take it easy, put one foot in front the other, no rush.

Over the last week Errol had him doing mainly cleaning work – tidying up the graves, clearing up rubbish people leave behind. He had start picking up little bits of stories about the graves too, piecing together things he learn from the headstones. At 3rd Street he let the fingertips of one hand touch the rough stone of Father Maurice tomb. McIntosh tell him the priest had come from Ireland and leave the priesthood for a Panyol woman he meet in the parish. Father Maurice, the woman he pick up, and all their children buried there. Nobody know how they let him have full title on the tombstone like if he didn't leave the church and make a boatload of children with a woman half his age, but 'Fidelis is a funny place,' McIntosh say, 'and them old Catholics had their own ways of resolving things like that.'

He reach 5th Street and stroke the low iron fence that bar off a full section of people that die from cholera long time ago. The gate that surround them have a plaque with all the names. He had start to pay attention to the ones that nobody go to. It feel a way that no one alive to come and visit them and clean the graves. Weeds grow all over the plots and he decide to clear it properly soon.

When Errol carry him around that first day he thought the order was clear – some places was where rich people bury and some places poor – but more and more he see Fidelis not so simple. Most of the graves here had small headstones: no marble, no mausoleums, just concrete or stone. Newer graves too: 1967, 1943, 1981. Civil servants, maybe teachers, shopkeepers, maybe even people like him, like the person he want to be. People who had work hard and get a bit of money together, maybe live in a nice house, nothing big, nothing fancy, a little yard in the front where they plant some flowers and maybe even some seasoning, some tomatoes, some sweet peppers, something that was just enough to make you feel happy when you reach home at the end of a day, something to make you feel like you didn't waste your whole life just struggling, fighting up for nothing. A good life.

And then sometimes in the middle of them one stand out – a mausoleum, a fancy gated-off set of graves – like this one name St Bernard. Plenty people bury here. Structure sturdy but the graves a little overgrown like nobody come to visit recently. He make a note to do some weeding there tomorrow too.

He duck down 11th Street and nearly jump. A man with long dreadlocks standing in the middle, but way off in the distance. Errol had tell him the point of walking around was to make sure nobody get left behind but he never expect to actually see anyone.

'Sir, we closing up now!' He throw his voice toward the figure. But the man don't even turn around.

Darwin call out again and start moving closer, lose his footing on a rough piece of ground and trip a little, right himself. And then the man not there. He stop and look around, but he can't see him nowhere. He shake his head. The statues and trees in this place could make you see things if you not careful. And it easy to slip away between the shadows.

He walk slower now and reach the spot where he see the man. On one side a dead house cover in vines. On the other, a grave with overgrown weeds, no headstone. His head start to spin. Maybe he not so sober yet. Between digging the grave, watching the sad little parade of mourners who come to support the old man, and now this. He think of the man who drive the hearse, the pastor in the white suit, the one who was help-ing the old lady. For all he know, any one of them could be his own family, any one of them maybe could resemble him if he look at them in the right light. Is not like he have a whole setta family to compare his features to. He shake his head. Swear this is the last time he taking a drink ever again in his life. He didn't think he swallow that much but drunk must be a thing that don't happen halfway. He breathe in the cool air deep and head back to the main road.

From the top of 12th Street, Darwin could see the flowers on Mrs Julius grave, the yellow and gold marigolds glow-ing in the late-afternoon light. And right up ahead, almost miss him, almost pass straight, stumble a little bit trying to make sure – this one real or is the puncheon? No. Real. Right there on the low wall where Errol had stand up directing them earlier – he squint to be sure – yes, was the husband, Mr Julius. He slump over like a bag of flour, the tall weeds between the graves almost blocking him from view.

Darwin walk toward him and try to think of what Errol would do, or McIntosh or Jamesy, but none of them here now. He have to figure this one out for himself. Mr Julius suit look as if he really slip and fall like his friends warn him, and his shoes that was probably black and shiny when he leave home this morning was covered with red dirt. The old man don't even look up and Darwin wonder if he know he not alone anymore.

'Greetings,' he call out soft, not wanting to jumbie him, 'Mr Julius?'

But like he was somewhere else. Maybe he was at home in his favourite chair waiting for his wife to come and sit next to him. Maybe he was helping her cook, cutting up vegetables while she stir the pot. Maybe he was listening to her laugh.

'Mr Julius, I am one of the workers. I was here earlier. I have to lock up in a few minutes.' He think about how the gate still open. Somebody coulda walk in by now and he would have to make the whole rounds again just to be sure. He study his good clean pants and then circle the grave and sit next to Mr Julius. The old man skin was a dusty black like charcoal. Not too much wrinkles. Is the eyes that really show his age. Deep, puffy bags under them and heavy like he see enough and tired of it all. 'You want me to call somebody? You have anybody who could come and stay with you home?' Still nothing.

The sun fading fast like it running a race with itself and the last thing Darwin want is to be still sitting here when it start to get dark. He don't know what to say to the man. He don't know nothing about death. Man like him does only deal with life. What happen when the body give out is a thing for the earth to decide. But he know he have to tell the man something. He could still hear the sound he make when he look in the coffin for the last time.

'Uncle, I don't want to say I know how you feel. Is not my place but . . . she not there, you know' – Darwin look down at the flowers – 'your wife. She gone somewhere else. It not good for you to sit here like this. What there in the ground is a dead. Is not your wife.' Mr Julius flinch like if he only just realize someone sitting next to him at all.

'Where your friends who come here with you?'

'Friends?' The old man say the word so soft that Darwin not sure for a second if he hear it at all. 'You married, son?'

Darwin shake his head. 'No, I not married.'

'Look at you.' Mr Julius study Darwin. 'You still have your mother's milk in your face. What you could come and tell me about where my wife is?' Mr Julius voice get strong, angry. 'Son, I married to Emily since before you born.'

Darwin look down at Mr Julius hands. A slim wedding ring on his left and a heavy gold guard on the right, the kinda ring people does get blessed to shield them from demon in this world and the next. He try to imagine that. Living with somebody for so long. He never even really see his mother with a man. Ms Enid neither.

Mr Julius voice start to tremble. 'I never spend one night away from her since we married. Not one night. You know anything about that, boy?' He turn away from Darwin and keep his eyes on the grave. 'You ask me about friend? That woman in the ground is my friend.'

Darwin don't say nothing, and they sit in the quiet. He know that only way Mr Julius leaving Emily here tonight is if he pick him up and throw him out, but he don't have the heart to do that. He look around at the graves. Upstairs in Mrs Shirley office was all the files with names and dates and numbers that say who bury in what grave, how deep, who they family was, but sitting with Mr Julius, listening to his breathing, the sound of a car driving past outside, bits of conversation over the wall, the stone hard beneath him, his muscles aching, the keys to Fidelis in his pocket, somehow, just for a second, all of it, the whole terrible day feel kinda like a gift.

'I have a son, you know.'

Darwin flinch. That is the last thing he expect the man to say. He feel like Mr Julius wasn't even talking to him anymore, not really, his fingers twisting the rings on either hand.

'Not with the madam. Before I meet her. I never tell her. Emily wasn't the kind of girl who family would have taken to that.' Mr Julius face spread into a smile. His teeth was good for a man his age, good and straight in the near-dark. 'My Emily? Lord! That girl was pretty like the morning! She never even used to be in the street without her mother. I used to have to time their outings to even catch a glimpse of her as she pass and send letter with the girl who clean for them.' He shake his head and look down at his feet. 'I don't know how I get so lucky.'

The smile fade. 'I used to send money when he was small. But it was hard. Hard to see him, you know? But I pay the embassy for the visa and the passage for them to go up to the States when the mother ask. I do my best, you know?'

Darwin don't know. He don't know at all. He feel something start to rise up his throat, but he swallow it down, deep. He don't want to put that on the grieving man. Not tonight. Sometimes when he not expecting it, a memory does come in his head, so faint he not sure if he make it up. A man who face was just shadow and smoke, dreadlocks big and thick like a lion's mane. When he was small he used to try and remember more, imagine he and the man used to play in the yard, or maybe that the man used to teach him things, talk to him, but after a while, well, is just so far he could stretch one memory. When Janaya was in a good mood, when they smoke something or music sweet on the radio, she let a name slip – Levi. She say it with a trace of a smile on her lips and it sound like spring water. Other times, when she think he not around and she and Enid talking, another name drop out her mouth – Carlton, this one hard like rock stone. He know, though he don't know how, that they was one and the same. He always tell himself his mother was enough for him. He never wonder until now, sitting there listening to Mr Julius talk about his wife, whether he had been enough for his mother.

Mr Julius reach out his hand and touch Darwin shoulder. 'The hardest thing in the world is to be a good man. You always end up failing somebody.'

The street lights around Fidelis flicker and switch on. Darwin stand up and try not to step on the grave. 'I going to leave the gate open, okay? It go look like it lock but if you just unwrap the chain you could push it open. So, you could stay with the madam a little while.' He turn to go. 'You go be alright, uncle?' He know is a stupid question, but he have to ask. Mr Julius just look up at Darwin and don't say nothing.

One of the bouquets of flowers tumble down off the grave and Darwin pause to fix it before he cross the loose dirt and walk away. He sure his pants dirty from sitting on the wall but he don't mind. When he reach the crossroads, he turn back and look at Mr Julius. The sky the same colour as the marigolds.

THE BIRD WOMEN

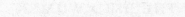

13

Yejide

The garden spring up around Yejide, green, lush and still. No blankets, no rainflies, no burning black sage. The mist was heavy on the hills after the rain and the sky like slate. Nothing in the forest breathing.

Yejide not sure if she breathing either. Beside her, in Geraldine chair, was her mother, Petronella, as if the last few days didn't happen at all. The grey leave her cheeks and instead of death whites she wore the same long green dress with the lace collar that Geraldine had on in Yejide dream three nights before. It spill over the sides of the chair and trail in the wet grass. A gold locket hang open around her neck; inside it a photo of Petronella and Geraldine as little girls in identical dresses.

Yejide tongue feel heavy and her eyes burn like somebody pack them with salt. She feel her body on the chair, the rough wicker on the backs of her legs, the wet grass beneath her feet and mud squelching between her toes. But she could also feel something else. The touch of hands on her face, the movement of air around her as people rush past, the brush of a skirt, then fingers, something round and cold in her hand.

She try to focus: the mountains, the riot of red ginger lilies, the slope of the garden, the forest at its border, her mother beside her. But at the edges: her mother's bedroom, Peter fanning her with an old *Daily Word* magazine, Seema holding her head in her lap, Agatha clutching the rosary beads. She look again, harder. Beyond the garden, beyond the room: a blue that twitch and pulse like muscle. She feel it more than she see it. Feel and see get muddled in her brain; she not sure of the difference.

Petronella reach a hand into her pocket, pull out a flat gold cigarette case, open it, take out a roll-up tobacco cigarette and then offer the case to Yejide. Yejide stare at her mother. Again, feel and see. How to separate them? Several faces superimpose onto one: Deborah's hair and upturn eyes, Maman's frown, Granny Catherine's pipe in her mother's slender hand – no, not a pipe, a cigarette thin and white. She try to make sense of it and centre her vision, but she can't hold it. It split and layer and multiply.

Petronella frown and flick the case at Yejide again. 'You were never the smartest child, but even you should know that when a dead woman offers you a cigarette, the polite thing to do would be to take it. Especially when that dead woman is your mother.'

Yejide reach out and take one. Two sensations at once: the hardness of the round metallic object. Peter? Yes, Peter had placed something in her hand. There, smooth and cold against her fingers, and here, the smooth paper of the cigarette.

Petronella rummage in her other pocket for matches, touch her cigarette with the flame and inhale deep. She cup her hand to protect the flame, lean over and light her daughter's. Yejide fumble with the cigarette – is years since she had one – put it to her lips and inhale a little bit. The smoke scorch her throat and she fight not to cough. It taste bitter and acrid, not like the stolen cigarettes of her youth, not like Granny Catherine's sweet tobacco that to her always smell like if blue had a scent. And there, under the taste, the smells from her mother's bedroom: the bay rum, the Tiger Balm, the sage smoke thick at the back of her tongue.

The mist murmur around them. Yejide don't know what to say. She sneak a look at her mother out the corner of the eye and pretend to smoke the cigarette. Today, somehow, while her mother face as different from her own as ever, something about the set of her mouth, the way she hold her head, cock to the side like she thinking, remind Yejide of herself. Her but not her. Catherine, Deborah, Babygirl – all their faces as one face, as her face.

'Are you dead?' Yejide ask finally.

'Yes,' Petronella answer.

'I dead too?'

'If you was dead you wouldn't have to ask. Dead people does know very well that they dead.'

Petronella take another drag of her cigarette, hold it for a few seconds and blow the smoke out slow. 'I can't taste a thing. I can't feel the heat, taste the sweetness. I can't even feel it against my lips.' She flick the ash in the grass at her feet, then relight Yejide neglected cigarette, which has gone out while she hold it. 'You could mistake plenty things but being dead isn't one of them.'

'I'll keep that in mind for when I die, then.'

Petronella grunt. Almost a laugh but like she forget how to properly make the sound.

Yejide try to come to grips with her senses again. A damp cloth on her forehead now, a cool hand on her cheek. Seema hand in her hair. The window still open, the green leaves wet on the windowsill.

Petronella study her. 'I can't see them. In the room. But I know you can.'

'Is this supposed to happen? I can see everything as if I still there, feel them too, but I here with you.'

'Of course this supposed to happen,' Petronella snap. 'Any damn thing in this whole house, in this whole family, not supposed to happen? You think we have control over anything that go on inside of here?'

The anger in her voice come off her like silver spikes. Yejide not sure how to respond. Is like she walk in on an argument her mother was having with someone else, an argument that had been going on for a long time.

Petronella settle and look out into the hills. 'Look, stop trying to see one thing, one place. You living Morne Marie all your life. You grow up in a house of dead people. Any place is ever one place?'

Yejide take a deep breath. Breath? It hard to say breath or think of it as breath here. More like a quietening, a stilling, an opening. Her vision close in, get narrow. There was just her mother now. She could still feel them – the room, the twilight – but she could close in her senses on her mother.

Yejide try another pull on the cigarette. The urge to cough was less. She wait for Pet to speak again.

'He good?'

'Who?'

Her mother look straight at her. That impatient look she always get when she expect her daughter to know what she was thinking without explanation.

'Peter?'

'Hmm.' The barest sound of assent.

'Peter is Peter. He is the same.' Yejide could see him in the room again. It was like closing one eye or adjusting a camera lens to achieve a sharper focus. Now he was picking up the leaves that were strewn on the windowsill, the floorboards, circling the bed where Petronella lay, not looking at her, keeping an eye on Yejide in Seema's arms on the floor. She could see her mother's body too – still, her mouth slack, eyes closed, white sheet draped over her small frame, barely there.

'He is a good man. A better man than your father.'

'Better than you deserved.' Yejide blurted it out, anger hot in her, suddenly spoiling for a fight. The evening around her pulse deep blue and then red for one second; the forest shine a deeper green.

Petronella nod and smile. 'That is good. It is best to be honest here. It will save time. But don't forget yourself. When you make a child –'

Yejide groan.

'– and have this burden to bear, then you could tell me bout deserve. Then you could tell me bout right and wrong and better and worse.'

'Right. Like I supposed to just go in the market and ask – What a pound for the man? Like it have man for sale?'

'Wait, you want me to tell you how to do that too?' Petronella steups. 'Look, you is a big woman. Is my job to tell you how to deal with the dead. After that you could figure and decide how you want.'

She flicked the ash from her cigarette again. 'Peter make his choice. I never tie his foot. He know what I am. If he want, he could choose different now.'

'Peter would never just leave us.' Yejide could hear the triumph in her voice, the recrimination, the pride. Peter would not leave her, Peter always been there for her. Even now he hovered over her body in her mother's room, doing the needful, clearing up, looking after them all.

'Don't assume you know what in a man mind, Yejide.'

'Is this you giving me relationship advice?' Yejide almost

laugh out loud. 'It's a little late for bonding, don't you think' –
she gesture around her – 'here in the afterlife and all?'

'You not in the afterlife.' Petronella stare at Yejide long
and hard. The cigarette forgotten, trailing from the tips of
her fingers. 'Just me.'

They lapse into silence again. Why you never love me?
Yejide feel the questions bubbling up behind her throat. Why
you never teach me? Why your grief for her was stronger than
what you owe to me? Instead she scan the sky for the birds.
They always come out after the storm and join the kiskadees,
the best way of telling when the rain well and truly over.
But there was nothing in flight. She look closer, focus on the
scene. Everything get slightly sharper, colours more vivid.

'You are a child still.' Silver spikes back again but more
gunmetal grey now, tempered. 'You still thinking that love is
something soft, something nice.'

'You could read my mind here?' Yejide have the urge to
cover her ears, to block her mouth, like if that could stop her
thoughts from leaking out to her mother.

'Here?' Petronella steups. 'Where you think here is?' She
look even more irritated now and gesture around to the garden
as if it was a simple thing to understand. 'This is your mind.'

Yejide watch the ash drop from the end of Petronella cigarette onto her green dress, and onto the grass at her feet, and
think of the deep red box of resentment in her inventory. Even
here, in what might be the longest conversation she ever had
with her mother, nothing she say or think or feel was good
enough.

'Since the day I make you I start to die.'

She say it so soft that Yejide not sure if she hear her at all.
'What?'

'Since the first day I feel you. Tiny. Faint. Like I swallow

104

a very small fish. Or a feather. I know. This thing we born with . . . At first, it make you feel you special, like if you one holding the whole damn universe together, your own woman body is the thing that keeping life and death in its proper place.' She come to the end of her cigarette, flick the butt in the grass and light a next all in one motion. 'Is a damn lie. This thing don't need you, not really. What it need is heirs. We born when it say, we breed when it say and die when it say. Repeat. Once it have someone alive to do this work, that is all it care about.'

'What "it"? God?'

Petronella cackle. 'See? Child. Big woman like you. God? Which one? Only children does ask about God. We is women.' She pause and glance at Yejide. 'You remember the stories Ma used to tell when you was small? All those stories about the animals and the war and Morne Marie. Every Sunday she would sit you down and tell you stories. You was young but I sure you remember.'

'Didn't think you'd noticed.' Yejide can't control the bitterness in her voice. 'Is not like you ever paid that much attention.'

Either Petronella didn't hear Yejide tone or decide to ignore it. 'You remember how the story end. The parrots ended the great war. They flew east toward the sunrise, turned their green feathers shiny black, and they changed.'

'Yes, I remember.' Yejide feel like she on the verge of tears, hearing Petronella tell Granny Catherine story. She had no sweetness in her voice, like she repeating the words by rote. Just sitting there as calm as ever, as if she don't care, not one bit, that she dead and leaving her, as if she didn't ignore her for the past year, for most of her life.

'The parrots wait for the dead and watch over the carcasses

and consume the flesh. They not concerned with no God and you shouldn't be neither. We come from Death, and Death older than all the gods no matter what they name. Death was done old when man start to look up in the sky to make God. We do her work.'

'So why you send me to church all those years? Why insist that we do Sunday school and Bible study and all that foolishness?'

Petronella shrug. 'I had to go. Your grandmother too. Just because we older than God, don't mean we on bad terms.'

Yejide look around: the garden, the hills, the sky – they all feel real. The room, her kin faces looking down at her, feel real too. Something else should be happening. This can't be it. After every hint that she'd picked up, every whisper of a great family legacy that she would inherit, she was expecting fireworks, hushed, urgent instruction. Not this. Just sitting and having an argument with her dead mother.

'So, what now?'

Petronella close her eyes and start to drum her fingers on her chest to music she alone could hear. 'You feel that?'

'I'm not sure . . .'

'Yes, you sure. There' – she reach out and press her other hand to Yejide pelvis – 'right there.'

Yejide feel the dusk press close behind her eyes and pulse to the beat of Petronella fingers on her chest. Her heart start to race and something pull her low in her gut like it had before. She fight to catch her breath. 'Yes. Yes, I feel it.'

'This is who we are – for whatever it worth. You feeling the thing that in my mother, and her mother and hers, calling to the thing that is you, and in your daughter if you ever get that together, and in her daughter and hers. Now look, see how I press my hand here, to my chest?' Petronella still drumming her fingers, lighter now like she was playing piano, one hand on her own chest, the other on Yejide, pressing. 'All our energies connected to the dead – you, me, your granny, everybody. When I go properly, you will feel it right there, sometimes like a cold wind blowing, sometimes like flesh pulsing, sometimes it touch light and sweet like a lover. See? We all have it. Born with it. That is why we die with the storm. It is just our way of gathering the energy to pass on. When I go from this place, it will pass to you.'

And then Yejide see it, or rather feel – how to see when is not your eyes working? When something in you seeing in a way you never see before? – sharp, shallow needle blues, placenta edges of pink and red and gold, flare then flicker and fade, like a bulb in a dark room.

Petronella grunt again. 'Yes, just so. You starting to see.' Almost sound like approval. 'After a while you will learn to separate the energies, the colours. New dead is not the same as old dead. New dead can be active, troublesome. Need plenty work. Plenty energy to keep them in the ground. Old dead different. Hard still, but different. They mostly gone on, but make no mistake, they still very attached to their bones and their graves and anything they buried with. Matter of fact, the older the grave, the more care it need. You have to make sure the body rest good, bury properly so they don't forget themselves and rage like they want to come back. We take care of them and they take care of us. Exchange.'

'How they take care of us?'

'How you think this house never fall down yet' – she gesture behind her – 'or no one come to trouble us, how no developers reach up the hill yet? Is the dead. The dead make us strong and we give them rest.'

'That sound fair. Like a balance.'

Petronella mouth twist like she taste something bitter. 'You wait until is you. Fair don't always mean good. Exchange don't always mean peace. Power don't always mean free.'

For the first time, something like fear touch Yejide skin and make all the hairs on the back of her neck stand up.

Petronella nod her head toward the deepening dark. It undulate like a cat being stroked, sides muscular and fur bristling. 'There. Focus on it.'

Yejide squint past the garden and the mountains, past the figures in the room, try to pull back the colours to her – the blues, the pinks, the dark purples.

'Not with your eyes, child,' Petronella snap. 'Some things spirit, and some things flesh.' She press low on Yejide belly again, rougher, hurting her now. 'Here. Look with here.'

14

Yejide swallow the dusk whole and feel it carry her up, up, up. All was colour. There again, the edges of pink and red and gold, sharp and drawing pricks of blood from her flesh, old rumbling blue rolling down a mountain, blue that black like molasses, roiling orange like harmattan, purple gloaming when the night separate into layers. And the dark is sex, pain, purple like dried blood on machetes, like blue over cane fields, like faint nothings, like heartbeats in sleep. She stroke it and it stroke her back, but it inside her and she inside it and she have no way to tell which way is up and which way is down and is like she a child tumbling in a wave, swallowing all the salt and sand and sea, teeth bashing ocean floor, nostrils filled with water. And then a hand pluck her out and she breathe deep and find nothing there but darker and bluer. Then another hand and another reaching out, grasping her as she pass. She open her eyes, saltwater sting, and pain, so much pain. Lancing pain on her back, leather and iron spines, cutting into her flesh, and she bawl out with a voice that is not hers. Molasses blackness and fire and burning, flesh dropping off bone, she in a vat of black heat and molten pitch. And now she skinless and fingers grip her throat and she hanging, hanging from the branch of a tree, breeze blow, and skinless she sway and below laughing, laughing. And she fall and then she small, small, and all around is red and muscle and warm and pulse and soft, she want to breathe oh God she want to breathe, and the hand that was around her neck is a cord and it choking, and then light and gone and mother. Cold metal at the back of her skull hard, feel it through her hair and knees grating against stony gravel, and a voice asking where the bag and the money and she don't know and then cold metal in her mouth break her teeth and blood and spit, throat gag and sound blast and nothing. White sheets, body paper-thin and lady in mint green, and metal bars and tubes and beep-beep-beeping and needles and blood and nurse let me die, just let me die, no more no more, and no, I don't want to die and pray for me please, doctor there must be something else, call the pastor, pray for me, I don't want to go yet, call my mother, doctor, call my mother, tired and can't do this anymore and this feeling won't stop and can't, and blade and skin and bubbles of blood and face against the cold tiles and the water come down and weep and take me, take me, take me . . .

Big black gates. Stone grey wall. Arches. And all the voices there, the oldest, the loudest, and she feel it in the centre of her and everything pour out and radiate into tributaries, out, out, out from the place Petronella touch her, out to the place beyond the gates, out to the city to pinpricks of energy all over the island and she is the centre. And she can't hold it and the hands keep reaching out, grasping at her clothes and her hair and her hands and her face, and the pain keep flowing through her and it come from the ground her feet stand on, up through her calves and thighs, and her pussy drip with it and her breasts feel full and heavy, and her throat close up and the top of her head burst open and up, up, up, sky and storm and cloud and wind and rage, and she put her hands on the cold metal gate and shake it, open! Open!

Everything still for a moment, like somebody turn the volume down on a radio, and something emerge out of the noise, coalesce into a single note, one clear sound from up ahead. Then it start to take shape – from sound to vague form, and from vague form to outline. It move down a wide road, come toward her, toward the gate, until she could see it now, clear, clear . . . a man. Tall and slim. His colour green.

She smell fear on him, wet and slithering; anger, sharp and sour; and under that, under all that, something familiar like bread just out the oven, the sound breeze make when it blow through bamboo in the afternoons.

A man. Like mountain, like cool river. Life. So much life in him. Still trying to walk toward her, hand outstretched. Light surrounding his head, spilling down his shoulders, down his arms, figures behind him roaming, their hands outstretched to her too, roiling blue at his back.

'We closed! Closed! Come back tomorrow!'

She reach out, without even thinking it, reach out like she want to touch him, and she see his face clear. She make out his features, the sketch of lines and colour and sense. He look up to the sky and then back at her and for a second she in her body and she feel everything – the hard, cold iron of the gate, her feet on the concrete pavement, the wind swirling around her head, rain on her face. And everything about him cut through the blue, cut through the dark. Like green bamboo, he don't break in her storm. He bend, and let her blow, let her rage, and he take it from her, set it down like is a parcel she holding too long and don't even realize how it heavy.

Then the gate gone, and the rain gone, and the concrete gone. Plush softness at her back. Familiar voices.

'Jide? Is me—'

'Don't—'

'Leave her. She will come back when—'

'Princess?'

Cool dusk. The flutter of the white curtains. A light, soft breeze through the window. No rain.

She adjust her vision. Feel it sharpen like Petronella teach her. The room come into focus. Start to separate the voices here from the ones she could still feel from before, from the other place, like they sticking her in her spleen. 'We closed! Come back tomorrow!' Then Agatha praying the rosary, Peter stand at the foot of the bed. Seema face looking down on her, taking her hand. 'What you see, Jide? What happen?'

'A man.' She barely recognize her own voice. It rasp and echo like she hearing herself from far away. 'I was in a grave-yard.' She could still see him. The sheen of his skin from the orange street lights, the fear, anger on his face, the green in his heart.

Seema frown; her fingers stroke Yejide hand but Yejide pull away. Her whole body feel heightened, sensitive, and Seema touch like thorns on her skin. But something in her other hand was cool, smooth and hard, and next to her body, something still warm. They had put her on the bed, her mother's body shrouded next to her, cocooned in death whites; and in her hand, the locket.

15

Darwin

Darwin never even finish his rounds. He lock up quick and head for home. The outskirts of the cemetery look like a small tornado hit – leaves scatter, a bin turn over, litter spread out everywhere. But the further away he get from Fidelis the more normal everything seem. The city still same way it is every evening when he walk home. Taxi drivers blowing their horns to attract passengers, people hustling from work and vendors setting up for the evening. Like nothing out of the ordinary happen. But he know what happen, he know what he see, and every time someone walk too close to him, every time a car horn blast, every time he hear the shuffle of a stray dog digging up in the bins, he spin round like somebody right behind him.

He didn't imagine it. He couldn't have. She was there. He know she was there. A woman in a white dress, her hands gripping the black gate. He couldn't really make out her face. Was like somebody now start to sketch it – an outline here, a little something shade in there.

Since that first time with Mr Julius, he meet a couple other people who get left behind by they dead. He know how grief does draw them back, looking lost, smelling haunted, half-convince that a grave is just a bed where their people would be sleeping from now on, that it would be okay to stay, to rest with them for just a little while. After a few times, he get better at it – how to talk to them, let them sit and then firmly move them along.

But she didn't look lost or haunted, not at all. She look damn vex, like she was ready to break open the gate or leap over it. And she look like she could do it too! Whatever stopping her from mashing in the gate he damn sure it wasn't him. It wasn't the height of the gate or the chain round it. He know that if she want she coulda walk in and a storm would blow round her ankles and move the dress just so, so he could see her brown legs, and the dust from the cemetery and the city outside would swirl, and she could pick up every tree out the ground from the roots, send headstones crashing down and blow the admin building clean over.

And the wind that come with her chill him down to his boots. Light at first, but the closer he get to the gate, the harder it blow, till it wasn't no breeze at all but like a hurricane come out of nowhere and centre itself over Fidelis. But no clouds rolling! The sky was quiet and black like a newly turn grave.

When he reach Bellemere, same boys on the corner under the dim street light, their faces half in shadow. He hail them as usual but nobody answer him. Just nod like he part of the ordinary scenery. By the time he reach home and see Ms Margo moving about the kitchen through the window, if he didn't know his own mind he woulda think that nothing happen in the graveyard at all, that he imagine the whole thing.

He head straight to his room. Can't manage any small talk this evening with Ms Margo or the couple who had move in. Dinner is the last thing on his mind. Every time the curtain flutter he feel like the storm coming for him again and the woman with it. He close the window, pull the curtain and think about the rolled-up bills in his bedside drawer that he put aside for Janaya. This is why man mustn't play with the dead. Never know what you go pick up in the cemetery and bring home. Never know what could raise up and come for you when you not looking.

But nothing about the woman feel dead. When she shake the gate, like she could capsize the whole thing, he remember he had the strangest feeling – just so, he wish he had a broom, like if he had know she was coming he would have sweep up the whole cemetery, the whole city, so it could be clear for her to pass. The wind had press against his chest till he couldn't take another step and, as he stand at the threshold of the cemetery and she stand holding the gate, everything in him had get quiet and still. Big man as he was – not frighten, nah, something else, some feeling he don't recognize – he can't do nothing but watch her.

Two graves to dig, and the day have a heat that Darwin know can't hold. He keep his mind on the work – bagging the empty rum bottles and litter left by visitors, careful not to remove the dead flowers, the handwritten notes, the spent incense sticks, the burnt-out candle stubs – clearing the way for the new graves. But no matter how hard he focus on the earth beneath his fingers, the rocks, the moss that grow in the cracks of the headstones, he can't shake what he see the night before. What – a spirit? The last thing anyone had to fear here was the dead, not when there was the living to contend with, but still he can't work it out: how an ordinary woman, small so, could even stand up in a wind like that, so strong it hold him so he couldn't move? And even worse, if nothing happen at all, if he just imagine out of nowhere a woman walking up to the gate of the bone yard with a storm round her head, what that mean for him? What this place start to do him already? He focus on the graves, his hands in the dirt.

McIntosh and Jamesy join him and they work in silence for a while. McIntosh on the wheelbarrow this time and he and Jamesy down in the ground. Errol nowhere around. Funeral this afternoon and the sky set up, rain drizzling just like he figure it would when he walk in this morning. It make the earth soft and digging easy, but if it come down any harder the ground would turn to slush under their boots and Darwin don't like the idea of scrambling to get out of the hole.

When they set up a good rhythm, he pick his moment carefully to speak. 'How long you working here, McIntosh?'

'Years. Not sure yes. Time does pass slow here. Fast too. Must be a good fifteen years now.'

'You like it?'

'Like?' McIntosh laugh out loud. 'What it have to like about work? Work is work. Allyuh young people always want to like something.'

Darwin look up at McIntosh. His cap shield his face from the fine rain, his eyes serious, brown hands gripping the barrow, his wedding ring stacked next to a thicker gold one. Back broad as he wheel the dirt away from the grave.

'You not so old, man.'

'Older than you,' McIntosh grunt. 'And young enough to still drink Jamesy under the table.'

Jamesy nudge Darwin shoulder. 'Don't study McIntosh. He does like to feel he in ting still. But he know Joanne does have to stamp he passport if he want to go anywhere these days. Bout drink me under the table.' Jamesy steups.

'Don't be on my wife nah.' McIntosh voice rumble. 'When allyuh fellas grow up little bit allyuh will see it have no shame in that. What Joanne say is law. Me eh vex. Twenty good long years I married to that woman. She never steer me wrong.' A big smile crease McIntosh face and the woman from last night drift across Darwin mind.

'Darwin boy, you ask me if I like this work? When you have wife and children to mind, you could tell me about like. Work is work and family have to feed. Schoolbooks have to buy. Them children does want ice cream when the weekend come. That is all a man could do. What he have to. If you lucky, you find a little extra hustle to make ends meet, you take a drink on a Friday, then come home to your children. Rinse and repeat.'

'Don't let McIntosh start up nuh.' Jamesy roll his eyes. 'We go be here forever talking bout the meaning of life like we on a blasted TV show.'

The rain start to come down harder and the grave only half dig. They pick up the pace.

'But allyuh must be see all kinda strange tings working in a place like this for so long.'

Jamesy shrug.

'Strange like how?' McIntosh pause carrying the barrow and glance at Jamesy.

Darwin stick the shovel in and watch the earth ooze down the side of the grave.

'I mean, right now I down inside a hole. Next to me on one side is a dead. On the next side is a dead. In a few hours we going to lower a next person inside this hole. Every grave-stone and headstone carrying the name of a dead. And this place old. Probably even older than any of Shirley records. Must be a strange place to spend your days. The kinda thing that does go home with you when the night come.'

McIntosh pick up the barrow, tilt it and watch the earth slide into the pile at the side.

Jamesy pause in the digging. 'You ever work the land, boy? Farming an ting, I mean?'

'Work a little garden up by my mother an dem. Get a little work on the government farms on the west coast. But nothing big.'

'Me, Cardo and Mikey meet working on a farm up by him. We grow up in the same area. Sweet potato, dasheen, seasoning, dem ting. Small farm. Working here I does just think of it as digging. Same work. Put something in the ground. Wait. Let the earth do what it does do. The sun, the rain. And things does grow. It simple.'

'But that different. When you planting, you getting something from the earth. Is about life. This here what we doing. Nothing does come back out the grave after we cover it over.'

Jamesy give him a half-smile. 'You sure?'

Darwin measure it out in his head – what to say, what to keep. 'Well, the way how this place is could make you think you see things sometimes. People sleeping in corners where you can't see them, visitors that don't want to leave after funeral when the place have to close up. A while back I thought I see a man just climb over the wall and disappear!'

Jamesy laugh. 'Well, that one you probably really see. Dem sprangers does move fast like they in the Olympics!'

Then Jamesy glance at him sharp. 'You ever see anything else?'

McIntosh wheel back over to the edge of the grave and look down at Darwin and Jamesy in the hole. 'Stop filling the boy head with foolishness, Jamesy. You go frighten him and he go never come back and we go have to train a next man. You remember the last one? I eh going through that again.'

Darwin not sure if Jamesy just teasing him or if he have something else behind his words but he decide to leave it. How to ask two big men in the light of day if they ever see a woman that don't seem like she really there?

'That deep enough, Jamesy?' McIntosh ask. 'Look like it to me.' They finish up with the base planks, the tarp for the sides, just as the rain start to get heavier. McIntosh reach his hand down to pull Darwin and Jamesy up. The ring catch Darwin eye again.

'Good timing,' McIntosh say. 'Lewwe get out of this rain. Unless allyuh want to drown in the hole.'

16

Yejide

And then the moths come. Tiny white cotton whispers that settle in Yejide hair, on the curtains, on Petronella armchair, on the banister winding up the stairs.

Large brown ones that fly straight at you when you trying to walk. Open a cupboard and they fly out like a small army, getting in the teacups when you try to make tea, sitting on the kettle until just before it boil. Then they scatter and fly to the bulbs, the lampshades, the light outside on the porch, casting shadows on the windows.

They gather in the Walking Gallery, on the flaking portraits of Maman; Deborah, with her laughing mouth, broad nose and upturned eyes; Babygirl, her face round like a small moon, her hair wiry and frizzy and near bursting out from under the patterned fabric of her headwrap. They gather on the photographs of houses that no one alive could identify – big dark-coloured houses with turrets and demerara windows, a tall slim purple house with an ornate black gate.

But the other kind of moths – black with white spots and a purple line running across their wingspan, big like bats – settle only in Petronella room: on her white-shrouded body, on the wardrobe, the sideboard. They plaster the windows and block out the sun, so the room stay in dusk-light even after the rain stop and the sky brighten.

'They come to see your mother home,' Peter tell her as he

brush one from his shoulder. He reach up and pull a tiny white moth from her hair and smile.

Yejide barely recognize herself. Every time she pass a mirror she do a double take. Her eyes glassy and wide with dark circles under them. Her hair spring out every which way and the white fluttering moths make her a tree in bloom. She find it hard to look at people straight on now, so she stare just past them. Everybody in the house like they split in two. She could see the Peter she had always known, a strong kind man who had never left their side, always looking younger than his years, the silent backbone of the house. But she could see something else now: a shadow around his body. The age. The old man he would become. Wasn't as simple as seeing his death. But she could see the time that would come to claim him. She see it around Seema too, even more so around Agatha and Angie. Mr Homer the darkest of them all. She wonder if this is how her mother had see everybody; her mother, her mother's mother, and her mother's mother before that. This gift, this curse.

They give her a wider berth as they pad around each other in the house, waiting for the ambulance from the funeral home. They can't take her wild eyes or her fixed gaze and she can't take the look on their face when they see her either. She find that if she stand very still, almost forget to breathe, she could look on at them as they all going about their tasks and they can't see her at all. Not invisible, just still, like she become part of the house, part of the air, existing in a dimension separate from where everyone else living.

When that wasn't enough, she sneak out the house, like she and Seema used to when they was young. She don't take Seema, don't even tell her. She can't bear the idea of anybody holding her hand. And later, when the outside feel too big, like she might drift away in it, she sit on Granny Catherine chair in the corner by the front window and watch Seema gather seasoning from the garden – no matter what going on, that woman always make sure there was food to eat. Just once Seema look up and toward the house like if she can feel somebody watching her, but she never give no indication that she see Yejide at all and Yejide head so full that she wonder if it might not be better so. When night come, she lock her door before she go to sleep.

The next day, Yejide stand on the porch waiting for the ambulance and Peter stand beside her. She feel him watching her out of the corner of his eye, like he worried the moths would start to flap and carry her away into the bright and sunny mid-afternoon air so different from the quiet, buzzing house. Her body feel rootless, her limbs soft and her head still in several places at one. She hear the beat of the moth wings like sails catching the sea wind, feel the elsewhere press against her chest.

And still she can't get the man out of her head. The green man amongst the dead. Who was he? Only light around him – nothing else. Light and forest and green and something strong and pulsing that draw her to him. How she travel there? And why? Wasn't something she could ask Peter about. How to tell your father – the man who as good as your father – that you see a man somewhere in a dream and know you have business with him, and he have business with you? Last night after the whole house gone to sleep, she sneak downstairs and sit in Petronella chair for hours, waiting, hoping. Trying to squint her eyes to make the garden look the way it had looked after the vigil, to somehow bring her mother back to her to ask her the questions that only she would know the answer to. But it seem like they only get one shot, one chance to say whatever else needed saying, and that time gone.

The ambulance drive up the hill and pull in front of the house. Three men get out, but the driver take one look at Yejide, standing on the porch, hair covered in wings, moths all over the windows even in the daylight, and get right back in the ambulance. 'Not me and dem devil ting,' he shout and lock the door.

Yejide can't blame him.

Two orderlies approach the house slow with the stretcher and she point them up the stairs. 'They not going to bite you. Is just moths.' They keep their heads down and carry the stretcher up. One make the sign of the cross as he reach the top of the staircase. Yejide leave Agatha, Angie and Mr Homer to deal with them and supervise the removal of the body from the bed.

She and Peter stand at the bottom of the stairs and look up in the direction that the orderlies had gone. 'Poor fellas. Was easier when it was Deborah. Mr Johnson from the funeral home, he used to us. He would just come for the body, deal with the death certificate and everything else and matter fix.' Peter look out the window at the ambulance and the driver's frightened face. 'Now they have to go through the drama with the morgue. It not easy for outsiders to understand how things does go in this house. Is not like when they cut her open they going to find any cause of death. Waste of time.'

They sit down on two armchairs in the living room where they could see the staircase.

'You talk to her?' Peter ask.

'Yes.'

He rub his temples.

'She ask for you.'

'Yes. She would.'

'She say other things too.'

'That is between you and your mother. You don't have to tell me that.' He reach over then take her hand. 'How you feeling?'

'You remember when you used to take me and Seema to the beach when we was small?'

'Hmm.'

'And we run on the sand and play whole day and then we would run into the water and wait for the big swells to come? And when it crest it would tumble us over and over into the sand and by the time we come out is sand in our hair and eyes red from salt. And for the rest of the day, even when we reach home, we walk around like if we still in the sea? Heavy but like we floating still? Salty tongue and red eyes?'

Peter smile a little. 'You always went further out in the water than I wanted you to. I used to be frighten bad. How I woulda go home and tell your mother that I let you drown?'

'Well. That is how I feel. Like I spend a day by the sea, and it take everything from me but give me something too, and I can't figure out how to use my body yet on dry land.'

'You look like her today. I remember when it happen to her. But I only see it from a distance. See her walking around in a trance for days. Then suddenly is like something else was filling her up that wasn't me, that wasn't even Geraldine.' Peter stare out into space. The longing and sadness in his eyes make her look away. The silence stretch between them.

Seema hurry down the stairs and stop short when she see Yejide and Peter. She have a question in her eyes that Yejide don't know how to answer. Last night she hear a knock at the door, the sound of a knob turning, then another knock, soft, once, twice, and then footsteps getting softer and softer. Yejide look away first; she never lock the door before. By the time she look up again, Seema already halfway to the kitchen. Is like a veil come down over Yejide now, and all the things she and Seema ignored, the things that they said would never change, thick in the air like the moths.

She feel Peter watching her. 'It does be hard all around when it happen. Your mother was a tough woman before she turn, so I had practice, but . . .' He reach his hand out and touch her forearm where it rest on the chair. 'Time does move a bit slower here, you know. Things take a bit longer. Just give her time. She will come to terms.'

The orderlies start to head down the stairs. Her mother seal up in a plastic body bag on the stretcher, moths trailing her. She and Peter stand up to meet them. The poor orderlies trembling so hard that she worry they might drop her. She feel Peter drift beside her, and she hold his hand to steady him. One by one, the inhabitants of the house come out to see her go. She feel Seema just behind her to her right, Mr Homer by the kitchen door, Agatha and Angie coming down the steps behind the body. As they cross the threshold of the house, walk through the door, a ripple move through all the moths like a small tornado. It take the white ones from her hair, the brown ones from the kitchen and the living-room curtains, the black ones that follow the orderlies.

If they could have run with the stretcher they would have, but they balance it carefully and place her mother in the back of the ambulance. The driver done have the engine running. All the moths cloud the air now in front the house, like tiny corbeaux circling. Yejide watch the ambulance drive down the hill. She don't shed a tear.

Yejide take a deep breath, squeeze Peter hand. She could see through the windows again, the curtains move in the breeze. Light flood the rooms of the house. She turn to her kin on the porch behind her. The look in all their eyes tell her that she wasn't the baby anymore. She wasn't nobody granddaughter, nobody daughter. She wasn't nobody Princess. They was looking at her, waiting for instructions.

'You still a child,' she hear Petronella voice talking to her in the garden. 'You still think love is something nice.' She let the words settle.

She look to Seema first. There were things to say between them, but they would have to wait. 'Start something on the stove. I sure everybody hungry.' Seema nod and disappear into the kitchen.

'Angie and Agatha? Can you make some calls? You know who need to know better than me. Mr Homer, I never keep a wake. I don't know—'

'You don't have to ask. We know what to do.'

Yejide love all of them in that moment – no matter what Petronella think about love, whatever she learning about it, she know she love them all, that they necessary to her. Till it hurt her to feel it. Just she and Peter left on the porch now. She grip his hand. 'Help me find the grave paper.'

SWEEPER

17

Darwin

Some days Darwin can't work out how long he in the city. The calendar say nearly two months, but Fidelis have a different kind of time – the hours longer, the days deeper, and digging graves and lowering coffins in the ground is like watching whole lives fast-forward beginning to end. Fidelis make him adopt its rhythm instead of his own. And is not just Fidelis. Port Angeles crackle and spit like oil on a fireside and he start to like how he could disappear into it, just another one of the many somebodies that come here for whatever it is they come for.

He learning that even death in Fidelis does work in sync with the city. Payday? That mean hospital, courthouse and graveyard. Heavy rain? That mean road accident for so and they too busy to even laugh and old talk. Then it have other times when something start to ripple through the city – the wrong man get kill, the blocks get hot and is only sirens blaring out through the night. Them times they digging grave three, four a day and have to send for temporary workers so they could do more than one funeral same time.

But now as it get closer to November, around All Souls' Day, is like the dead and the living come to a kind of a truce. All the graves quiet and sometimes he don't see the other gravediggers at all for a couple days. He know they does work other jobs and get little contracts when things light in Fidelis, but nobody let Darwin in on the cut. True, he could use the money, but he don't mind. The days when it was just him, even the weight of the keys in his pocket make him feel good. And when the street lamps come on, the outer edges of Fidelis gild in borrowed light, he stand at the crossroads right at the centre of the cemetery in near-darkness and feel his whole body relax, like how a man must feel when he finally reach in his own home after a long day and smell food cooking. Not that he ever know that feeling but he figure it must feel a little bit like this, like Fidelis at twilight.

Maybe everything does just get easier the longer you do it. True, some nights he still dream the heavy scissors in his hand, his head getting lighter with each cut, his locks spreading out amongst the zaboca leaves in the dirt yard. But each time he shave his head over the sink, he get more used to his reflection in the mirror. He make sure to gather every last strand and put them into a small clay bowl, say a prayer, strike a match and set it on fire. The bitter scent of burning hair somehow make him feel restful and safe. He was a man without law, without vow, but he was still his mother's son.

But no matter how much he feel like he getting used to it, his life always half in shadow. Errol still giving him a little extra after each burial and he still taking it, although each time he feel a bit more uncomfortable. He tell himself, the same way somebody have to clean the streets, and somebody have to collect the garbage, and somebody have to pave the road, somebody have to bury the dead. He say it over and over till he believe it, and think of the envelope for his mother in his dresser drawer, getting fatter through the weeks and then slimmer each time he deposit some in her account, praying her pride don't stop her from withdrawing it. He put his uncomfortable feelings in the envelope with the hundred-dollar bills and try not to look at either of them too hard.

Fidelis half in shadow too. Parts of it he could see plain, like how to dig a grave – how deep, how wide; how to deal with the grave paper; how to keep enough distance from the grieving so he there but not there; how to leave the stray dogs to sleep in an old crypt when he see them but run the lovers who looking for a little action; how to recognize the young boys who want to vandalize or stay in the cemetery at night on a dare.

But other things about it he not so sure, not sure at all. Like one day he clearing up on 4th Street and he notice a grave looking fresh, earth piled high. The rain fall for the last two days straight, and everything else flatted down and water-logged, but this one look like they now finish fill it. And it wasn't the first time either. He ask McIntosh about it and the man look him dead in his face and don't answer, just move on to talking about something else like Darwin never ask him anything at all.

A next time he notice a concrete angel fall off the pedestal and smash on the roadway. Grey stone splinters scatter along the path, the face of the angel bash in. He look around and it don't seem like anything missing. Just the statue tip over. It don't make sense. He remember Errol talking about people breaking in an trying to steal things but nothing looking like it gone. The grave was old; he don't think anyone bury in there for a while. He sure it eh dig while he was there so what knock over the angel?

He find himself looking over his shoulder, peering around at the graves, searching for anything out of place. He know it not possible to remember everything exactly the way it was, but he get into the habit of marking them, trying to memor-ize details, his eyes combing over the plots to figure out what was real and what was not. Maybe if he just look sharp enough he will catch the answer lurking just out of the corner of his eyes.

One week before All Saints' Day, he at Fidelis first thing like always. He push one side of the iron gate all the way open and then the other so cars could drive through. He fetch the name, plot number and funeral time from Shirley since yesterday. He have maybe about fifteen minutes before the boys arrive. Half an hour if he was lucky and they all late.

He unlock the admin building and enter Shirley office. Everything neater since he fix the filing cabinet and bring in another one that he scavenge from an office throwing away old furniture down the road. They could put in a request for a new one with the regional corporation but, with everything strapped and stressed, finding new things for people who does deal with the dead wasn't a priority. He was glad to see Shirley face light up when he bring it. He even fix the broken clock above her desk and help her put the files in order so she could get them easier.

He get a mug and the nice Jamaican brew she like from the cupboard, and set up the timer on the coffee maker so it would be ready for her when she come.

From Shirley window, the hills that surround the city look clean and lush and Fidelis peaceful with nobody there but him. But no – a figure catch his eye, someone that not supposed to be there. The dreadlocks man he see before. How he reach here so early? Darwin wonder if he make a mistake closing up yesterday, miss the man sleeping among the graves and leave him here overnight.

Darwin feel kinda irritated that somebody else there to disturb his peace, but the man just walking around the graves, no scene. It early but sometimes people does come to visit their dead before they go to work or use Fidelis as a shortcut from one side of Queen Isabella Street to the next. Something about him, though. Moving in no regular pattern but fast, flowing strides like he almost running. Passing behind the mausoleums and miniature spires, in between the statues of the Virgin and the cherubs and the thick stone crosses, disappearing and then reappearing further away, each time just a little further than Darwin eyes expect. Even from high up, he could see the set of the man back, the dread, the way he walk, legs long and lean. And then he stop, turn back toward the admin building, look straight up at Darwin. He hold his eye unblinking for a long moment. And then he raise his hand.

Darwin don't even know he decide before he running down the stairs, bursting out the admin building and taking off after him. The man stepping over each grave like it easy, not sticking to the roads at all. Darwin try to follow him, but he can't bring himself to run on people grave. He try to get ahead of him, run two streets up on the main road then duck back in, cut him off, but he lose him for a second time. Where he going? Darwin sprint back to the main road – he must be able to see him if he look down each street – but every time he catch a glimpse he lose him again, first behind two huge mausoleums, then again behind a big samaan tree. He must cross one of the streets sometime, just a matter of waiting him out.

Finally, he spot him. The man emerge onto 12th Street and stop. He standing with his back to Darwin, looking down at the first grave Darwin ever dig. The memory clear. The old man, the white lilies, the way the marigolds had blaze gold in the late-afternoon sun. Whatever remain of them long gone now. And yet even from here he could see Mrs Julius grave look fresh, the mound of dirt still high and round like if someone just finish it.

Darwin don't dare call out. His heart beating so loud he feel the man could hear it all the way across the road. If he shout, maybe the man would turn around and he could be sure, he could be sure of what he seeing. But he never turn around and Darwin start to feel like a fool just standing there staring at a stranger. He force his heartbeat to slow. Stop being foolish. Is a good thing. Just somebody come to visit Mrs Julius grave, a family friend, somebody from their church. Must be that. He shake his head and walk away. This place making him crazy. Running behind people just minding their own business this hour of the morning. He almost reach the main road when he turn, just one more look before he head back to the office. The man gone.

Shirley meet him sitting on the steps of the admin building in a daze. 'Morning, Darwin! Nice day, eh?' Her voice sunny like somebody who never give a second thought to whether they going mad.

18

Funeral done and the boys in high spirits. They start drinking from about four. Nobody bawl down the place and try to jump in the hole behind they dead. No stubborn family wandering around afterward. No storm woman in white. Darwin and all feeling good. He can't see where them boys planning to put more alcohol before the day done but they insist that he working with them too long now and is time they carry him out to lime.

He almost don't recognize Errol. The old man come out from the admin building looking crisp. He even take a shave, slick back his hair, little bit of grey at the temples. No dirty overalls. Suede shoes brush, shirt clean and looking new. Mikey and Jamesy clean up too. Darwin change out of his overalls, but he can't afford no fancy clothes like them fellas. He have better things to do with his money than that. The thought start to get him a little bit nervous. He hope they not going to some place on the waterfront the way Errol dress up. He never went no place like that. But the rest of the fellas look casual enough, so he feel a little better.

'Yuh passport stamp, McIntosh?' Jamesy laugh.

'Joanne gone out with she sister and the children by they grandmother. Both a we passport stamp tonight!'

They walk out Fidelis into the evening and Darwin lock the gate behind him. He take one last look inside, scan the road reaching away into the dark.

'You expecting somebody ah what?' Errol ask him. 'How you peeping back in the cemetery so.'

'Just checking.'

'You eh have no business in there right now. Play fass and make thing have business with you nah. Come,' Errol clap Darwin on his shoulder and shove him forward. They follow McIntosh, Jamesy, Mikey and Cardo down the road. 'Lewwe go and drink.'

They leave the wider streets of Port Angeles behind – past the big shops and outdoor market stalls and parking lots, past the grand squares and parks run to seed, past the vendors with clothes hang out on closed storefronts. Night-time Port Angeles is a parallel economy. No shops open but people selling and buying still. And everywhere they pass people hailing Errol. The foreman look about a decade younger, barely limping at all, shaking hands and nodding and waving like he is mayor.

Darwin fall into step with Mikey. 'Is everybody know Errol ah wha?'

'Everybody who need to.' Mikey smile.

He look around at the boys. Cardo and Mikey like twins although they don't really resemble at all, pacing almost in time with each other, same haircut, clothes near-identical. McIntosh tall like the leaning lamp posts that they pass on the street, Jamesy like a shadow behind him. Somehow in the street-light flare, he start to watch them fellas and wonder about their lives, if like him they have things that they hiding, soft selves that they don't want anyone else to know.

The streets get narrower and the street lights fewer; water run slow in the drains and piss stain the walls. They in the Old Quarter now. Stone buildings, board houses that standing since before the century change. Old men sitting on long wooden benches smoking cigarettes, a table pull up outside another bar with some fellas knocking cards, a next one where they playing dominoes. The clack of the dominoes hitting the table and the men bawling out appreciation mix with the music booming from big speakers park up outside on the pavement. Whole street in a sound clash.

People talking in a sound clash too. Plenty Spanish, some Hindi, some languages he never hear before. He pass two old ladies selling chives and green seasoning bundles on a roll-out mat talking long-time patois. The smell of charred meat coming out from a BBQ shack make his insides churn a little bit but the dumplings frying in the Chinese shop actually smell good to him. Every single part of this city have its own secret, its own language, and no matter where you from, it seem like everybody, at some point, does end up in the Old Quarter of Port Angeles. And now he here too.

He follow the boys into a low wooden building with murals of men in old-fashioned suits holding microphones, people beating steel pan and a big faded sign at the top say LUCKY. The rest of the name fade out, paint peeling. As they step in, the light change from the hard orange street lights to a softer blue, air full of smoke. He smell some good grade and his spirit ease. White plastic chairs scatter around, Formica tables laden with bottles of white rum, bowls with ice, cutters. In the middle is a kinda dance floor and booths line the walls in the shadowy corners. Tall black speaker boxes in one corner, heavy dancehall bass booming. Some fellas knocking pool, dim bulbs hanging over the green felt tables.

Maybe is the light, maybe is the swirl of people, or maybe is just the last few weeks, but the whole place have a haze that make him feel dizzy. Can't make out nobody. Man could be right there, and you still feel like they sneak up on you. Even the Fidelis boys look strange and unfamiliar in here. Like any moment he could look again and realize they was somebody else the whole time.

They head to the bar, Errol leading and the others in his wake. Something about it feel like a movie he and Janaya used to watch when he was small, bout Shaka Zulu. He had sit down between her legs while she rub oil into his scalp and stare at Shaka and he warriors go into battle. They carry long shields that look like locust wings, block they whole body, and they move in a unit, shield first, like they was all one body carrying one shield. He can't even remember now if they win the battle or not but that image of black men, like him, with shields and spears and moving in a unit, make him think that it have nothing in the world that could ever beat them.

They move through the room cool-cool and the crowd part for them. They eh going into the battle but as people see Errol the energy of the whole place change. Wasn't like the people on the street who hail him casual – here is like Errol is a surge gathering force, ready to spill over and wash away everybody in the bar. And McIntosh and Jamesy and them riding the crest of it, and Darwin part of it too, right along with them.

'Sweeper!'

Even above the music Darwin hear the man hail Errol as he pass by. Errol stop to talk, and the fellas stop behind him. The man tall, nearly tall like McIntosh, but he broad like a fridge and even in the low blue light the gold round his neck and on his fingers glint.

Sweeper? Is not a strange thing for a man to have all kinds different name, but the way the stranger say it just reinforce the feeling that everything about Errol was a cover for something else. The limp that come and go when it convenient to him; the milky-white eye that make you feel like he don't see everything; the wide, gleaming grin that you could mistake for friendship. People watching him with something that look like respect? Fear? Darwin not sure. But if Errol was Sweeper here, and the boys was warriors out of a movie he see when he was small, then what that make Darwin?

They finally reach the bar and Cardo and Jamesy start to call for drinks. Darwin catch the eye of a quiet-looking girl and ask her for a Malta.

'You not drinking, darlin?' she ask him and smile as she bend down and pull the cold black bottle from a tub on the floor.

'No, Empress. Not as far as I could avoid it.' He look over at the gravediggers in high spirits, properly drunk already. 'But with these fellas I don't know how long that go be. Better you give me two.'

'You moving with Sweeper and dem?' She raise her eyebrows as she pop open the bottle at the edge of the counter. 'You don't look like the type.'

'And what type is that?'

She shrug and nod toward Cardo and Mikey, Jamesy at the bar. Post up like big men, hundred-dollar bills passing free and what look like a never-ending stream of bottles coming back to them across the counter. 'That type.'

Darwin don't know how to respond to that but he make a point to ask if he getting paid less than the rest of them because the way they pelting out money he swear they wasn't doing the same job. He turn back to answer the woman when he feel somebody watching him. Hard. He scan the room. Nobody he know here. Then he catch the eyes that stick on him. Young fella he don't recognize standing up further down the bar. When he and the man eyes make four he look away but not before he see surprise in the gaze.

'You know him?' Cardo had come up to stand next to him when he wasn't looking.

'Nah, I don't think so. He little familiar, but I can't place the face. I don't really know nobody from up here.'

'You want us start him?' Cardo voice was slurring already, looking for fight. 'You rolling with us tonight. Nobody can't give you no trouble.'

'Easy nah, Cardo.' No call for all that. 'Everything cool. He must be mistake me for somebody else.' When he look back to the bar the man gone, disappear into the crowd.

They head to a table near the edge of the dance floor. Some girls come and sit down with them, Cardo pull out a pack of cards and next thing All Fours in full swing. Darwin don't know the game, so he hang back watching them. He look around for the youthman who was staring at him but like he gone. Errol at a table over the way in the corner talking to a man Darwin don't know. Except he look again and recognize the face this time: same man he see at the gate of Fidelis, back when he first start, giving Errol something – an envelope or a package. He can't remember now. He tap Mikey on his shoulder.

'Who is that Errol talking to? I think I see him before.'

'You mighta see him on TV or something. Councillor for the area. We does get small contracts an ting from him. Small construction, roadworks, dem kinda ting.'

'Oh. So that is the boss who does pay us for the work in the cemetery then?'

Mikey pause in the middle of taking another shot of the white rum. 'Eh?'

'I mean I see him before in Fidelis with Errol.'

'You always asking some outta timing question eh. I tell you everybody know Errol. Not strange to see him talking to all kinda people.'

McIntosh jump in. 'You must be make a mistake, Darwin.

No reason for him to be in Fidelis. Is the TV you see him on.'
He pour a generous finger of something brown and smooth
in a tumbler and shove it across the table. 'Take a drink, boy.
You ever play cards? No? You sure you from here? How a big
man like you never knock no card? Come look. Lemme show
you. Relax nah, boy, is Friday.'

The weird orange-blue light glint off the glass and Darwin
take it.

He stumbling home. Head bad. Again. Something bout these
fellas does make him forget himself and end up drinking when
he don't intend to. But it feel good to be with them outside
Fidelis, somewhere normal, somewhere with real people and
real life. He bend the corner into Bellemere, walk on autopilot
through the familiar streets. He reach the sentinels under the
street lights, faces in shadow like always. He almost pass them
when one step out so he could see his face.

It click. Is the man from the bar. He don't know how he
didn't recognize him before. Self-preservation sober him up
quick. He eh know what this man problem is; they pass each
other with no issues before. He eh looking for no war, but if
war find him . . . He hold the man gaze, arms loose and ready.

'Evenin, the boss.' The man nod and the other fellas
mumble and nod too. Darwin almost spin around to see who
else in the road that they could be talking to. But is only him
and them and the broken, flickering street light and something that wasn't there in their eyes before. Respect. It make
Darwin shiver.

19

The next evening Ms Enid walk up Margo driveway and
Darwin feel like weeping to see her again. But he know that
the fact that is Enid and not his mother mean that she still eh
forgive him.

'Emmanuel.' She hug him, squeeze him tight, then pull
back and scan him from head to foot. Run her hand over his
short hair. 'How you doing, boy?'

'I alright. Just working. You know. You didn't have to
come all the way down this side. I tell you I would come and
check you by your work.'

'Well, it give me a chance to see that you settle. See Margo
too.'

He take her hand and walk her up the drive and they sit
down on the gallery, looking out into the street. 'Plus, I know
if you come in between work hours you will make some excuse
bout you can't stay long.'

'Is not that.'

'I know, I know. You busy.' She watch him sideways like
she looking for more words in between what he eh say.

Darwin pull out some spare papers from the folds of the
Bible on his lap, and start to build a spliff. Sun eh gone down
yet and the day have a golden glow. Every now and again a
car drive by. Or somebody walk up the road heading out for
the evening. He could smell Margo cooking food inside. The
onions and garlic simmer, the sound of a sharp knife hitting a
cutting board, the chadon beni and celery in the air. The radio
playing and Margo humming along out of tune, chattering

away at Jerry and Keisha, the couple who come to stay. They had all get well friendly since they move in. He glad for that. Margo don't focus on him so much again and he could come and go with nobody in his business.

'You look alright. You look good,' Enid finally say.

Darwin glance at her, light the spliff and take a deep pull.

'Well, what else you want me to say?'

'Nothing.'

'You want me to come quite here and sit down and tell you nothing? Just stare at each other like strangers? Wait for Margo to finish cook and make small talk around the table?' Enid smooth down her skirt, take her handbag off the chair next to her and put it on her lap. 'We could do that if you want.'

'Here.' Darwin take the envelope out his back pocket and hand it to Enid. 'I set up an account for her but I check the balance and I can see she not spending what I putting in there. But if you give it to her . . .'

'You know your mother don't want any of that.'

'She win the lotto since I here?'

'You know your mother.'

'Yes. And you know her too, so make sure she take it. Even self you have to pay the light bill for her or buy the groceries and leave it in the kitchen, so she think is from you.'

Enid take the envelope, open it and rifle through the cash. Her eyes open wide. The envelope disappear into her handbag. 'Emmanuel, where all this money come from?'

'I have a job, aunty.'

'A job? That is what they calling it now? You come here to get yourself in trouble? You want me to go home and tell your mother that her one son come in the city to get himself in trouble?'

143

'I not in any trouble.' Darwin think over the last few weeks. Nothing happen. He could say, well Ms Enid, I see a woman walk out of a storm and disappear. My boss have some kinda shady dealing with city council, gunman on the corner watching me like I one of them, and old graves looking fresh and new like something come up out of them. Is not the kind of conversation a sane man could have just so.

'I see Marcia last week.'

Darwin flinch at the sound of the name. He hope it don't show. 'Finally tired of the cold?'

'Nah. She come home to see her sister. Not here for long. Remember Marina? She just had a next baby.'

He nod, not trusting himself to speak. Marcia never here for long. She never look for him them times either.

'She ask for you.'

Last time Darwin see Marcia she was walking away from him rolling two suitcases, handing her passport to the immigration officer. She didn't turn around. He didn't expect her to. He couldn't go with her and she wouldn't stay. A good nurse like Marcia could get visa easy. Nurses always in demand over there. Not so easy for him, hustling work all over the place. It used to be he and Marcia walking to school and back home every day, taking each other up in test, memorizing song lyrics on the tiny radio in her room – couldn't listen to that kinda music in his house. He was there at her sixth-form graduation, he was there when she get the letter saying she didn't get into the medical school in the university, when she make the decision to be a nurse instead. Nurse just as good as doctor, she used to say, better even. He was there to take food for her in the hospital, make sure she eat in between shifts. When she get the visa and he get denied, they know they reach the end of a road. Know each other too long to say they would keep in touch.

The light get soft. The green parrots fly overhead squawking in a squadron across the sky. Evening time. It don't happen often but still, sometimes, he wonder how his life would have been if he had get that visa. He and Marcia shivering in the cold somewhere in that grey place, holding hands and sliding on pavements cover with ice, sitting on a bus avoiding eye contact with other people like he see they does do on TV, finally coming home to each other, wherever they living the only warm place because they together in it.

He eh vex with Marcia. So things does go. But he can't pretend that it don't sting a little. That he don't wonder sometimes too. 'Well, hail her up for me next time you see her. Give her my best.'

Enid shake her head. 'You know, if she had try harder, allyuh coulda make things official, so you could apply again as—'

'Leave it, Enid.' He hear the irritation in his voice, the rising volume, and feel her bristle beside him. Every time Marcia back in the country, they come to this conversation some way or other. 'What is for me is for me. I not riding nobody coat-tails for no visa. Marcia have her life to live. I have mine.'

Enid sigh, reach out and touch his shoulder. 'You right, Darwin. You always been like that, always do your best. Since you small. Lewwe not talk about it anymore. I sorry I bring up Marcia.'

He look up at the parrots in the sky. 'Aunty, you remember my father?'

Enid pause. 'Yes. Remember when he come and remember when he leave.'

She remember more than him. But the man he see in the cemetery yesterday morning, something about him. Is like

145

Fidelis pull the memory from his brain and bring it to life –
a stranger who shoulders broad like his own, who legs long
like his own.

'Springer, right?'

'Eh?'

'His last name. I know she used to call him Levi or sometimes Carlton. His real name was Carlton Springer?'

'By the time I meet him, he was just Levi.' Enid shift in her
chair like she little uncomfortable. 'I didn't know Janaya tell
you too much about him.'

'Nothing wrong with my ears. Is not everything she have
to tell me.'

'Listen,' Enid sigh, 'you can't blame your mother. Working in graveyard is one thing, that allyuh is Nazarite is another,
but this place . . .' She shake her head and look out into the
street. 'She feel like this city seduce that man and she never
see him again. Is just frighten she frighten to lose you, Emmanuel.' She reach over and take his hand and squeeze it. Then
her eyes change, and she look at him sharp. 'Why you ask?'

He think of old Mr Julius telling him about the son that
he hardly ever see, how that boy could be anyone walking
around in the world now. Mr Julius coulda meet him on the
street and never even know. A cool breeze blow and snatch the
flame from the end of the spliff. He flick the lighter. 'Nothing. No reason.'

20

Yejide

She drive the car in slow and park on the central road. On one side was a concrete building with a few men lounging on the steps in workmen overalls. She scan each one. None of them was him. On the other side was white marble like bleached bone, dark-grey mottled stone, rusted galvanize at the top of latticework frames, rusted gates falling off their hinges, sightless angels, pitted crosses, fresh flowers, dried ones and tall weeds blowing like cane arrows in the breeze.

How to explain the feeling of coming back to a place that you see before in a dream? Was that what she should call it – a dream? Not the right word. But there: the tall black gate; there: the grey stone walls; there: the dead. Muted now, like something leach all the light from what was technicolour.

She remember everything from that night. The memory so vivid that it eclipse the few times she actually visit the cemetery for real. Falling, flying, falling. Drowning in the needs of the dead. And as she here now she feel them again, like cats rubbing up against her, their bones creaking in their coffins, vibrating, migrating from grave to grave as the earth shift, as water unsettle the layers, as time have their way with them. Some so faint that they less than a whisper, but rooted deep still. Old dead. She remember her mother words and nod, yes. She feel the truth of it.

But something else. Not just old dead. She focus harder. Not just new dead either. She take a deep breath and hold

on to the steering wheel. Something in her stomach feel
alive. Like the feeling when you take the first bite of food
that gone bad. Your system know it as it hit the back of your
throat, no matter how good the food look. She don't know
how she miss it the other night – something struggling, angry.
Wronged. The word surface in her mind in her own voice,
clear amid the voices of the dead. Something here had been
wronged.

The feeling ache inside her like a cramp she steeling her
whole body against. Instead of fighting it, she let herself sink
into it and the pain hold her close. She feel something in her
reach out like a mother's hand soothing a crying child. Hush.
Hush. I here. The spasms still, quiet, and pool in her like a
lagoon, dull and heavy.

Darwin

The sun high, and the heat burn his scalp. Jamesy and Mc-
Intosh standing by the front steps with Errol, playing music
from Shirley's tiny radio. Darwin hear them talking as he get
closer.

'She come driving or walking? You see?' McIntosh ask.

'Car there.' Jamesy nod to a sleek navy-blue car on the
main road.

'She come to bury her mother,' Errol say. 'Old-money
people. Must be. They here long enough. 6th Street. Allyuh
know it. She burying this week.'

'Nice. And she sweet too.' McIntosh snicker.

Darwin reach them on the steps, 'Who sweet?' and something in the air change.

'We just checking out a lady come to see Shirley. We know

that eh your scene.' McIntosh laughing but face closed down now and Darwin know that there was something else in the conversation that wasn't meant for him.

'You is a good boy nah. Serious.' Jamesy join in. 'Matter of fact, we never even hear you talk bout any woman. You is a monk ah wha?'

'Leave him. He have work to do. Allyuh only like to sit down and old-talk whole day. At least the boy does handle business.' Errol light a cigarette and lean back on the wall. He turn to Darwin. 'She up there for a while now. They must be almost done. Carry her to check out the plot when they ready.'

Darwin walk up the stairs to Shirley office. Two voices – one raised, the other one soft and soothing. He know Shirley's is the softer one. She know how to talk to people when grief eat them up and the last thing they want to hear about is paperwork. He slow his step to give them a bit of time to wrap up, and wait until he hear a pause in the conversation. He squeeze past the filing cabinets at the top of the stairs and step into the office.

He almost trip over his own boots. Like somebody cuff him in his chest – is the woman, real as judgement, her back to him, sitting at Shirley desk. She pause in filling out the form, her body rigid. He don't need to see her face to recognize her; swear that he could hear the wind.

She turn slow to face him. They stare at each other and time stop. She real. He can't believe she real. No storm. Just a woman. Her handbag on the chair next to her. And she looking right at him.

'Ah Darwin, I glad you come,' Shirley start. 'This is Ms St Bernard. Her family plot is the one on 6th Street. The one like a house with an awning? I was trying to explain to her that . . .' Shirley keep talking as if she absolutely fine with people who become storms and then become people again, like if he eh forget how to move any part of his body, like if is a normal thing to meet a beautiful woman who look like that just so, on a Tuesday afternoon.

He search her face – skin brown, eyes dark like the longest road. Rust-red headwrap. He want to see her hair. Somehow he can't remember if he see her hair that night. He wonder what it would smell like, feel like under his fingers, but same time he glad he can't see it. Without it there was just her face, bare and clean like river water. And in her face – she couldn't hide it. He know she recognize him too.

'Darwin? You will carry her?'

'Carry her?'

'To see the plot and to explain about the problem?'

Darwin have no idea what problem Shirley talking about, but he figure he could wing it. He trying not to stare and know he failing bad.

Shirley look back and forth from the woman, still turned to stare at Darwin, to Darwin standing by the door. 'You know each other?'

'No—'

'Yes.' Darwin keep his eyes on her.

'Uh huh.' Shirley mouth twist in a half-smile. 'Well, I will let you two go ahead and decide on that one.'

Next thing Shirley waving them out and they walking down the stairs, past the boys, Darwin working as hard as he can to put one foot in front of the other, not daring to look at her.

They walk in silence, Darwin skin humming. Her dress black today, and her sandals flap against the soles of her feet.

'So that is your name? Darwin?' she ask.

'Emmanuel. Emmanuel Darwin.'

'Emmanuel. Like the Israelite. You here to save the world, Emmanuel?'

He look over at her expecting to see a smile. But her face serious. He offer his name but she eh give him hers. 'Why you tell Shirley we don't know each other?'

'We don't know each other.'

'You know what I mean.'

'You want me to tell her how we know each other too? You want to explain that one?'

'Well, you could start by explaining it to me.' He trying to read her, get some kinda vibe about what she feeling or thinking, but she look away and her face lock up tight. 'I didn't think you was real.'

'Well. I real. You disappointed?' She almost bite the words out. And it make him feel like he suddenly take a wrong turn, look up and find himself in unfamiliar territory.

'You asking me or accusing me?'

'You do something for me to accuse you?'

He feel himself bristle before he can catch it. 'Okay, ma'am. I ask a simple question and now you have me wondering when the argument start. I eh the one who show up by a cemetery like a jumbie.'

She don't answer, and he feel his stomach clench. He gone too far. Silence between them except for his boots crunching on the asphalt, the faint sound of traffic outside.

He trying to find something to say, anything to smooth the way between them. 'So, you from around here?'

'Look, Emmanuel . . .' Her tone soften a little and her voice calling his name is like a shaft of light in the dark. He want to ask her to say it again, to ask hers too so he could say it back to her, to see how it feel on his tongue.

'All I want to do is figure out how to bury somebody, how

to have one less thing to see about today. I really not up for small talk right now.'

It feel like a slap but the door of her face open just a crack and he see it – the weary. She look just like so many other haunted ones; her eyes puffy from lack of sleep, head full of lists and death announcements, trying to remember all who she forget to call. He imagine her sorting through photo albums, looking for pictures for the funeral programme. And his bristle smooth. He want to comfort her but somehow he know she wouldn't take it. They settle into the silence. Every now and again he see pain in her face. A twisting; her eyes flutter. She stumble on the path and, before he even think about it, he put out a hand to steady her.

'You alright?' Electric. Just touching her skin.

They reach her family plot on 6th Street in silence, his fingers still tingling. Shirley was right to say it look like a house. He know it well. Over eight feet tall and, instead of walls, four stone columns; at the top a pitched roof just like one of the old houses in Bellemere with white fretwork design. 'ST BERNARD, 1870' carved just below the roofline. Underneath is several graves next to each other, each with its own headstone and cover over with small grey stones, green shoots pushing up through them. The whole thing surrounded by a low fence with a gate. She pull a small set of keys from her handbag, unlock the gate and walk inside.

Darwin don't question what a gate that anybody could just step over need a lock for. He stand outside and watch her. He count nine plots, nine headstones, some with several names etched one beneath the other. No parting words, no last names. He scan some of the names, the ones not too faded to read: Maman, 1870; St Pierre, 1880; Patricia, 1900; Sandra 'Babygirl', 1910; Victor, 1940; Charlotte,

1960; Harold, 1965; Deborah, 1979; Catherine, 1990. The most recent is Geraldine, only a year earlier. On the back wall was another marble slab with more inscriptions but he too far to read them. The traffic sounds outside get thin and it feel like it was he, the woman and her dead, alone in all the world.

'Your family here a long time.'

'Yes.'

'Who . . .' How to ask? He don't ask them too much anymore, no matter how sad they look. No point asking when you can't help anyway. But she shake him up and settle him down same time, so he decide to just go ahead. 'Who die?'

'My mother. Petronella.'

'I'm sorry.'

Her laugh come out like a bark. 'I'm not.'

'You wasn't close?'

'No.' She pause. 'I not sure what we were. I just know I have to do things a certain way. Things about the burial.' She glance back, seem to want him to understand. 'The woman in the office. I tried to explain to her. My mother, Petronella, she has to be buried here, in this plot. See here?' She point to a grave next to the one she standing in front of and Darwin cross the threshold to look closer. 'That is Geraldine, her twin sister. They have to be together. But the lady said the grave was too new. I don't understand the problem.'

What Shirley had been trying to explain click into place for Darwin. He feel on more sure footing. 'We try not to dig a grave that come up right against another one when it so new. If the first grave dig to nine feet then the new one could dig to seven feet and it have no chance of the two graves collapsing into each other. But Geraldine bury seven and with the rain coming is a chance that when we digging for your mother . . .'

He pause and look at her, expecting to see her face fall when she understand the problem: the wet earth could crumble as they dig; a shovel could hit rotting wood, sometimes so rotted that the shovel would spill the contents of the coffin. And even a coffin can't hold the dead for long. Sometimes a shovel don't hit wood, but bone.

She stoop down and brush her hands against the low growth of weeds on the space with no headstone. 'You have to bury her like how I say. That is all I know. It have more to grave than your numbers and measurements. I understand what you saying, but it have to be like how I tell you.'

He don't know what to say. 'I just working here. I am not the boss. I just dig the graves and lock up in the evening. Nothing more to it.' As soon as he say it, he feel uncomfortable, but it is the truth. He have no choice in how these things work. He just do things how Errol and dem say to do it.

Her face darken. 'How you could be working in a grave-yard and don't believe in death? In the ritual of it and what it mean? Death is your trade.'

He try to think of something to offer, something to take away the bad-tasting words he just say. 'Sorry. I don't mean to sound any kinda way. It might not be my place to say this, but I think it don't matter to your mother where she is now. It don't matter to her sister where she is. It don't matter to the Most High where none of them flesh is. Why it matter to you?'

He turn to see her staring into the distance, like listening to something only she can hear. He lift his gaze to where she looking. Nothing there. Just graves and more graves, tall palm trees with shaggy fronds that look like beards, statues of angels and winged babies.

Yejide

Don't look, don't look, don't look. She say it over and over again but all she want to do is look at him. She glad she facing away from him. Everything about him make her feel unsteady. Prickly. Like a heat coming from under her skin and she can't take it off to get cool. Like the perfect opposite of when Petronella send her to the dead. That was a dry wind, this is a humidity wrapping around her, a heat radiating inside her, like walking in the forest just before rainy season when the air heavy and warm. Like when she and Seema run in the bush behind the house and count lizards and climb the tonka bean tree and lie down in the leaves on the grass below.

She pull herself together, straighten up and turn to him, focus on the matter at hand. 'You know your work, but I know my work too, and what you know about grave and what I know about grave is not the same thing.' She hear herself and she know she probably sound crazy but she can't think of no other way to explain. 'They have to be close, up under each other like always. Geraldine waiting for her. Is not a good thing to disappoint dead people. They does take it hard.'

He standing away from the graves, giving her room, like he in the gallery of her house, wanting to be invited in. She want to wrap up herself in something thick and heavy so he can't see her, so she can stop this building need she have to touch his arm like he had just touch hers, to see what his skin feel like, to stop this urge to tell him everything that worrying her and ask him everything that worrying him, to blurt out things that she never say aloud to anybody, not even Seema.

She wipe her hands on her dress, and stare at the trails of dirt she leave. 'You know I almost hated her when she was alive.'

'Your mother?'

'My Aunt Geraldine.'

'Why?'

'They were close. There was no room for me.'

'So why you care?'

'Why I care about what?'

'Why you care how they bury?'

How to explain to him that her mother is a womb and a grave; a cage and a pair of wings; a feeding tube and a noose. 'I don't know. I have been trying to find a word for what we were that sit right on my tongue.' She take a last look at the graves and then turn back to him. 'We weren't close. But we were bound. Like duty. Like vows.'

'I know about vows. Know about breaking them too.'

She walk toward the low gate, toward him. 'Are you the kind of man who does break vows easy?'

Darwin seem to think about it. 'No. Not easy.'

'So, you understand.'

'Understand?' He throw his head back and laugh, and she let herself just look at him – throat taut, mouth wide, hair cut close to the skull – and for a second she think of how a wolf does stretch his head up to howl at the moon, or to call to its kind far away. Something lonely.

'I don't understand nothing today, ma'am. Who are you? How you come here the other night? You going and tell me what going on?'

'You wouldn't believe me if I tell you.'

'I think anything you tell me right now, I believe you. I know what I see, and I know you here right in front of me.'

He grin slow, and everything else recede for a moment.

'You could at least tell me your name. You really going to make me go back to Shirley to find out when you could just tell me?'

His voice low and warm now like she could touch it. She too close to him, close enough to touch his arm. Close enough to lean in and whisper a secret. No. No way she could tell him anything more. He would think she was a crazy woman and he would run away, far and fast in the opposite direction. And somewhere inside herself, she already know she don't want him to run away.

She smile back at him, shake her head, close the gate and lock the small padlock behind her. They walk in step to the main road and, for a little while, she is just a woman, and a man was walking her to her car.

'What you see when you see me?' His voice serious again and she not ready for it. She turn to look at him. He so tall. She itch to reach her hand up and touch his head. He could use a better haircut. Something softer. But scraped bald make the bones in his face stand out – cheekbones like they carve from an ebony tree. Eyes tired, though. Kind, sharp, but tired. He don't miss much, don't just let things rest. Something hadn't been letting him rest much either. She know what that feel like.

When they reach her car she almost feel relieved. She close the door and turn the key in the ignition, and he step away. The engine rev up and she feel him watching her. Don't look, don't look. She wind the window down. The words bubbling up in her throat, all the things she could say but sure she should not. 'What if I tell you that what I see in you that night make me know I was going to come back for you?'

Soon as she say it she feel like an idiot. Who says something like that to a stranger they just meet? But his eyes look thoughtful, careful. Considering her.

'I think I was waiting for you to come back.' He don't smile when he say it. If anything, he look even more serious.

She nod, drive off slow, and watch him watch her in the rear-view mirror, while she turn the car in the crossroads to head back out the gate. Before she could talk herself out of it, she pause again. 'Emmanuel.' His name on her tongue sound sweet and grave. 'Don't call me ma'am. Call me Yejide.'

Darwin

Yejide. Her name like a prayer in the dark and he want so badly to echo it back to her, shout it loud as her car drive away. Stupid. He should have ask her for her phone number. 'What you see when you see me?' What kind of question was that? How he going to see her again now? Next time she come to Fidelis would be her mother funeral. He can't move on her in her mother funeral! He should give her some time after the burial done. When her life settle. He can wait as long as he have to for her. But how will he find her later if he don't get her number at the funeral? And he still don't know how he going to persuade Shirley and Errol about the plot for her mother grave.

He stay watching the exit to the cemetery for a long time. In his mind he could see her car heading down Queen Isabella Street, turn on the main road, weave through traffic. He think of her sitting there, small hands on the steering wheel. Maybe she switch on the radio. Maybe her mind turn to lists again – the things she have to do. Maybe she thinking of him like how he thinking of her.

'She gone, boy. What you waiting for?' Jamesy call out.

Darwin forget they was there, watching him.

'Like yuh score, boy!' McIntosh laugh.

Errol watching Darwin careful.

'Is not like that.' Darwin shake his head, walk over to them. 'I was just trying to explain the problem with the grave. She want to bury her mother next to the sister but the grave too new, too close. Especially with the rain nah. I explain it to her but that is how she want it.'

McIntosh grin. 'Eh heh and the fact that she pretty have nothing to do with it, right? You feel we born yesterday?'

'Is my job.' He shrug. 'She seem like a nice woman.'

'All a them nice, boy. I never meet a woman that eh nice yet.' McIntosh shake his head. Then his face get serious again. 'Listen, it not good to get too close to them people, Darwin boy. They go home and they don't think about you again and you there holding grief that don't belong to you. And where you going to put it? You think we could do this work if we used to study every person who want burial a certain way? Every pretty face that come crying to you to solve their problem? Take it from me. Best to forget about that.'

Errol grunt. 'If she want to risk disturbing the next grave then that is her business. It don't bother me. We go do it how she want. But leave that woman alone.' He walk away without another word.

McIntosh watch him go, then turn back to Darwin. 'Take what we telling you. When she go back to her people she eh go remember you. When the grief fresh you does look like the saviour. But when it heal and scab over all you go do is remind her of pain and death. Best to remember that we is your people now.'

'I hear you.' Darwin nod. He understand what McIntosh

mean. It make sense. And is true he not sure what to make of Yejide, but the others eh see her bring a storm to Fidelis. They eh been dreaming about her since that night. McIntosh give him one last look and follow Errol. The others drift off too and leave Darwin standing by himself, staring out the gate after a car that long gone.

21

They just start to dig on a plot by the south wall on 15th Street when a police car bend the corner and squeeze itself down the narrow lane, blocking it entirely.

Darwin stop wheeling the barrow and watch the jeep crawl toward them. Cardo reach over and grab him by his arm. 'Look him here, officer! Look the criminal!'

Jamesy and Cardo burst out laughing but Darwin shake him off. Babylon wasn't nothing to joke about far as he was concerned.

'I tell allyuh to stop work?' Errol growl at them.

Cardo carry on digging but McIntosh and Jamesy keep watching the jeep. It finally stop and two officers step out and walk over.

'Morning,' the taller one call out. Neither them in uniform. Darwin figure that if either feel any kind of way about being in a cemetery they doing a good job of hiding it. Although, he guess they see plenty worse.

Errol smile at the taller officer, like if police rolling up on him was exactly what he hope would happen that day, and extend his hand. 'Errol Jardim. I am the foreman. The care-taker. How can I help you gentlemen today?'

The officer shake Errol hand. 'Errol. Yes, Councillor Ancill mention you.'

The other officer look at each of them in turn, and then his gaze come to rest on the shallow grave.

'We following up on a missing person's report. One Mr Beresford Julius.'

Darwin nearly drop the barrow on his foot. The shorter officer flick his gaze over sharp.

'Julius, Julius . . .' Errol looking up into the sky, frowning. 'Nah, that name don't ring any bells.'

'His wife was buried here almost two months ago. Mrs Emily Julius,' the tall officer continue. 'We eh find much in his house when we look around, but we did find the paperwork for the burial. Sitting right there on his kitchen table. Ring any bells?' The shorter one keep his eyes on Darwin.

Darwin feel a sinking feeling. He remember. The old man was grieving, falling apart. How long he keep Emily grave paper on his table, like if the house itself a cemetery? His friends never go and look for him? Check in? Then he remember what the old man had say – my friend is lying there in the ground. Darwin shoulda checked up on him. He think of Mr Julius so many times, but he never study to ask Shirley to see the records, to find him and make sure he was doing okay. Eventually, he realize with shame, he just stop thinking of him altogether.

'Ah yes! I remember now!' Errol reply. 'Old gentleman. He was in a bad way. Ent, Darwin? You remember how he was?' Errol turn to him, his one good eye flashing, the other dead white.

The questioning officer focus on Darwin. 'You know Mr Julius?'

Darwin swallow the lump in his throat. 'No, officer. Just see him here. At the funeral.'

'And what would you say his state of mind was?'

'He look sad. I mean, he just bury his wife, so he was sad. He had a couple people with him. They was pulling him back from the edge of the grave . . .'

'Sad? Right. Anything else? This was the last place he was

seen. So, any actual information you can remember about what happened that day?'

Darwin mind racing now. Mr Julius missing all this time? Should he tell the officers that the old man was here after hours, that he let him stay? But then Errol would know he leave the gate open whole night. He would lose his job.

Jamesy step forward. 'Well, officer, you know how it is. We just take a two drinks after we was finished, after the funeral. Then we went home.' He lean up on his shovel. 'Nothing unusual. Just a normal day.'

'When was the last time any of you see him?' the tall officer ask.

'What time we finish?' Errol turn to Jamesy.

Jamesy pause. 'Mus be bout three thirty? Four?'

Cardo nod. 'Yes, it was about that because I had to go and pick up my girl from the hairdresser for half past four and you and me leave same time.'

'And did any of you see him leave, or who he left with?'

Darwin see it coming but he too late.

'Well,' Errol turn and look over at Darwin, 'you was the last one here. You see him? When you was locking up at the end of the day, I mean?'

He swallow. 'Nah. I just make my rounds as usual and lock up like you tell me to, boss.'

Errol smile again and turn back to the officer. 'He now join the crew, officer, but he is a good boy. Team player. Does work hard. I could vouch for him.'

Darwin sure the officer would get out a pad and pencil, take notes, ask him more questions. He sure at any minute he would break. He ready to explain that it was his fault, that the man was sad, so sad, and that he leave him even though he know he wasn't supposed to leave anyone in the cemetery. He was the only one who know what weight the man was carrying. It was his responsibility to check for him. But he leave him here. He went home. They could ask Ms Margo.

'So just to confirm, when you locked up at six thirty Mr Julius was already gone?' The shorter officer open his mouth for the first time. He not letting that one go so easy.

Darwin back into a corner. 'Yes, officer. The old man wasn't here when I lock up.'

'You sure?'

'Yes, sir.'

'Shame,' Jamesy mutter and shake his head. 'I hope allyuh find him, officer. It so hard for old people when they get left alone.' But then he turn back to Darwin, where the police can't see his face, and smile slow, shovel in hand. McIntosh and Cardo keep their faces straight, but Darwin don't like what he see in Errol good eye at all.

Errol shake hands with the tall officer again. 'I will tell Councillor Ancill I see you today. Good to see police doing their job, man. Allyuh does get a bad rep but it have hardworking officers on the force.'

Darwin watch them go, the jeep rumbling down the narrow street.

'Alright, boys, back to work.'

McIntosh take the barrow from Darwin, his rings glinting in the light. And suddenly everything terribly clear. Darwin know where he see that gold guard ring before. He seeing it on McIntosh hand for weeks. It the same one he see on Mr Julius hand the day of his wife funeral. Darwin stomach heave and he stumble back from McIntosh on the loose earth.

Errol look over at him. 'Watch yuh step.' He not smiling anymore. Nobody smiling. Errol one good eye black like asphalt, the other flat and cloudy.

The men start to work again. Darwin back away from them, the sound of the metal scraping the dirt and the creak of the wheelbarrow in his ears. He whisper something about needing to take a piss, turn a corner out of sight and vomit on a grave cover in sharp purple leaves.

The light already start to fade. In the distance over the hills, corbeaux circling. He there for hours, in the Carmelite quarter of Fidelis, where the nuns bury: a little enclave down a street that branch and divide and lose its own logic, almost like a separate graveyard nested in the main cemetery. The headstones faded but the flowers always fresh. He might be the only person who does come here, other than the nuns. He hear the sounds from the funeral in the main cemetery, the hymns, the cars driving in and out.

He could run. Just slip away. He must find work somewhere else. He make enough for Janaya and him to get by a bit longer. Thank God he set up that account for her before he leave. At least the money still there, even if she decide not to spend it. And what he give Ms Enid. But even so, how long that could last them? Suppose he don't get nothing else? He would be back in the same jam as when he start.

It have no way the police buy his story. Where one old man could disappear to at his age? And the way they ask, like they know already that he see Mr Julius after six thirty. None of it matter anyway. The police know the councillor, the councillor know Errol, and Errol eh protecting Darwin over his crew, if it come to that. So is Darwin who the last person to see Mr Julius alive.

The old man ring. McIntosh rob a grieving old man? Or worse? Darwin spend a good while with these fellas by now. They kill a old man just so for a gold ring? Them fellas go really set him up for one small piece of gold? He think of them all standing round with the officers, like in a theatre, and everyone know their lines except him. Shirley was right. They have him proper and well tie now.

He try to weave all the pieces together but something missing, and he can't figure it out. Say McIntosh find Mr Julius in the cemetery and attack him just because he can. But why he going back there after hours in the first place? He take a deep breath. At some point he going to have to go back and face them. He feel exposed, out in the open and surrounded by snipers with nothing to defend himself.

He will wait them out. He have the keys anyway and he have to lock up, so that would buy him some time. Until he know what to do, until he decide what his next move would be, better to lay low.

When the darkness properly fall, Darwin unfold himself from among the graves and head toward the admin building. He make his way by habit, and by the faint glow of the street lights beyond the cemetery walls. Fidelis quiet. It occur to him that the last time he was here this hour was when he was with Mr Julius, and even then it wasn't this late, wasn't full dark.

But as he reach the centre road he realize he not alone. The tip of a cigarette glow in the distance and the lamp outside the gate silhouette five figures, shovels at their feet. He walk down the road toward them, his shoulders stiff and heart pounding. Everybody here – Errol, Jamesy, McIntosh, Mikey and Cardo. It remind him of the first time he come in Fidelis and they watch him like a little boy.

'Wham, Darwin?' Errol take a draw on his cigarette and nod at him when he pull up.

'Boss,' Darwin reply.

'Lil extra work. Bigger cut than usual. You want in?'

'Cut? I don't want no cut, boss. I on my way home.'

Errol laugh low. 'Well, I thought you was smart but like I give you too much credit. Ent your mother living nice now, Darwin? And her medication buy? And she have groceries in her house? Where you feel that money coming from every week? How much you feel gravedigger does make? You think any of us eating on the corporation salary? You cut in already. No going home now.'

A pair of headlights slice through the gate half-blind Darwin and then shut off. Cardo open up and the car roll through slow. McIntosh, Mikey and Jamesy walk over wordless and Jamesy open the trunk.

Errol smile and spread his arms wide like he embracing the whole of Fidelis. 'Is not any kinda man does come to work in a cemetery. From the time I see you I know you have a something in you, same thing it have in all of us.'

Mikey, McIntosh and Jamesy walk toward them with something wrap in a blue tarp. Long. Bulky. And blood. He could smell it. They handle it easy, like they accustomed.

'And too besides,' Errol continue, 'who you think the police going to remember when they never find Mr Julius? Who you think they going to look for? How your mother go feel when she find out her son is a killer?'

He hear the car trunk close but can't see who close it and then the car slide out of gate like shadow. A white envelope pass from Cardo to Errol, who put it in his pocket. Errol reach down and pick up a shovel from the ground and throw it to Darwin. He catch it by instinct.

'What is that, Errol? What it is allyuh doing?' But he know. God he know.

'You eh hear they does call me Sweeper? Come nah, man

Darwin, you working in Fidelis so long and you eh know a dead when you see one?'

They walk in a line down 15th Street. Jamesy, Mikey and McIntosh up front holding the body, Cardo next with a torchlight, then Darwin, and Errol bring up the rear. Nowhere for him to run. Not an option anymore. Everybody seem to know where they going with no instructions and they move easy through the dark pathways. Eventually Jamesy and them stop walking, rest down the body in the tarp. They standing in front of the grave they dig earlier that day. Cardo and Mikey start to move the flowers – the marigolds and the roses and the lilies and the carnations. Put them careful on the next plot along so they don't get crush.

Then Errol push Darwin toward the grave. 'Dig.'

And so Darwin dig.

'Do quick,' Errol say. 'Nobody have time to be here whole night.'

The grave empty fast; the earth still loose. The sounds of breath in and out. No one talk. He can't even stretch his brain to the evil of what he doing. Who it was wrap up in the tarp? Who he cross? He think about the boys on the block who call him 'boss'. They know what Sweeper and dem does do in the cemetery after hours? What else it have in the world right in front of his eyes that he don't see?

The loud thud echo in the darkness. His shovel finally hit wood. 'I can't.' He don't even know he saying it out loud. For the first time he really feel like he going to collapse. 'Nah, I can't.'

'Boy, dig the fucking hole,' McIntosh growl.

He grit his teeth and keep going. Scrape the shovel along the length of the coffin till he catch a glimpse of the wood below, the ends of ropes thick with wet dirt. Cardo shine the torch down into the hole and Darwin squint up at where the fellas stand above him. He can barely see their faces, the circle of torchlight like a small moon blinding him. His chest start to pound. They could bury him here too. Knock him out with a shovel and just cover him over. It take everything in him to stay calm and not try to claw his way out of the grave.

'Rope.' Errol voice cold.

Darwin peel them from where they lie tangle on the lid of the coffin, rough and gritty, heavy with soil, and toss them up one at a time. Finally, Jamesy reach his hand down and drag him out. The fellas form up around the hole. Each one take hold of one rope end and they pull, heave, the weight of the coffin like the weight of all the world. The torch lie on the ground, shining toward the grave, but the scene around them dark and Darwin feel more than see the coffin rise to the surface. They slide it onto the solid earth.

'Right, boys. First thing first.' Errol reach for the torch and shine it toward the coffin. Jamesy and McIntosh pick up two long pieces of iron that Darwin didn't notice before, wedge them under the lid and press down. The crack of the lid, the creak as they open it in the quiet dark, nearly make his knees buckle. What the hell they doing? He don't want to look but Errol swing the torch beam onto the body like a spotlight. Is a man. Face like wax, perfect and terrible. He could have been asleep, except when people sleeping there is still something of them in their face. Eyelids flutter. Mouth slightly open. This face just still, frozen. Nothing in him at all.

Jamesy squat down and stick his hand in the coffin, searching around for something. One by one he pull them out. A small silver box. A roll-up wad of hundred-dollar bills. He pass them to McIntosh. Push his hand under the man collar. A gold chain. Lift the man head and unlatch the clasp at the back of his neck. Check the man hands. Rings. He pull each one off. One stick, too tight. He pull and pull, turn around on the man middle finger till it pop off. Hand it all to McIntosh. Now he pat down the man whole body. Pass his hands down legs, chest, arms. 'Daz it dey. Done.'

'Not bad,' Errol nod.

McIntosh help Jamesy to lift the lid, rest it back on the coffin. 'Come, boy. Nearly done.' He hold out the rope again, almost sound apologetic.

They lower the coffin back into the hole and then Darwin step away. Exhausted, shaky, sick. He want to be as far from the grave as possible. The back of his ankle brush the tarp, cold and slightly sticky on his skin.

'Take the legs,' Errol tell him.

Everything slow down. Darwin feel like he moving through quicksand. Can't get control of his limbs, don't even know how to start. He stare at Errol.

Mikey push past him. 'Do quick nah, man. We wasting night.' He grab one end of the shape on the ground, heave it up casual, rough, like lifting a bag of flour. Darwin reach down, numb, and lift the other end. They stumble to edge of the grave.

'Drop him.'

And Darwin let go. The body hit the side of the grave as it go down, earth tumble down with it; then a horrible muffled thud, and silence.

They shovel earth back into the hole. Everyone help now and the work go fast but the quicksand feeling still there and Darwin shovelling and sinking, shovelling and sinking. Halfway through, he look up from the barrow and see Errol standing at the head of the grave. He not digging, he not even watching them. He sorting the bills they find in the man coffin, checking the envelope Cardo give him. He put the chain in his mouth and bite it hard, to see if the gold real. He nod and slip it into a small bag along with the rest.

The grave fill and they cover it back with the flowers. Errol distribute the cash. Hand the gold to McIntosh. When Errol offer to Darwin he can't even move his hands. Can't take it. Errol walk up to him slow and push the money in Darwin shirt pocket.

The money feel hot like it burning a hole in his chest. He hear himself asking Yejide, 'What you see when you see me? What kind of man you see?'

ALL SOULS'

22

Yejide

Dusk drape her head like a shawl. For the last nine nights she carry Petronella locket cold on her breastbone and Granny Catherine pipe heavy in her pocket. The smoke don't bother her now and the burning tobacco taste sweet behind her throat.

Since she small these three days – All Saints' Eve, All Saints' Day and All Souls' Day – always feel special to her. Wasn't till she was in high school that she hear some of the other girls from town talking about going to Halloween parties. Whatever other people call it, the holiday have a magic on Morne Marie. Agatha and Angie would cook and they would all gather in the living room. Granny Catherine would tell stories and Mr Homer would play music. Was those days she would hear about Deborah and Babygirl and Maman and all their lovers and their sisters and their kin. And so for Petronella wake to fall on those sacred days – she couldn't have plan it better.

Yejide leave the locket open so Petronella and Geraldine faces out in the cool air. Mr Homer turn to her. 'We could make a start whenever you ready, Jide. Although' – he look up to the sky – 'we should catch it before full dark.'

She tap the pipe against her thigh and nod. They gather on the front porch of the house, all dressed in white – Seema, Peter, Agatha, Angie, Laurence and Mr Homer. Each carry a handful of white candles. Mr Homer hand Yejide the first candle and she pass the flame from Granny Catherine silver lighter on the bottom to soften it. She pause and look up at

Mr Homer – I doing this right? Is this the way? He nod and she crouch down and press the candle into the step. Then Mr Homer raise his voice and speak into the night air: 'And now let us call the ones who have come before us, who are here still with us and will be here after we are dust.'

Yejide pass the flame once more round the bottom of the candle to make sure it stand steady on the concrete, then light the wick and watch the wax pool, melt, then run down to the gallery step. 'Petronella Mavis St Bernard.' She say the name soft into the flame. 'She of two faces. She was here with us and not at the same time. She grieve and grieve until it too heavy to carry, look to the gathering storm and take to her bed, her sister's name on her lips.' The flame buck and sputter then swell and hold.

Yejide look to Peter, now waiting on the step below her, candle in hand. He follow her lead, taking the light from her candle to his and pressing it to the ground. 'Catherine Adara St Bernard,' he whisper into the flame, 'the dear one. Stop the car in the middle of traffic on the way to town to check inventory for the coming week, unlock the door, look toward the hills and the darkening sky and walk in the direction of Morne Marie. She speak to no one until she had come all the way up, through the village, through the hallways of the old house and into the master bedroom.' This flame don't sputter one bit, just burn strong and steady.

Seema hands shake before she light her candle with Peter flame but her voice smooth. 'Deborah Moriah St Bernard.' The flame swell big and wild, nearly catching a lock of Seema hair before coming down to size again and burning quietly. 'Her brown legs was wrap around the hips of her long-time lover. She pause in mid-stroke, sniff the air, climb off him, put her clothes on and walk out of his house. The wind had already start to set up before the man could even pull on his pants.'

Yejide think she could hear a little of Seema old self in those words, a touch of mischief and laughter, but before she could catch her eye Agatha cup the flame in her hand and light the next candle. A small sputter and the flame burn blue. Her voice a smoky croon, 'Sandra Babygirl St Bernard. She was telling her daughter the best way to soak the fruit for black cake one Christmas when she stand up from her chair on the front porch, kiss Deborah on her forehead, pull a wad of rolled-up bills from her brassiere, and hand them to the child just as the wind began to blow.'

Angie sit on the last step. She barely touch the flame to the wick but it catch with one word – 'Maman. The first. The one who bring the fire. One minute she was clearing bush outside with a three-line machete sharpened by her own hand, and the next had look up at the gathering clouds, drop the blade, leave the bush half-cut and take to her bed.' The black smoke from the tip of the flame soar into the dusky air.

Mr Homer walk to the bottom of the steps and Laurence walk behind him, candle in hand. He pick up his goatskin drum from the ground and stand on the grass in front of the house. 'We say their names together on this day to make sure they stay with us, that they don't forget themselves and the promises they have made. We have promises to keep too. We speak only of the manner in which they died. We speak to no one about how they lived, or how they learned to fly.'

He point his body toward the valley and start to beat a slow rhythm, his old hands firm and heavy. The drumbeat echo soft with the crickets and the frogs singing in layers, the fireflies making pinpricks in the dim.

The rhythm sound like she know it all her life. Not sound – she remember the way Petronella tell her – not sound, feel. Something guiding her like the way iguana know how to burrow through the bush, like how a fish know the way to part the water when it swim. Mr Homer start to walk and the group follow him, lighting candle after candle until the flames trail along the driveway, then curve they way back, surrounding the borders of the land. Together they make a road and the road say to the dead: *Here. This way. Come home.*

Mr Homer still drumming and at last Yejide hear a faint rhythm answer back from the darkness. The breeze snatch it away and she raise her head to listen harder. It come again, louder, and she can't tell if the wind draw it closer or if the hands that beat it were coming up the valley to meet them.

Peter come to stand beside her, his hand cupping a flickering candle. 'You wouldn't remember from last time. You was so small when Catherine die.' He nod in the direction of the faint sound. 'But they always know.'

'The villagers?'

'Yes.' He bend low to press another candle into the soft earth. 'News travel fast down there.'

'They know what we are?'

'No. Well, they know enough. The old know more than the young. That is always the way of things.' Peter voice drift off as he look into the dark. 'Whatever they know or don't, is enough to answer the drums from the hill, to come and help lift the spirit, make sure it don't settle in the valley and forget.'

'Like if any of us could ever forget.'

'Hmm.' Peter nod. 'I suppose not.'

Yejide eyes drift to Seema. She walk from candle to candle relighting the ones that blow out in the breeze. Every time they passed each other in the last few days she touched Yejide on her shoulder, smile – tentative and unsure. But the veil between them still there. Yejide keep her bedroom door lock at night and she hear no more knocks or footsteps outside it. She hadn't told Seema about the conversation with the man in the graveyard either. Emmanuel.

'How you meet Petronella, Peter? I never ask you.'

The flame in his hand light half his face. She can't tell whether the question hurt him or not, if it was the right time to ask, but he still here. Still here with them in this crazy house even though she gone.

'She never tell you?'

Yejide frown at him then realize that he can't see her face in the darkness. 'She never tell me anything, you think she would tell me this?'

'True, true.'

The drums get closer, and Mr Homer rhythm get louder. She only see his back as he stand down the slope of the drive-way, calling the drummers up the hill.

'Is Geraldine fault,' Peter finally reply, and laugh a little.

'Geraldine? How?'

'I found your mother at the shop. You never meet my mother – she gone a long time now, Marjorie was her name – she teach me to make my own clothes since I was small, so I used to go to the shop to buy cloth, zippers, buttons, them things. Is me who make all the curtains in this house, you know that? I always make sure I see about myself. Ma always used to say learn to take care of yourself so no woman can't make style on you.'

'Good advice for a life with Petronella.'

Peter frown. 'No words against her tonight, Princess. Not tonight.' His voice hard like a slap she didn't see coming.

She almost want to cup her hand to her cheek to soothe the sting.

'I sorry, Peter. I didn't mean . . .' She drift off and his face reassemble into the peaceful look he always wore.

'First time I see her she was directing some workers in front of the shop. They was offloading boxes and long reams of cloth. And big men yes ma'am-ing and no ma'am-ing her like she was an army general. I was across the road and I just stop. Hold up people on the pavement and had them cussing me. I didn't even need anything that day but best believe I find myself crossing the road, all the while making up what I was going to say I needed, figuring out how to ask for the boss lady. I don't think I had more than ten dollars in my pocket. But by the time I reach the door I get nervous and I just walk past.'

'You walk up to the shop and just turn back?'

'Like a fool,' he laugh. 'I make the whole rounds down Isabella Street, all down by the market trying to get brave, before I finally come back. By the time I walk in the door and spot her by the cash register, I was ready. I wait in the line, was only about three people in front of me. When I reach her, I say, "Good afternoon, miss, my name is—" and before I could say anything else she just say, "Wrong sister."'

Yejide stifle a laugh. Don't feel right to be laughing at a time like this but even she didn't see that one coming. 'You take Geraldine for Mummy?'

'Girl, is shame I was shame.'

'But how she know you wasn't asking for her? How she know you wanted Petronella?'

One of the candles blow out and Peter start patting his pockets. Yejide reach out and hand him Granny Catherine silver lighter. He kneel at the candle and Yejide follow him.

'Geraldine just point toward the back of the shop. All I

could see was reams and reams of fabric, curtains hanging from the ceiling. Those days the shop wasn't as fancy as how it is now. Was just cardboard signs with prices and rolls of chiffon and sateen and cotton and polyester and rayon like a maze. I didn't even know where she was pointing or why, but I walk in the direction Geraldine send me, still feeling like a fool. And then there she was – standing at a table with the measuring tape round her neck and a big sewing scissors in one hand slicing through some deep blue fabric. Twins. Same face. But the second I see her I can't imagine how I mistake one for the other.'

Yejide feel her breath catch. Peter not even there with her anymore, just kneeling on the grass staring into the flame.

'She let the piece she cut off drop to the table and fold back the rest onto the spool, her face serious. And I say to myself, Lord, I make a mistake. This woman hard. No way, no way I have a chance. And then she look right at me – right at me, yuh hear. Straight face, no smile and she say, "Take you long enough. I say you wasn't coming."' Peter unfold his body and stand up. Yejide stand with him. 'And that was it. I following her ever since.'

Did her mother see Peter coming like she had seen Emmanuel? Had she been as confused, as sure? Had she known what she was sending her daughter to when they met in the dream garden between the living and the dead?

'Look.' Peter point ahead. Pinpricks of light like a swarm of fireflies roll over the crest of the hill and start making their way up the drive. Mr Homer beat the drum louder and now there was no way to mistake it. The drums that answer him coming up the hill toward them, coming from the swarm of light.

Agatha join them and take Yejide hand. 'Come. You

supposed to be standing on the gallery.' The others join them on the front steps. Suddenly Yejide mind flick back to the Walking Gallery. A black and white picture just like this – a gathering of men and women standing on the front steps, their faces barely visible, eyes like black points, and the light faded as though early evening. It shake her to the core. She had seen this moment over and over again from the time she was a child, passed it every day, not knowing that it was the image of her own future.

She can make out the people in the approaching crowd clear now. People carrying candles in Styrofoam cups, the light casting patterns on their faces; others carrying big flambeaus. Young people helping the elders on the rough road in the fading light; children running in between the feet of their parents; drummers wet and glistening with sweat, their drums singing out into the night. Two women to the left of the crowd holding hands, clutching rosaries: 'Hail Mary, full of grace, the Lord is within thee. Blessed art thou amongst women and blessed be the fruit of thy womb . . .'

Mr Homer walk forward to the group, his hands a blur. As he move closer to the gathering crowd, is like he fling off his old-man self and age backwards. The younger drummers break out of the group and follow the candle path toward Mr Homer just as he following it toward them. When they meet, the prayers and muttering voices crescendo with the drums and Yejide see so much light and colour surrounding each one of their heads – some dark as pitch, some deep purple, some saffron yellow – full of life and restless energy.

Then out of the forest, from beyond the borders of the St Bernard land, they come: one by one, faces from the paintings in the Walking Gallery call to life. Maman, tall and broad like the columns of the house, striding across the grass. The strength of her gaze make Yejide feel like she about to tip over, but a hand take hold of hers, squeeze tight, and she know without looking that it belong to Seema.

Then Babygirl come, her face smiling and open, full of mischief. She walk dainty and quick and join the throng, gather close to the women saying the rosary.

Deborah walk out the tonka bean tree, like she had been sitting in its boughs just waiting for her turn, and march up straight to the drummers and start to dance. Her body sway and sweep, low to the ground then on tiptoes like she ready to take flight. She touch the back of one of the drummers and his body bend like a tree in the wind and his hands start to cut a rhythm that sharpen everything, set a frenzy in the crowd, and what was a mournful dirge start to resemble a Jouvay morning at daybreak, with laughter and movement and waists and hips and arms in the air and song.

Deborah circle the drummers again and Yejide almost can't see her body in a blur of sparkling gold. She shine so bright it seem impossible that nobody else can see her, and Babygirl hold the ladies with the rosaries and their prayers get louder and more ardent; sound like song, like they want to lift themselves to heaven with their prayers. Maman stay standing steady on the outskirts of the crowd, her feet taking purchase on the earth like she alone holding the whole world together, like she grounding them all in the land that she pay for in blood and fire.

Yejide smell tobacco in her nostrils even though her pipe gone out long ago and she know is Catherine. Her granny float out of thin air and walk toward the throng. Her eyes bore into Yejide's and she swear she see tears, happy tears like she glad to be back. Yejide break free and start to run down the steps, hands trying to hold her back and failing,

'Granny Catherine, Granny Catherine!' She run straight into the crowd, scattering people left and right. She could hear the frail voice of one of the elders in red say, 'The child in spirit. They come for her. Leave her, let her go,' and the hands no longer try to restrain her. But before she could reach her granny, something start to stir in the air in front of her. Like motes of dust circling, coming together, trying to form something solid. And out of the dust and candlelight and the thick, steady drumbeat come Petronella.

Yejide stop in her tracks, between the spectre of her mother and her grandmother. Petronella, who was always so sure and so stern, look lost and spiderweb thin, like she barely there at all. And when Yejide look closer she see something that she had never see before – bits of herself in her mother face. Something of her in the wide-set eyes, the way she tilt her head, how her collarbones jut out, her bony shoulders. She imagining it? Some kinda wish fulfilment? Her mother, who was always larger and more beautiful and more terrible than could be real, now stand almost the same height as her daughter. But something else too. Her face narrower, longer than she remember, her arms more spindly, oddly proportioned – too long for her body. She hold them in close by her side, not like arms at all. Like wings. And she not dancing like the others, she not even really moving, as if her body can't quite remember how.

'Is you who giving her life now.' The smell of blue smoke, sweet tobacco float past Yejide nostrils and she feel the baby-powder presence of Granny Catherine standing behind her. 'Just like how every daughter exist in her mother womb long before she is even a thought. Is the daughter who make the mother an ancestor when she die.'

Yejide think of Mr Homer words when they start the ritual:

we call their names so they remember. She see her mother spindly frame, the bird way she hold herself, the way she frozen
staring at the dancers, and she know what she have to do. Petronella can't be an ancestor in this halfway form; she need to
remember that she has not always been a winged thing. It was
not just the drums that call her to the land, to the house; was
not just the candles that light the road and bind her to this
place. It was Yejide, the child, the heir, who must remind her
mother spirit that she was also a woman. Once she lived and
she was a woman.

Yejide body start to sway. The people that had parted to let
her pass gather round her and make a circle. She see Agatha
and Angie at the edge of the crowd but she can't see Seema.
Peter alone on the gallery, his face barely visible in the dark but
she know he looking, looking, his head turning this way, and
that way, feeling Petronella there and searching for her still.

But none of them is Yejide business now. Her business here
with her mother, to make her whole, to flesh and ground her,
to make her woman again. One by one her foremothers walk
toward her and draw close and she feel her throat open and
she speak with their voices and it come out in a song:

*Fold your wings in close to your body. Shift your power to your
legs. Feel the muscles stretch and lengthen, grow strong to walk
the long distances that you will need to cover.*

*Use the sickle of your beak to pick the feathers from your body.
The first, like plucking the very heart from your chest. The second,
like gouging an eye. Steel yourself. The others will feel like mere
pinpricks until you don't notice the pain at all. Bury each black
feather in a secret place. If you can find a bush fire, drop a feather
in the flames. Do not stay to watch the blaze singe it to dust. The
black smoke is part of you now. Leave it be.*

Petronella start to fill out. The motes in the air combine

and form themselves up into something solid. The colour return to her skin, her face compose itself and the green of her dress become luminous like mangrove river.

Think yourself long. Think your body bigger than itself. Your sinews will remember; you know the meaning of sacrifice. You will see others that look like you remain small, remain bird. Do not mind them. They have their work and you have yours. Not all can come where you must go.

Feel the chords in your throat reknit themselves, hum, vibrate. Test your voice. Not all beautiful things are pretty and yours is small and croaky from lack of use. But use your throat. Sing.

When the last feather is gone, and your woman body has grown full, remember that you remain a bird inside. You have not forgotten how to fly. For what is more woman than holding death and life, sky and earth in your body same time, to fly while earthbound?

Her eyes come back last, flashing sharp like she know herself again. Petronella. And Yejide feel her heart fill up, feel like a long line that connect Maman to Babygirl to Deborah to Catherine to Petronella finally include her now, after all this time. She gaze in her mother eyes. They brim with emotion, more loving than Yejide had ever see them, growing rounder even as she look upon her daughter, and finally her voice emerge, raspy like sandpaper.

'You shoulda run.'

'What?' That was the last thing she expected.

'You shoulda run while you still could. Take your man. Make your own damn life. Leave me, leave all this. Let me fade away. Find a different kind of death.'

And she realize what she see in her mother eyes isn't softness, isn't love. Is regret, bitter like gall. Yejide so angry she could almost laugh. What the hell Petronella have to be bitter about? When she had a mother to love her like any ordinary girl?

'But you was happy here. With Peter. With Geraldine. I know it, I saw it.'

'Where it say anything about happy in them stories Granny Catherine was always filling your head with? You remember anything about corbeau living happily ever after? No. I woulda make sure you understood that, if it was me telling the story.'

'So why you didn't tell it then?' Yejide feel like Petronella still have talons and they ripping her heart from her chest. 'You coulda warn me if you didn't want this, didn't want to be called back. You think I trying to disappoint you? How I suppose to know what you want?'

Pet steups and her mouth twist in disapproval.

Yejide know that face well and it send her over the edge. 'You hold this against me my whole life! Just because you wanted a different kind of fate? Because of something that have nothing to do with me, that I couldn't even help?' She hate how her voice pitch high and whine like she a child again. It come out like a question, though she don't want it to.

Petronella sigh and it sound like distant wings beating, like the whole forest moving in the wind. 'This is our life, and this is our death. Is how it is. It don't matter now. From this side . . . none of it matter.'

'So, you never love me then?' Yejide almost in tears now.

'Spirit and flesh, Yejide. Don't confuse one for the other.'

The dead women of Morne Marie gather round her then, and fold Petronella into them. The voices they had give to Yejide dry up in her throat. Together they shrink and darken and lengthen and beaken and claw and wing and they take to the sky, wings black-brushing her head. And her mother go with them, leaving words small like a breath in her ear, 'Run. Take your man, take yourself and run. Let the dead bury the dead.'

The last drumbeat cut and the crowd – voices and bodies and spirits that was in full flight, energy high – start to settle and come back to earth. Yejide collapse on the sweet grass, her body alive and tingling and slick with sweat. And she could hear the crickets sing and the frogs croak and the life under the soil writhe and burrow and creep.

23

Darwin

'Yejide . . .'

Darwin wake with her name on his lips.

The sound of drums shake him from sleep but now that he sit up in his bed, chest heaving and body slick with sweat, the only real sound is the morning drizzle tapping on the galvanize roof and the clinking of the little glass charms in Ms Margo window that sing every time the breeze blow.

For hours he toss and turn with dreams. He had been back in the pickup that had brought him to Port Angeles, watching the corbeaux circle the city, but this time somehow he jump out the truck and follow them and end up in Fidelis standing next to a grave and he know it belong to Mr Julius. Six corbeaux sit down watching him with beady eyes, head cock to one side like they waiting for him to do something. He grab a shovel and start to dig. He can't let the old man suffocate in the ground and he dig and dig and dig till he feel like his back breaking. Errol and the fellas appear too, and they laughing at him, and when his shovel hit wood he start to scramble the dirt with his hands till they bleed, and his nails rip away from his skin. But when he open the coffin, is not Mr Julius at all but Yejide. And her skin pale and grey and ants crawling out of her eyes. He hold on to her body and scramble it up, try to carry her away, to get her out the coffin. If he could just get her out, he could save her, just get her out of the hole, but he feel hands grabbing at his shirt, grabbing him and hauling him out, and no matter how he fight them he can't get to her, can't do nothing for her, nothing at all.

In another she was in a clearing in the middle of the forest and she was dancing, in a big multicolour dress, spinning, spinning, spinning till the skirt float out around her and she was all brown legs and thighs and skirt, and he feel like his heart going to jump out of his chest. He start to walk toward her, to reach out and take her hand, but she lift off into the air and float like a balloon till all he could see is a speck in the sky leaving his hands empty and his heart sick.

Fear settle in him and coil like a macajuel. He sit up and put his feet on the ground – dreams wouldn't let him sleep anyway – and welcome the cold of the floorboards, the chill of the early-morning air. Used to be that dawn was a promise, a new day that mean he could always start over; no matter what going on, once he have life, two good hand and two good foot, he could always start over. But two good hand and two good foot don't make him any less safe, wouldn't do him no good in jail. Two good hand and two good foot don't help if it have man like Errol in the world willing to take them from you.

He still don't know for sure. Is not like he see them fellas kill Mr Julius or anybody else but what he see was enough. What he help them do was enough. Errol was right. He in it as deep as them ever since he come to this place. Maybe is something to what Ms Enid say after all, that his father come to Port Angeles and the city pull him under.

His father.

He know it don't have any sense to think that that man he see is his father. It have no way. Big man like him, long past the point of wanting a daddy. What he want to find him for anyway? He go help Darwin out of this mess? Tell him how to raise a man from the dead? Tell him how to claim a woman that appear and vanish like a storm and leave no trace behind her?

He run his hands over his head. New hair come through again. He still wasn't used to way his head felt, the shape of it, the nakedness of it. He never think about his hair as a thing that does change so fast but with his head bare and open he feel it all the time now. Every scratchy prickle of new growth announce to the world that time passing, that things changing, that he not only make a choice once but making it over and over again.

That choice bring him to Yejide. A woman he only see twice in his life and each time have him more confused. A woman who invade his dreams. It have nothing good that could explain that. Nothing that come from God could explain that.

He should be fighting for his life, packing his things, leaving a note for Margo, heading back out in that long line in Wharton – give me another job. Any other job. But as the sky outside start to lighten, streaks of pinks and blues and purples as the day wake up, all he could think is that her mother funeral was tomorrow. He feel a thrill that he would see her again but how to look her in her face knowing what he do last night? And what if dem boy dig up in Yejide mother coffin too as soon as she turn her back? Should he warn her, 'Take all your mother things, don't leave her with none. Matter of fact, bury her somewhere else'? He can't do that without implicating himself and he don't know how to see her again if he just never show up to Fidelis at all.

He know he should run. He was never a stupid fella. For everything that he was, he was never stupid. Better to go home and hope his mother forgive him. He shake himself and get off the bed, straighten the sheets, fix back the pillows and head down the corridor to the bathroom. He lock the door, look in the mirror and think of the first time he had see his face after he take the shaver to his hair, the scissors to his beard. His face even harder now – eyes looking hollow. His beard fuller and more ragged. He look like one of them pipers he used to see on the block. He been so many different men since he get off that truck. Is like all his selves – past, present and future – colliding and going to destroy him in the process. 'You always do your best, Emmanuel,' Enid had say. He wish he could believe that still, could see that man in himself, the same man Yejide was so sure she would come back to Fidelis for.

He turn on the water and cold splash on his face brace him for the day. He hear the first sounds of Margo moving around in the kitchen – the screech of the kettle, the smell of onions sweating in the pan. All Saints' Day. Whether he ready for it or not, is morning.

Enid work a few days a week taking care of old people in a place name Sweet Home. She was a nurse working in the health centre when he was growing up, and it serve her well, so even though she retire a good few years now she could still get work when she want it. Rich people have no shortage of old parents that they have too much money to mind themselves. And those who not so rich does work so much they don't have the time or the space to put them. Between them Enid was never short of work; they too glad to have somebody like Enid Phillips do the needful. Sweet Home sit just outside the city proper in Wharton. Darwin can't work out what could be sweet about your family sending you somewhere to die but he suppose whoever name it so was hoping that the big green yard, the neat rose bushes and the converted colonial-style mansion would cover up all those other parts.

The security guard at the entrance nod at him as he pass, and he almost change his mind and turn back; even fake police make him jumpy. And then, when the receptionist sitting at a desk big like Margo whole kitchen table smile at him and offer him a seat while he wait for Nurse Phillips, it was almost too much. He don't know how everybody who look at him not pointing they fingers and accusing him, how they can't smell the stench of dead on his skin.

'Emmanuel.' Enid smile at him as she walk over. She look like a whole different person in her uniform, fit in like if she was more at home here than in Dalia Street. She sit in the chair opposite him, tuck in a corner with a little coffee table and a window. 'I tell you I don't mind passing by you for it. Give me a chance to sit with Margo a little bit anyhow.'

'Nah, is okay. Easier for me to pass on my way to work. And we could still spend a little time.' The last thing he want is for Enid to come back round Bellemere again, with the boys on the corner still nodding to him like he some kind of gangster. The more distance he could put between his life now and his Dalia Street family, the better.

'If you say so.'

He hand her another envelope and she put it in her pocket quick.

'Lord, these people going to feel I in some shady business now with you handing me envelope like a blasted drug dealer.'

'You know I not no drug dealer, Enid!' Darwin feel his face get hot. The receptionist look over in their direction. He say that louder than he mean to.

Enid eyes open wide. 'Who you raising your voice at? You better pat down when you talking to me, eh.' Her voice low and steely. Then soften. 'I was just making joke with you, Emmanuel.'

'Sorry. I just . . .' He rub his eyes. 'Didn't sleep so good.'

'You looking like you eh sleeping so good for a while now.'

'Just work, Ms Enid. I okay.'

Enid lean forward close to him, her eyes bright. 'Emmanuel, you know you could always come home. If you in trouble, if things not going how you plan here, you could come home.'

'Everything okay. Don't worry. Is just a few nights. I handling it.'

'Well, alright. If you say so. You is a big man.'

'Ma good?'

'She good. She miss you.'

'She say that?'

'No.'

Darwin think about the last few days. Better so. 'Alright. I gone. I nearly late. What time you finishing?'

'Just now. Just doing changeover for morning shift. If I don't watch these new girls they will kill out all my residents. Keep you busy.' She glance at him, her smile crooked and teasing. 'Too soon?'

'See you later, Ms Enid.' He could feel her eyes on him as he walk out the door.

He don't like to give these town taxis his money when the traffic heavy, he could walk faster than they could drive, but it early enough that he hoping the route not jam up yet. He flag down a car at the junction up the road and jump in. From the backseat window he watch the fancier houses get smaller and less fancy. Then the houses disappear and is more apartment blocks, then those go too and is only stores and offices and restaurants and workers hustling to get a start on the day. They taking a route he not familiar with but then he see the Governor Square up ahead and get his bearings again. The car slow down and stop, a line of traffic in front of it. The driver lean on his horn, the next man in front stick his hand out the window and cussing everybody. A headache start to brew like a storm. If they keep this up best he get out and walk.

And then he see her. Yejide. She sail through the crowds of people on the pavement like a fast-moving schooner in white – loose-fitting pants, a white T-shirt and sandals, white headwrap covering her hair. If he didn't actually talk to her once already, he woulda swear he hallucinating her again.

He start to tell the driver, he will take it here, pull out his money to pay the man, when he get a flash of the blue tarpaulin, the loose soil, Errol teeth biting down on the dead man gold chain. Best to leave it. He put his wallet back in his pocket. She don't need the trouble he have riding with him. Same time the traffic start to move and his driver stop grumbling. He take one last look and out of nowhere he get a feeling, certain in his gut, that if is anybody who could deal with the trouble he in, is that woman right there. But the car picking up speed now and the crowd closing in and he lose sight of her in the distance.

24

When he reach, a line of cars park up waiting for Fidelis to open. All Saints'. He open the gate and let them in.

'You think this is something?' Shirley say while they drink a cup of coffee together upstairs, looking on at the people milling around. 'Used to be more! Long time this place used to be buzzing for three days straight. Council used to give a special grant to clean up the whole place, we paint all the monuments, power-wash the mausoleums – even the ones where the line die out used to get a little something. But these days. Well, you know how it is. The old ways does die out. Now everybody have to ketch they own ass.'

He only half-listening to her. For his part he glad things busy enough today, so he get to avoid Errol and McIntosh and them. So many people around – young boys come to hustle a dollar for the dead season, families bring flowers or put a fresh coat of paint on their ancestors' crypts – and Darwin easily melt into the bustle alongside them. All day he clearing brush, painting kerbs, weeding the plots, mixing cement to repair broken headstones. Everywhere is the smell of incense and candle wax and fresh-cut grass. At one grave he see a couple hold each other and cry. The headstone was small. Little angel wings at the top. At another, about twelve people gather around, a car door open and music blasting from the radio. Red cups line up on the low wall that surround the grave and a man empty out a little bit of the rum on the ground before he start to top up the cups.

But now and again he pass one of the crew, moving in

another direction, and he feel their eyes on him. It have a waiting in the air: they show their hand already, what the real work in Fidelis is, and now they watching him struggle to get out the knot they use to tie him, wondering when he would stop trying.

It feel like how it was in the beginning again – them as one unit and he on the outside looking in. Except this time, he don't want to be let in. He hoping they forget he even exist.

He working down in the south-east corner, cutting back the bushes, when Cardo sidle up to him. He don't say anything for a while, just watch the blade chopping, the brush collecting at their feet. Then he clear his throat.

'Darwin, boy. It doh have to be like this. Listen, bredren. I understand. We from the same place, two ah we come from country, grow up with nothing. People shouldn't bury with all them things anyway. Where we from people who would be glad to have a little piece of what them fools want to put into the ground.'

If the thing wasn't so dread he woulda laugh. If talking that make Cardo feel better bout himself then good for him. But Darwin don't turn around, don't stop what he doing, and after a while he hear the big man shuffle away.

By the time the sun on the descent on the other side of mid-afternoon the tension have him on edge. He decide to take a walk in the city, find a bench to eat a late lunch. He head to clock out and right there on the steps is McIntosh, smoking a cigarette. Blocking his path. Darwin stop in his tracks. He almost turn back and forget about the whole thing but that would be too obvious. He keep going, trying to look casual.

'Darwin.'

'McIntosh.' He nod. 'How it stay?'

'Alright inno. Sun hot today.'

'Yeah. You taking some shade?'

'Yeah, a little something.' He slide the pack of cigarettes from his pocket, hold it out to Darwin.

He shake his head. 'Might have a little drizzle later. Cool things down.'

'Nah, boy.' McIntosh slip the pack back in his pocket but keep hold of the lighter. 'This kinda heat does stay. Weatherman say it going to get worse.'

'Yeah?'

'Yeah. Heat for so from now till whenever. Ting does dead in this heat.'

McIntosh start to flick the lighter on and off. Darwin could hear the scraping sound of the metal ball under the man rough thumbs, the click and whoosh of the flame coming to life in the cradle of his hand. 'Might be a good idea to put some more water on them ixora in the evenings so they stay good. Smart thing to do nuh. Make life easy for yourself down the line.'

'I don't think so.' Darwin look from the flame in McIntosh hand to his face and hold his gaze steady. He like that, as tall as McIntosh is, he have to look up at Darwin slightly from his seat on the steps to talk to him. 'I don't think so. Ixora tough, man. You ever realize you don't see them dead just so?'

'Eh heh?'

'They eh easy to kill.' They look at each other a little while longer. Darwin know that they eh talking about no blasted ixora but he not going to give McIntosh an opportunity to make his meaning plainer.

'So, you is a smart fella eh. Know about plants and ting?'

'Nah. Not smart, McIntosh. Just know a little something.'

'Right. Right. That is good. When people feel they too smart sometimes, it doh go good for them, you know. They don't like to take advice.'

'Well, that is not me at all, as I say. I from country. Just a simple fella.'

'Mm hmm.' McIntosh keep his eyes train on Darwin. Then his cell phone beep in his pocket.

Darwin abandon his plan to clock out. As McIntosh answer the phone he turn and walk down the main road, out the gates and into the street as slow and casual as he could manage it. The breath that he was holding come out in a rush. A single car park up alongside the cemetery. Navy blue car, windows tinted. The hair on the back of his neck stand up. He tell himself be easy, just cool. Nobody will attack him in broad daylight. Even so, he decide to cross the road.

But then he look closer and realize he know the car, and he can just make out the driver. A woman, dark shades almost covering her face, shielding her from the late-afternoon sun. Before he could start to walk toward the car, it roll forward slow to meet him. His heart racing different now.

The driver's window slide down. 'Hi.'

'Greetings.'

Everything he decide fly clean out his head at the sight of her. Her skin deep brown and smooth, her hair uncovered for the first time, thick coils that he want to bury his hands in.

'You busy?'

'Right now?' He think of the people in Fidelis with their candles and prayers, the keys in his pocket. He supposed to be back there soon. He think of Errol. What message it would send if Darwin disappear in the middle of the workday? But she was here, right here. For no other reason. She come for him. 'I not busy.'

He can't see her eyes behind the darkers but he know she just staring at him, like how he drinking in the sight of her.

'Do you want to go somewhere?'

Darwin look down at himself, his overalls, his dirty boots. 'Where?'

'Does it matter?'

It seem a foolish thing suddenly for him to worry about how he looking, if he would dirty up her car, if she would want to be seen with him. He remember that first day, when them fellas tease him about not wanting anybody to know that is a cemetery he working. But is here she meet him. It have nothing he could hide from her.

'I don't want to be alone right now.'

He see her fingers tighten just a little bit on the steering wheel, like asking for something she need was a hard thing for her to do. He walk around to the passenger seat and get in.

The car clean. He wince a little to see dirt flake off his boots onto the mats. She even Armor All the dashboard and the steering wheel to protect them from the sun, so everything look black and shiny. Purple and silver rosary beads hanging from the rear-view mirror. Faint smell of spiced wood. He wonder if is the oil she rub into the dashboard but when she lean slightly closer to him to adjust the mirror he realize it coming from her. Perfume? Something she put in her hair? Or maybe is just how her skin smell to him. Like sandalwood. Cedar.

They pull off, join the main road and the slow crawl of all-day traffic in Port Angeles. He watch her grip on the steering wheel, light and sure. She small but lean all the way back in the seat, right hand steering, left hand on the armrest. It take everything in him not to reach over and put his hand next to hers.

She drive careful. Not frighten, not uncertain, just steady. The light turn yellow as they reach an intersection and she slow down. The car next to them zoom past. Nearly smash into a next car trying to beat the light from the other side of the crossing. Car horns blare out, the man in the middle of the intersection stick his hand out the window, pelt cuss behind the car that nearly run into him and then drive off. All this before the light even properly change red. Darwin shake his head. Is people like that does keep Fidelis busy.

He about to make some comment about bad drivers and car accidents but as he turn to her he wonder if she even notice what happen. He still can't see her eyes, but just the way she hold her head, the way her mouth set, he could tell she somewhere else. She shouldn't be driving. Her mother funeral is tomorrow. But she didn't say she want to talk. She just say she don't want to be alone. He could do that. Just be with her. He lean back in the seat.

They turn off the main road and cut through back streets, through a series of neighbourhoods mazed with shortcuts. He don't know these routes at all. He just been walking from Bellemere to Fidelis and back. Not too much free time to explore anywhere. He can still hear the city noises, the traffic, the car horns, but they seem to be always one step ahead of it, the sound far off though they can't be out of the city yet.

She know her way around. On autopilot, her mind far. He look out the window. Some of the streets look like Bellemere – family houses, little front yards. They drive down one with some boys playing cricket. As the car get closer one boy grab the stumps and the bat and he and his friends scatter to the sides of the road. Darwin nod and hail them as they pass and some of the smaller ones run behind, waving and laughing like is a game they play every time a car come this way.

Darwin look at them in the wing mirror and smile. Remind him of Dalia Street. Not like they used to include him in their games too much when he was small but he remember seeing them from his front step or when he was going market with Janaya. When he look front again he catch Yejide glancing at him just for a second before she turn back to the road.

They leave the crush of the city behind. Less concrete, fewer tall buildings and apartment complexes. The bigger houses get fewer and further between. Here, children splashing each other with water from a garden hose and a standpipe running into the drain outside; people sitting on concrete benches at roadside bars under umbrellas with beer-company logos, Styrofoam cups scattered on a table; a line of people outside Melinda's Kitchen winds its way down the pavement; two men walk out of Ali's Last Stop Rest and Bar, one carrying two big bags of ice to his car trunk, the other hefting a red and silver gas tank on his shoulder.

Her left hand move from the armrest to the gears and he feel the engine turn over as the road start a slow incline through the mountains. Before long everywhere turn green and the air feel cool, and the road open into another world. On one side is rock folds and moss-green trees and tiny springs trickle out of the cracks. On the other, lush valleys, the golden glow of the afternoon sun and big open sky. Is not like Darwin never see mountains before, not like he never see the world splay open in green and gold and fire and softness, but somehow here with her, driving in a silence that don't feel like silence, it hit different. He keep his eyes on the view outside the window, reach toward the armrest in between their seats and catch hold of her hand. Her fingers stiffen, then fold themselves into his. He breathe in the cool air, feel the last rays on his face and close his eyes.

25

Yejide

The breeze from the open window ruffle his scruffy beard slightly. She resist the urge to stroke a rough spot on his palm in case it wake him up. She can smell the earth on his boots, that unmistakable man smell after a long day. Not unpleasant. Just what it was.

She always like driving. The rumble of the engine, the way her car hug the corners as she drive around the bends in these hills. She know the roads like the back of her hand, but still. Some of the corners so sharp and blind that she would not see an oncoming driver until they were right on top of her; or a group of hikers could emerge from a path in the mountain, just so; or an agouti could dart across the road forcing her to mash brakes, or, if another car was too close behind her, to feel the sharp, distressing bump under her tyres. Driving make her experience death like any other person in the world – always a possibility, something to guard against, something to fear and the little thrill of escaping it for another day. Driving make her feel ordinary.

But nothing ordinary about holding the hand of the sleeping man who will bury her mother tomorrow. Even the shades can't stop her from seeing his cool green glow, his light, his life. It terrify her. How to feel this way and then know that any time together would mean watching that light change, watching it grow darker and deeper until she could see his death, maybe down to the exact moment? Her mother and Granny

Catherine suddenly seem lucky that they went first, leaving Mr Homer and Peter behind. But she wonder about Deborah, about Babygirl, about Maman. Had they outlived their lovers? Another thing she didn't know to ask. How had they borne the inexorable knowing, the waiting? How to say to a man – as he wash the dishes in the house, dig out the sweet potato from the backyard, carry a child on his shoulders, read a book in the gallery, hold you close, bring you tea – that you will miss him soon when he is dead? Her mother words echo in her head. *Take your man, take yourself and run.*

But Emmanuel. No death at all in him that she can see. What that mean? Maybe they could live their whole lives, neither of them knowing the year, the month, the day, the hour. She could be normal with him and he never have to know. She could convince him that what he see that night was just a dream, that whatever god was his and all the gods that was hers bring them together and that was that. She could leave Morne Marie.

She look over to see his eyes flutter open and turn lazily toward her. God, he beautiful. It take plenty effort to keep her eyes back on the road.

'I see you earlier today, you know. In town.' His voice thick with sleep.

'Where?'

'Francis Street. Just past the square.'

'Why you didn't say anything?'

'I was in a car heading up the road.'

She sneak another quick look. He could have got out the car.

'And I had decide that maybe it wasn't a good idea.'

'Why?'

'Just . . .' He sound careful, like he measuring her, weighing his words. 'My life real complicated right now.'

Before she could even realize it she burst out laughing. He sound so earnest and so worried. 'Man, you have *no* idea.'

He chuckle deep and low and then his eyes widen a little, surprised, like is a while since he really laugh.

'Well, at least I know you don't snore,' she smile.

His hand tighten around hers.

The road broaden and they turn away from the view and continue uphill. Up ahead Annie standing in her usual spot, at a folding table on the pavement, stirring a big silver pot, a rack of roast corn on the side, charred black and yellow. The smell float into the car. 'Hungry?' Yejide ask.

'I could eat.'

She slow down and pull off the road next to the vendor. 'Afternoon, Annie.'

'Afternoon, dear. Your usual?'

'Yes, please,' she say, with such eagerness that it make Annie laugh.

'And for the gentleman?' Yejide watch Annie look boldly at Darwin, sizing him up. Within the hour the network would be activated: Ms Pet daughter bring a man up Morne Marie.

He smile. 'Two roast for me, auntie. And if the soup taste as nice as it smell I will take one too.'

'Ask Yejide and she will tell you. This is the best soup you will ever eat.'

'Well, give me a big one then and put plenty dumpling.' His grin nearly break Yejide apart. It is the first time she see him smile, really smile. Annie blush and look at him somewhere between a mother gazing on her favourite son and a siren wondering how soon she could lure him to her bed. He had that quality. The kind where you don't know if to take him home and feed him or just take him home.

Annie hand their food through the window and Yejide

pull off, holding the corn with one hand and steering with the other.

'So, you from around here then?' he ask.

'Higher up the hill.'

'But they know you in the village?'

'Small community. Everybody kinda know everybody. Even if just by face.' This is the opening to tell him everything. But she enjoying the moment – the smell of the roast corn in her hand, the steam rising from his cup. She don't want to break it.

'My mother used to make a wicked corn soup,' he say. 'This one not far off.'

'Used to?' Are they the same in this too?

His smile falter a bit. 'Well, she probably still making it. We eh talk in a while.'

'I'm sorry. Mothers are never an easy thing.'

'The other day when you come to the cemetery. You sound like you know a little something about that.'

'Yes.'

'You want to talk about it?'

'Right now, all I want to talk about is this soup.'

He nod. 'Soup easier.'

They drive on for a while until she find the spot she had in mind. She pull off the road again into a wide-open area. A few cars already there, but they park plenty far apart. Yejide get out and walk toward the edge of the clearing, and he follow her. From here they can see all of Port Angeles. The squiggly streets, the sprawling gardens, the tiny parks, flashes of silver and rusted brown, the spires of cathedrals, the red and yellow poinciana trees. She feel him just behind her and for a crazy moment is like they could walk off the edge right into the blue sky. He move to stand beside her and she watch his eyes widen as he take in the view.

She run her eyes over the city until she find Fidelis – pale grey and stone. It wasn't the only one. She could see others – smaller dots of bone white, punctuated by green or stone or brown earth. And she could feel yet others – those without headstones, without markers, without signposts, places that had almost forgotten themselves, it had been so long that someone had gone to mourn there, places that prickled her temples with their anger. But Fidelis was the centre. Like all the other places were connected to it, a power radiating outward from the same source. She could feel it pulsing. 'Look,' she point. 'Where we met.'

He follow her gaze and find it, his face steady, but his eyes – so much happening behind his eyes. 'When I first start to work there, I used to look at it from the office a couple floors up. It was so big. So much bigger than I imagine it. But today, from here, is just another thing in the city.' He point in another direction. 'The Greens bigger. People playing football, coconut vendors, tents, cars park up on the strip. I pass it on my way home sometimes.' He turn to her and smile, a kind of relief in his eyes. 'It feel good to see Fidelis looking small. Make me feel better.'

Yejide don't have the heart to tell him that is not only headstones that make a place a burial ground. Under the Greens, under fancy restaurants that used to be plantation houses, under the government buildings, under the housing complexes, under the shopping malls, is layers and layers of dead – unknown, unnamed, unclaimed. It don't have a single place on this whole island that don't house the dead.

They sit on one of the concrete benches and eat in silence. She feel him sneaking glances at her in between surveying the view, then the smallest of touches, a nudge on her arm. 'Hey. Could even see the sea from here.'

She see it. Muddy brown, then slate grey and then blue, then the sky orange and pink streaking away from its surface.

'I was thinking the other day that I should go by the sea. Just breeze out. You know, I is a man believe in life; and life simple – live good, work hard, help somebody when you can, keep your heart clean, thoughts upfull, but this last season . . . I don't know, is like I get lost along the way in there and I don't know how it happen.'

She turn to him fully, not worried anymore if he see her looking at him. His stubbly scalp, his bearded face in profile, cheekbones like an artist take his time and carve it out from a tree. His long, lanky body folded on the concrete bench, leaning forward, forearms on his knees, hands clasped, staring at the sea. She feel like she see everything in him he eh even see yet. The boy he used to be, the man he want to become. Trying to find his way in this city, trying to be good. Trying. She feel him bursting with a thing he want to say. And she will him not to, because if he say his thing then she will have to say hers.

'Maybe some saltwater could help me make sense of things.' He turn to look at her. 'When last you went by the sea?'

'Used to be all the time, but the last few years . . . I guess I grow up. You know how it is. When I was small we went nearly every weekend. Peter – my stepfather – used to take me and Seema when we was small. Nervous the whole time, always keeping an eye on us. He used to say if any of us drown on his watch better he just walk in the sea one-time than have to go home and tell my mother he lose her children.'

'Seema is your sister?'

Sister. She roll the word around in her head. Her Petronella boxes was one thing but she never thought that her relationship with Seema would be something that she'd have

208

to find a box for. Sister. What other word was there? How to explain it to him? 'Yes. We grow up together. She's my sister.'

He nod.

'One time I remember so clear. We spend the whole day there. Eat sno-cone, collect chip-chip, go in the sea – Peter holding our hands tight. We build sandcastles with some other children up the beach. Then the tide start to come higher and the beach get quiet. Just a few people left. Probably couples looking for a private spot – didn't think about it like that then.' A trace of a smile in his direction; the teasing in his eyes right back at her. 'Peter wrap me and Seema up in a big towel and we just sitting watching the sea, our hair full of sand. It was a perfect day.' Just remembering that feeling make her feel full. 'I almost drown that day too.'

'What?'

'Peter take his eye off us for a second to pack up our things and in that moment I hear somebody calling my name. Or that's how it sound at the time. I didn't know any better. But it was coming from the sea.' He turn to her fully, mirroring her position, like his whole body listening.

'I get up and start to walk toward it. Seema grab my hand. That's how I realize she couldn't hear it. Only me. I walk right into the sea, feel it rising from my feet, my legs, my chest, until it close over my head. And then the breakers start to churn, undertow pulling me out like the sea decide to keep me. Hair in my eyes. Sand swirling. I wasn't afraid. I was just trying to hear what the voice was saying. If I could just relax long enough, I knew the murmuring would come clear. Then I feel a hand yank me by my hair and Peter was holding me and running with me out of the sea. Seema on the shore bawling her eyes out. First time I ever see him look angry. I didn't know at the time that when a parent look like that is because the fear so deep it look like rage. He bundle us in the car quick-quick. No time to even wash off the sand from our feet. Me and Seema in the backseat wrap up in the same towel, our hair dripping, in silence all the way home except for Seema crying.

'By the time we drive up to the house, Mummy was already flying out the door, down the steps and pulling me out the car. She grab my arm and drag me in the house, into the bath. Rub the salt off my skin with a washcloth like she trying to tear it off. The whole house in uproar. I only hearing people asking what happen? Petronella, what happen? Peter, what happen?' Yejide drift off. Her mother words in her head still like an echo: *Not yet. You not ready for that. Not yet.* 'It never occur to me then to wonder how she know about it before we have chance to tell her.'

By the time she look up, the other cars gone. She nearly forget Emmanuel there for a second, but now they sitting so close that their knees touching. He reach over, take her shades off and stick them in his pocket. She glad for less light, hope he can't see the tears that she fighting. The last rays of the afternoon sun disappear; the first few electric lights start to dot the valley. Emmanuel skin shining blue-black in the fading light and his voice low like the hum of the city that spread out below them. 'You say you eh want to talk but I don't think I ever meet somebody who want to say the hard things so bad.'

'Don't you have hard things?' She don't know what it is about him that does make her want to tell him things she don't even remember she holding on to. 'Things you worry would change everything, if someone knew?' In the semi-dark she can look right at him without shame and she know, even though she can't see it, that he looking right at her too.

'Well,' he exhale. 'Life full of those. And yeah, maybe

some things you say them and they change everything. But that don't have to be a bad thing.'

They so close now that the only thing between them is breath and dusk and promise. 'Far as I concern,' his voice so warm she feel like she could touch it, 'this thing what happening here with us, it past the point of easy. And I okay with that if you are.'

26

Darwin

By the time they back in the car, the night thick and deep around them, Darwin know that it have nowhere she could take him that he would not follow. Every time they pass under a street light the brief flash bright up her eyes. They don't look troubled anymore. Whatever else was on her mind, whatever was behind the story about the sea, gone now.

He know he should be studying other things – what he going to do about tomorrow, about Errol, even about the fact that the keys to the cemetery jangling in his pocket and no one at Fidelis even there to make a pretence of locking up. But the night warm, the air smell green and sweet, not a drop of rain falling, and he still holding her hand as they wind their way uphill. It make him feel brave. And the words start spilling out.

'I grow Rasta. From small. When things get hard – you know how it is – I come to Port Angeles because I needed a job, any job. Well, they give me any job. Rastaman can't work with the dead. But I needed to take care of my mother. And I needed to . . . needed to make some kinda life on my own, to get some answers to some things.'

He pause. He don't think he ever say that part out loud before, not even to himself. He glad she focusing on the road. 'Death is a thing that I don't study too much. Better to look toward life. But working in Fidelis, is hard not to think about it, not to think about all the bodies under my feet, their lives, whether they still there in them boxes, whether they hanging around the place somehow. It hard not to care about that.

'One time I bury a man wife, an old man name Mr Julius. Emily was her name. It was the first time I bury somebody, first time I dig a grave. First time I ever really see a funeral. Mr Julius was in a bad way and afterwards I stay with him. We sit down right there on top where his wife bury. I stay with him for a while just talking to him, trying to say anything to help but I can't.' He feel it choking him, trying to say it out loud, the thing that haunting him. 'These days I feel like death all over me, like I can't wash it off my skin.'

She turn on the brights and the forest hug the car as they drive up a narrow road – the sound of tyres crunching on the uneven ground, frogs singing, branches brushing along the sides of the jeep.

'I can't see no death in you,' Yejide say quiet.

Darwin swallow down guilt. 'Just because you can't see it, don't mean it not there.'

'But I can see Death.' Her voice so soft, almost like she talking to herself alone.

'How you mean?'

She take a deep breath. 'When we talk before, when I come to see about my mother grave, you ask me why I care how she bury, what it matter if two dead women rest beside each other. But I could hear her sister waiting in the ground for her. I could hear and feel every single body in the cemetery, new and old, feel them like they in my blood. Is something from my mother. From her mother. Now it pass to me.'

Darwin listen, turn it over in his head. So many moments he shoulda just run, from the first day he jump out at the city gates and step over a man sleeping rough on the concrete. Even before that, from the first day he take that scissors out his mother kitchen drawer and make a new man of himself, one that he don't recognize. From then he shoulda know that he was walking a road that he eh bound to come back from. Like his soul sinking, sinking. But he sitting in a car with a woman who tell him she does deal up in necromancy, and somehow he feel like is here he supposed to be more than anywhere else in the world.

'Since my mother dead I see each person death stalking them like shadow. Being around people, looking at them is hard. Disorienting. Is like walking around and being able to read every mind. Even when it far away, to know the day and the hour that death coming for them. But you? You, no. No death. You just feel like life. Make me feel to hold on to you, make me remember what normal feel like, or to drink you like something sweet and cold, keep me here in my body, just a person, not like I belong in the dark with things that I can't even see.'

The last words come out in a rush, like she want to say all of it before she get scared and change her mind. He want to reach over and kiss her right there and then but she have two hands on the steering wheel now, the car still winding along the road, pitch-black beyond where the headlights reach.

Then he feel them run out of road and start driving down a dirt path that get wider and wider the further along it they go. A soft orange light up ahead glow through the trees. They make a last turn, the darkness thin and then he see the sky again, the building fullness of the moon, so many stars, and the shhh of bamboo as a light breeze blow through the patch. They come to a clearing surrounded by forest. A house. He never seen one like it. No part of it match the other. Parts wood, parts concrete, part he can't see in the darkness. How it hang together don't make no kinda sense at all. She pull up behind an old-model jeep and cut the engine. Darwin look around at the house and the forest and yard and he feel the strangest thing, like he been here before, like he know it.

'This is the house my family build. Long time ago. All here used to be cocoa estate. Thirty-six enslaved Africans labour on that land – pick the cocoa, dry the seeds, all to make chocolate they would never get to eat. Until Maman come.'

'Maman?'

'They just call her Maman. She is the first of us that anyone remember. When I was small my granny used to tell me a story about talking animals and a great war. In the story the world was being torn apart by death, the living have no way to balance with the dead. So the ancient birds became corbeaux – carrion birds – and they devour the dead. Balance restored. They save the world.' She smile, soft like she remembering her granny voice. 'It was my favourite story. I never dreamed it was true.'

True? Darwin shift in the car seat but stay silent.

'Two African enslaved here try to run away – a man and a woman. She was pregnant. When the overseers catch them, they string them on the thickest branch of a silk cotton tree for everybody to see so nobody would try again. They hang there, rotting in the sun, and nobody was allowed to cut them down. Then one day one big corbeau start to circle the estate. And when night fall, a strange woman appear standing below the bodies. She tall like a balata tree, her skin black like midnight, but when the people try to get close, to ask her what she doing there, she disappear. Next day, the bodies gone. Well, the place tun up. The planters vex, the overseers vex and punishment start to share. Then – and nobody for sure know when it happen or how, because everybody have a different

215

version of the story – the house catch fire. When night fall, the house standing and by daybreak is black soot and crumbling ruins. Nobody eh see no fire, nobody eh smell no fire, no ash descend the hills. Nothing but the selfsame balata woman standing in the ruins of the house.'

He could see it, picture it in his mind the way she tell it – somebody who face look like hers, stand up in front a burning estate, hair like flames.

'Well, you could imagine how the authorities call for obeah. But how you could charge a woman for a fire that never happen, a woman that only sometimes there at all? No survivors to question, no heirs from Europe come to claim the spoils. Some people didn't want nothing to do with her or the house after that. They run away and leave the cocoa and the remains of the estate. They say it strange how the fire never spread, and the land never burn – just the house. But a few say the woman save them. They say when she want she does take to the sky, and that the dead under her protection. They call her Maman and together they build the first version of this house from the remains of the old one. Some people who hear the stories come to seek her and they stay too. Each generation grow it and we living here ever since.'

'She really fly?' He feel excitement quicken in him. Enid used to tell him a story when he was small, bout how long time it had some Africans who coulda fly. That some of them fly all the way back home to Africa too and leave the plantation behind. But after a while we forget how – something about salt. That because they give us salt to eat, we get heavy and can't fly again.

'Maybe. I don't know. Yes, she really fly. All I know is since my mother die I could send my spirit out my body. And

216

my spirit have a shape that is not a woman at all. And I feel the dead calling and I see death coming before it reach.'

'But not for me.' He stare at her, mesmerized.

'No,' she smile. 'Not you.'

They get out the car and she reach for his hand to lead him toward the dark house. He should feel frighten after what she just tell him but he totally calm, like nothing could touch him – not the dark, not the light, not no jumbie waiting in the forest. His head spinning with her story, the way it call to Enid stories, echo like old truths. How much more stories all of us hear when we was small actually true?

He can't see one thing in front of him but her steps sure and he follow close behind, keeping hold of her hand. He think about snakes and glad he still wearing his boots and overalls.

The front-porch light flicker. Potted plants scattered all over. Mother-in-law tongue, basil, rosemary, chadon beni, shining bush, lemongrass. Maidenhair ferns hanging from the balcony and just a little way off from the house two chairs side by side in the yard.

He hear her breathing next to him, as they stand on the porch, looking out into the darkness, and Darwin suddenly realize what this place is.

'I see here before.'

'What?'

'I see you here before.' He think back on the way they came – the open grass, the trees, the bamboo. 'In a white skirt. Or a dress. Dancing.' He turn to look at her. She looking at him too. The whole world shrink. The pulse in the hollow of her throat, her skin in shadow, the only light coming from the low porch ceiling, tiny insect wings buzzing around the bulb. 'And then you float up in the sky, still spinning, still dancing. I try to reach out to hold you before you fly away but I couldn't. You just gone past the clouds, past the stars.'

He reach his other hand out and place his thumb where her skin flutter at her throat. 'I thought it was a dream. I feel like I dreaming since I first see you in Fidelis but all of this real. Everything that happening to me real.' And before he could lose his nerve, he stroke the soft skin of her throat, pulse beating faster, lean in and kiss her – cedar and sandalwood; forest and sky – and she pull him past the threshold of the house.

27

Yejide

Yejide don't think she even lock the door. Up the stairs, holding him so he don't stumble in the dark. The house asleep; she hadn't considered, hadn't thought, what would happen if anyone downstairs when they reach, but it don't matter now. The landing, the door. Her mother room that was now hers. The bed broad like a raft to take them someplace that wasn't here. She let go of him and her hands ache – but the windows, she want the windows open, want the night inside. Step out of her shoes, flick the latch on the louvres and open them wide. The singing frogs and the crickets and the stars and him behind her, hands at her waist, lifting the thicket of her hair, lips at the nape of her neck.

Clothes too heavy, chafing against her skin. Buttons, zippers. He slide her dress from her shoulders. His overalls stiff and rough under her fingers, then his skin so smooth but warm, alive. She kiss the hollow of his shoulder. He gasp and she catch the sound between her teeth. She taste the dust and the dead on the length of his skin, a heady swirling thing, molasses-thick, tobacco-sweet.

He step back and she watch him unlace his boots, kick them off. Then his undershirt gone, drawers gone and it is just him on the bed, his skin against the pale of the sheets, and his fingers drawing her down, then her skin on his. The short swirls of his hair in her hands, the rough of his beard against her face, his tongue in her mouth, then on her throat, her nipples, the river of her navel, the thick of her waist, the broad of her back, the soft undersides of her arms, her fingers. He look up at her and his eyes like stormy elsewheres, drowning, and she slide her palms down, down. She feel swollen, carrying more water than the small body of her could hold, and he move down between her thighs and drink in the rain of her, and the raft of the bed begin to lose its moorings and him faster and deeper and more and more until her body burst its banks and flood the world.

The room press close and the air thicken. And she feel them, the dead, pressing in on her same time he press against her. Yes, she nod, and her yes isn't just for him but an open permission. The room fill and teem with colour and fear and joy and heat and death and dying and life and birth and she carrying worlds between her thighs. Too much, too much. The moths flutter and multiply in her throat and their wings beat against her eyes and she roll him over and grip his hips with her thighs, her hands brace on his chest, his hands on her hips, and they lift off the raft, float past the ceiling and past the roofline, past the forest below them and into the endless sky, and black wings sprout from her back and her throat grow small and tight and voiceless, her fingers talon into his flesh and she drop a single feather as they fly, don't even see as it scorch the earth below.

28

Darwin

When he wake up the night thin outside. The last of the dark filter through the gauzy curtains and soften everything in the room. Her skin indigo in the slow hours before dawn, their limbs tangled. He shift beneath her, his hands still in her hair. She breathe into his chest and they fumble closer to each other.

'We could leave.'

'Mmm?' She half-asleep.

'After we bury your mother we could leave.'

He feel her holding her breath against him, her body still.

He know this word 'we' even bigger than the word 'leave'. 'We' say that this is not just some kinda obeah thing between them. 'We' say that they doing this for real. That he know what he doing and he asking her to trust him. This one big small word saying things that he not sure how to back up. She have a whole house here, a whole life. If is anybody who need to run away is him. What reason she have to go with him? He half-hoping that she gone back asleep and didn't hear it. Give him time to consider, time to figure out his next move.

He feel her exhale, her lips against his skin, soft. 'Where we would go?'

His heart start to beat. He think fast. 'I have some money put aside. We could put some gas in the car, head down to the south coast. I know some people. It have a boat that does leave from somewhere there. Don't even need a passport. Nobody really checking the traffic on that side. Only if you going airport, going up north, but south is like open waters. You know is centuries people going up and down in them pirogues. Up and down, from the islands to the mainland and back. We could do it.'

He feel her smiling against his chest. 'We could row a pirogue?'

'Is an example.' He laugh. He actually laugh and squeeze her tighter. 'I mean people was doing it in pirogue long time. Them big boys and dem transporting guns and ammo all now, so how hard it could be?'

She giggle and he feel like something in his chest open up big, big. It make him start to dream out loud. 'Down there it have plenty land. Big river, big waterfall. The soil so good that things does grow easy. And they even find oil there the other day. I read it in the papers. Going to have plenty jobs soon. I could get some land and get a little farm going. You could—'

'I could open a next shop. A different name. And let the dead see about the dead.'

'I like that. Yeah. Let the dead see about the dead.' No Errol, no Fidelis, no more sleepless nights over Mr Julius.

He pull her closer and feel her breathing settle. It could be real, they could do it. He don't speak no Spanish but he could learn. The thing was that she accept the 'we'. It give him a kind of hope that he didn't dare to have, that he don't think he ever have.

They drive in sleepy silence. He try to convince her to let him get a maxi home, she have a hard day. But she wasn't having it – no maxi don't come up here, she say. With no traffic on the road, what had feel like hours getting here fly by. When they leave the mountains was still inky-black and street lights dot the highway. But now when he look out the window and back toward Morne Marie, the first fingers of dawn start to lighten the navy sky in the hills. Up ahead, over the city, the night still reign. They pull up outside Ms Margo house and he kiss Yejide again, just once, and then stand in the middle of the street watching until her red tail lights disappear.

Darwin heart feel light and he not even sleepy. He just want to sit for a while, smoke something and remember the feel of her skin, the taste of her, smell sandalwood on his fingers. He might even reach work a little late today.

He don't see them coming. The first blow send him to his knees. Reeling, he pitch forward, hands on the cold pavement, turn to get up but they already on him, two or maybe three of them. Blood blurring his vision, he curl into a ball, protect his head and wait for it to be over. They don't say a word but they rifle through his pockets, his face pressed into the drain. Take it, he say, take it. Is just money. But they leave his wallet still in his pocket; they don't even pull it out. Whatever they searching for, they don't find it, and eventually they leave him on the concrete, one last kick to his stomach before they walk away.

Darwin don't rush. He don't sleep either. Instead, he use the last of the night to plan. Clean his cuts, put some soft candle on his bruises, drink some garlic tea and avoid Margo in the kitchen when the daylight stream through the windows. Most of the blows was body shots but he can't hide the wound above his eye, or the swelling. He take out the rucksack that he come with and pack what necessary.

By the time he walk through the gates of Fidelis his heart clear and cold. The bone yard feel different to him today. Rain in the air after the last few dry days and his skin feel electric, like his body tune to a frequency that his ears can't hear yet;

walking on the edge of a three-line, everything in him sharp and primed and aching.

Errol and the boys waiting in they usual spot and as he walk up to them he feel like when he used to walk into the schoolyard, locks long and loose, the eyes of the other children waiting to see if they could bait him today, feeling him out to see what they could get away with.

'You late, boy,' Errol start.

McIntosh look him up and down. 'Like you had a hard night.'

Darwin don't say a word. No old talk today.

Mikey and Cardo sprawl on the steps. He look down at their hands as he approach. No bruises, but as he stare they turn away, actually look uncomfortable, shifting so he could pass. He take the steps slow and steady.

'Morning, Darwin—' Shirley jump up from her desk, mouth open. 'What happen to your eye!'

'I alright, Shirley. Some youthmen jump me in Bellemere and take my wallet.'

'No! This town getting worse and worse, eh? Lemme see.' She touch her hand to his forehead. 'It not looking too bad but it must be hurting. You want anything to put on it? I might have some plaster here, some Mercurochrome.'

'Nah, I sort myself already. It look worse than it is.'

'Well, you watch yourself today, eh. Maybe sit it out? I will make sure your timecard fill out still.'

He shake his head. 'I okay to work today, but thanks.' He take the timecard from her and stamp it. Sign his name.

'You sure? You don't have to play no hero with me.' She touch his shoulder and he flinch, the spot tender.

She pull back, purse her lips and stare at him hard. 'Listen, Darwin, the surest way to end up in trouble is not to know when to pack it in and save yuhself.' She shake her head. 'The dead done dead already and the living following them soon enough.'

By the time he head down the stairs again the cars start to arrive. First one by one then in a long line till they block traffic on the road outside. All Souls' Day. Families with flowers, food and offerings, come to visit their dead. And extra workers, mostly young boys and street children, hoping to earn some change for painting the fences around the graves, pulling up weeds. One of them carrying a bag of cement; someone was getting a new headstone.

Every time a car door close, Darwin look up to see if is her, even though he know it too early. All now so she probably in the church. He think of her sitting in one of the front pews, her sister next to her, the priest saying prayers, the pallbearers bringing the coffin. But after a while the rhythm of All Souls' take him over and he find himself lost in watching. As he walk around he see a group of women crouched by a grave, lighting incense and candles; nuns in their habits heading to the Carmelite quarter. He see a man with a small garden shovel at his feet, pressing a golden lantana plant into the soil of a new grave; another man sitting in the front seat of his car, just staring. A couple holding hands, passing a cigarette back and forth between them, lighting another almost as soon as the last one done. Children in their school uniforms looking bored, like their parents drag them here and they would rather be anywhere else. And hovering above all of them a low drone of voices – cries and moans, the up and down cadence of prayers, the mundane chatter and sometimes even laughter.

When is time the gravediggers pick up their tools and start heading toward the plot. McIntosh and Jamesy lag behind and

Darwin can't shake the sensation of being exposed, his back to them like a target. His mind fill suddenly with the image of McIntosh with a shovel raised, bringing it down hard, Darwin skull breaking apart like is nothing.

They stop at the St Bernard graves. The problem of digging a new one so close to the old seem like minor matters now.

He turn around and wait for Jamesy to mark out the plot but Jamesy just drop his tools and stand there looking at him. McIntosh face blank, Cardo staring at his shoes, and Errol smoking a cigarette, smirking. The boards, the rope, the tarp already lay out next to the plot. So, this how it going to be? Right. He go to the tool bag and find the spray himself, take it out along with the yard-length Jamesy never use. Mark the grave in thick, straight lines, go back for his shovel. And he start to dig.

Yejide family graves. Catherine, Deborah, Sandra 'Baby-girl', Maman. And many more names listed on the headstones. For a second he wonder what would happen if he break through to Geraldine casket after all. But the more he dig the more the rhythm of the names drown out the fear. He feel calm, safe, strong. Maybe he only imagining but he sense they there with him, all those women down in the graves. The men around him seem to disappear and is only Darwin, in his body, in the hole, digging the grave.

'Alright, boy. Alright.' Errol voice cut through his thoughts and when Darwin look up he already deep in the pit and the rest of them, watching him from high up, looking almost worried. Then Cardo come forward, pass him the boards to lay and the tarp to seal, but he won't put his hand to help him out. None of them do. So Darwin scramble and crawl out the grave himself. Is only then he notice that the cut over his eye open up, his vision blurry and bloody. McIntosh seem nervous but Errol look damn vex; Darwin realize he never see him actually angry. His mouth twisted and tight, his eyes narrow to slits. It make him seem more dangerous, and yet somehow that make Darwin glad – powerful, to know that he could piss the old man off. This must be how she does feel when she fly from down the mountain and make a storm.

'Watch yourself,' Errol murmur. 'People does disappear in this town every day. Nobody eh go miss you.'

Darwin know he should be scared now but the pain and the exhaustion make him feel reckless. He and Yejide go be gone by tomorrow anyway. He just have to get through the rest of the day.

29

Yejide

Before they leave the house that morning, Mr Homer pull Yejide and Peter aside and hand them each a tiny vial.

'No, I good. I will be okay.' Peter try to brush him off but Yejide know that Peter far from okay. He look frail, shaky. Of the two of them there was one person who would miss her mother more and she know it wasn't her. She almost feel guilty.

Whatever Mr Homer give her to drink bitter and oily and she don't think she will be able to keep it down. But then it settle into her warm and slow and everything else feel like a haze. She know she in the church, she know Peter holding her hand. She can see faces of people she vaguely remember, some from the village, some that had passed through the house over the years. A carousel of white-robed mourners, hymns and purple roses.

She listen to the priest saying things about a woman she don't recognize, a pillar of the community, a successful business-woman. *You still thinking that love is something soft, something nice.* The stained-glass windows over his head start to swim, all the colours melting out the wooden borders and float in the air above her. Loyal friend, devoted mother. *Since the day I make you I start to die.* Generous parishioner, true pilgrim. *Only children does ask about God. We is women. We come from Death.*

She grip the hard edge of the pew, feel it dig into her palm. She having a hard time linking what her body doing and what she actually feeling. Which Petronella the priest talking about? Devoted mother to who? The giggle start bubbling up before she can stop it. *You shoulda run. Take your man, take yourself and run.* Peter look at her, his jaw slack. Titters from the pew behind her, eyebrows raised over fans, the priest arms outstretched carrying on like he rehearse his lines and wasn't going off-script for nothing. The giggle turn into a snort and then, before she know it, she laughing out loud, the sound echoing in the cavern of Sacred Heart Cathedral.

'None of you,' she can barely catch her breath she laughing so hard, 'none of you know who the fuck we are.' She feel dizzy like if she spinning around and around very fast with her arms fling out. Is not until Peter cradle her cheeks and wipe the tears with his thumbs that she even realize she crying.

The incense burn her eyes and she fight not to sneeze while they wheel the coffin out into the street. She and Peter stand at either side of the head with the priest alongside them, then Mr Homer and Laurence, then Agatha and Angie and Seema bring up the rear. And around them surge the procession of mourners, and drummers winding over the puckered asphalt, trailed by angry drivers and the horns of stopped traffic, a blur of singing voices that rise and fall with the rhythm of their steps and the beat of the drums:

> *'Abide with me; fast falls the eventide;*
> *The darkness deepens; Lord with me abide.*
> *When other helpers fail and comforts flee,*
> *Help of the helpless, O abide with me.'*

She feel for a moment like she looking at the procession from far above – and it look like a wave cresting, foamy and inevitable – the mahogany casket like a raft bobbing on a white sea.

They approach the gates of Fidelis, and as they cross the threshold the buzz of the place pull at her feet – but held at bay, not overwhelming. Whatever Homer make her drink push everything into a box that she can wear around her neck, next to her mother locket. Close and present but contained. Down the main road of the cemetery, turn into the narrow street where the mausoleum stand, tall and marble white. There he is – sharp in focus in the midst of every other blurry thing – standing at the side of the plot on a high mound of dirt, waiting. What happen to his face? Puffy, swollen in places. Bleeding? She feel her body lurch toward him but he give the smallest shake of his head that say, No. Not here.

The drums sound far off and the priest voice is a low drone. Peter and Mr Homer holding on to each other, Mr Homer like he reliving Catherine funeral all over again.

The gravediggers open the casket and she look down and see her mother face, same as it always was. The white lace collar high at her throat, the pearl earrings at her ears, the deep green dress in folds down her body. Her hands clasped on her stomach, the plush velvet of the lining bulging with offerings. From far away Yejide hear someone start to moan, louder and louder until it is a broken wail. Then she realize the sound not far away at all but right next to her. Peter, God, Peter. His face working and distorted. She try to reach for him, embrace him, but he disappear into the crush of bodies and voices and hymns and drums. No one hear her cry out for him.

They close the lid and start to lower the coffin. She feel hands pull her forward, closer to the edge of the grave. And it hit her, like the slow roll of an earthquake, from the ground at her feet up through her legs, her body and fill her head, burst through the haze. Sadness, grief overwhelming, but it don't belong to her. It come from the dead. The lowing, keening sound begin at Petronella grave and radiate throughout Fidelis, and Yejide sway, head heavy, half-step out – gripped suddenly from behind, pulled back from the edge, Seema voice in her ear saying, 'It's okay, it's okay, you okay.'

They fill up the grave and then the mourners step forward in ones and twos and threes, with purple-blue roses, carnations, lilies. She watch the women from the shop linger for a moment and then retreat. Watch Seema and Laurence murmur some words as they lay down a bright spray of marigolds. A woman she never even see before come forward and touch the soil; a young man take a folded piece of paper from his pocket and stick it amidst the flowers.

'You okay?' Darwin voice just behind her, quiet in the thick of the crowd, people still moving forward and back with flowers, with offerings and prayers.

'What happen to your face?'

'It don't matter.' He brush her fingers for the briefest of seconds and relief flood her, pushing against the keening, holding it at bay.

'Just come with me. Let's leave now. Forget all of it. Can we leave right now?'

But he don't answer, and just then she see a face staring at her from the edge of the crowd, one eye milk white and the other deep black like a well, malice coming off him hot on her skin.

She reach into her pocket and stretch her closed fist behind her so no one can see what she holding. But Darwin close his hand over her opening fist, press it even tighter shut and whisper in her ear. Then the space at her back empty and her mother in the ground and she feel the malevolent eyes still watching her, the dead grasping at her from below her feet.

ALL OUR LIVING AND
ALL OUR DEAD

30

Darwin

Darwin look out at Fidelis from his spot by the south wall. He perch on an old crumbling table tomb that look like the craftsman change his mind halfway through making a simple flat surface, and last minute decide to add a little raised plinth and something looking like a grotto with a statue of the Virgin Mary inside. Was hard to see from afar if you not looking for it, so close to the boundary wall and partly hidden behind raised tombs and headstones.

At first he thought he was the only person that used to like to come here, but then he start to notice the burnt-out candle stubs on the ledge every now and again, the flowers at the statue feet, or behind the Virgin, tucked further in the grotto. Never any flowers on the graves below, though, like the family line die out long before. He like sitting there. Low enough that he could pull himself up without too much effort, high enough that it give a little extra vantage point to see Fidelis. But his aching ribs, the threatening dizziness and nausea make it harder to climb today. At least no one would ever come down to look for him here.

All over Fidelis is the orange glow of candles in the blue-black evening haze. The graveyard stay open a little later for the season but even so is nearly closing time. He just don't have the heart or the energy to walk around and tell the people to wrap up, run them home. Not yet. Let them stay with their dead. Let them light their incense and sing their hymns and arrange their flowers and pour that first capful of rum out on the earth. Let the music play from open car doors, let the widows pray, let the widowers whisper the things they never say when she was alive. Let the children who don't even remember the person who name on the headstone stay as long as they feel to. Let the families tell stories. Let the dogs roam around sniffing for a bit of offering left behind. Let the vagrants find shelter in abandoned mausoleums a little while longer. Let the lovers stroll, searching out a corner where the light don't reach. How many end up here before time with no one to mourn them, no one to visit them, family don't even know that they dead? Let the dead have their company.

He been trying to work out when it happen, how it come that when Shirley tell him the names of the people to bury he find he could hear them without feeling sick to his stomach. Maybe it was Yejide, the way she move through the place like if is her backyard, the way she squat right on the ground where they was going to bury her mother and insist that the dead deserve to rest the way they want to, just like the living. Or maybe it start even before he meet her.

'Is a nice kinda vibes these times, eh?'

Darwin almost fall off his perch. Below him, the outline of a figure leaning up on the wall, looking out at the darkening cemetery, but the voice clear-clear like he sitting right next to him.

'Yeah. Peaceful.'

'Almost make you forget where here is for a little while.'

'Hmm.'

A snatch of laughter come to him on the breeze and he make out two small children running down the main street, ducking into pathways, in and out of the few graves left with tall weeds.

'See what I mean? To them is just a place to play. On a normal day, all now so they father probably about to tell them is time to come inside – street lights on. Time to do homework or go and bathe before bed. But this come like a little magic time where they can just be free. Headstone, grave, none of that don't matter to them.'

'True.' Darwin don't know how he feel about a strange man hanging around a cemetery to watch little children. He hope he just lonely. Some people who pass through Fidelis, the only family they have does be in the ground. 'You visiting?'

'My son. He here.'

Darwin heart suddenly feel tender for the man. 'I sorry for your loss.'

'Yes. You never realize how much you miss, you know? Always think you have time. I never get the chance to get to know him.'

They sit in silence for a while. Darwin feel bad for the man like how he had feel bad for Mr Julius, but he have too much on his mind already, and he don't want to get into no long conversation, and have yet another person grief to be responsible for.

'I think he is a good man, though.'

Something about how he say it make Darwin uncomfortable. And irritated. How this man come quite here to find him, when he just trying to get some time to himself? And so shifty, spying on people from the shadows? It make him ruder than he mean to be. 'Why you standing there in the corner like you hiding?'

The man laugh. 'Is now you want to see me? Why you don't come down from there so you could see me good?' His voice sound teasing but there is something measured about it when he turn to look up at Darwin.

Is the man he had see near Mr Julius grave, the man he had see standing at the crossroads and running among the headstones. And he have Darwin face. The cheekbones a little less sharp and he taller, a little broader – his back, his shoulders. Dreadlocks fall down his shoulders and his back like a waterfall. But the way he hold himself is like looking in a mirror.

Darwin head swim. He grip the small statue next to him, suddenly feeling like he about to fall right off the tomb onto the graves below. He get a concussion from when them boys beat him up? He hallucinating? He must be imagining the resemblance. The jagged stone of the statue digging into his palm steady him. He hesitate. 'Levi?'

The man nod slow, his face solemn.

Darwin swallow hard and pitch himself forward, jump down from the tomb. A smile start to spread across the man face, his teeth white against his dark skin.

It make Darwin whole body feel cold, frozen. He don't know whether to laugh or cry. To hit him or to run. This man. All this time. 'What you smiling for? You find this funny?'

Levi smile falter a bit.

'You was here? All this time?'

He answer simply, 'Yes.'

'You never call, you never say anything? Just living here good all this time?' He back away, can't stand to be this close to the man. If he stay this close he don't know what he might do. 'You know what she went through. What I . . .'

Levi face don't change. He just look at Darwin, wistful. Calm.

Darwin can't stand it. 'What you doing here? Here, of all places? And don't even pretend is just by accident. I see you here before.'

Levi taking in every inch of Darwin face, like he trying to

commit it to memory. Then his voice come smooth and even. 'Emmanuel. Is me who name you, you know that? Is me who cut the cord when you born, right there in the house when she take in with labour pain. Ambulance take forever to come and I was frighten bad. But I just know that is me who have to do it, me who have to help bring you into the world. Is me who lift you up to the world and say you is my son.'

'And is you who walk out the house same way and leave your son.' He want to spit the words, wish he could rinse out his mouth from the word that bind him to this stranger. 'Who tell you I here? I know is not Ma. How you find me?'

Levi shake his head slow. 'Find you? Jah know I never leave you, Emmanuel.'

Darwin try to keep his heart steady but his head pounding. 'How you figure that? You tell Ma that you would . . . You just leave and you never call. You never send no message. You leave.' He feel off-balance, dizzy. And something else welling up in him, past the anger. 'And when I see you here before – you run like a damn coward.'

'I wasn't no coward!' Levi voice boom loud like it come from deep inside him, his eyes flashing, anger bright in them.

The anger hot in Darwin too and he square himself up to the older man, feel himself moving toward him, too many emotions swirling in him to endure.

'I was young.' The tension drain out Levi voice, his body, like the weight of holding it was too much for him. It hit Darwin like a bucket of cold water.

'And I was stupid. When a man leave he woman home, baby have to feed, and say he gone to look for work, for money, he can't come back hands swinging. I meet a man who say he could link me with a hustle. One thing lead to a next thing . . .' He shrug.

Darwin heart still beating hard. He swear he could feel it squeezing and releasing in his chest. Levi had look taller when he was staring down at him but now that they side by side they almost the same height. They stand for a while staring at each other, then out at the darkening cemetery. Tiny flames dot the whole place now – on graves, lining the roadways, the smell of incense floating in the air, a low hum of voices, hymns. It dark enough that he can't see faces anymore. Anyone that look this way probably wouldn't see him either, or the man beside him who say he his father.

He don't know what to say, whether that explanation is enough, whether he can forgive him. Maybe it eh matter now. Levi say he was young. Darwin can imagine it. He must be near enough the same age now his father was then.

Levi cast around and find a low wall, beckon Darwin to sit. 'Plenty thing I thought I was clear about back then, Emmanuel. But is all a piece ah foolishness. Only thing that matter is what a man stand for and how he right his wrongs.'

'Easy to say now, after all this time.'

Levi chuckle. 'True, true.'

Anger still rumbling in Darwin but he quiet it, push it down. 'And it harder to do.'

'Well,' Levi pause and look at him. 'I trying. You have wrongs that need righting?'

Darwin consider how to answer. If anyone understand how it feel to do a wrong thing without meaning to, it is his father. And he owe him. The man owe him. Maybe is the candles flickering in the near-dark, the sadness in the air, the prayers whispering on the evening breeze, but despite his anger, all the things he feeling, he tell him. He tell him everything. And when he done, they just sit there in the quiet a while, and he don't feel so dizzy anymore and some of the pain in his muscles ease. It feel good to finally say the whole thing out loud.

'Hadda be someone I can go to,' he say eventually. 'Sweeper and them can't be so big-time that he above everybody.'

Levi shake his head. 'Is not whether they so big-time. Is that people like me, like you, like this man Mr Julius, we so small that it have nobody big who really care if we living or dead. When I didn't come home, babylon start any manhunt for me? They had pictures of me in the papers?' He gesture to Darwin black eye and bruises. 'If you never walk out of here, you think they would even waste the time on the paperwork? You know, Janaya used to say that Port Angeles had no life, only death. She wasn't wrong, but she wasn't right neither. When I come off the bus and land up here, I find more life than any place I ever see – small lives, you know? Rubbing up on each other, living on top each other, eating and starving, robbing and killing, loving and working and making babies and music and singing and praying. And dying. I mean, a small life is a life still ent?'

Darwin look at the sky and realize that dusk long pass and the night black. He can't hear voices no more. He look out at the cemetery. Almost all the cars gone. Some of the candles still lit, but most blow out on their own. He been talking to his father for hours. It make him calm. He eh afraid. 'I have to get back to work. Is time to lock up.' He get up and start to weave through the graves, back toward the spine of Fidelis, toward the gate that always calling him in or out. 'You coming?'

'Depend on where you going.'

'I have some time. I figure we could find some food, talk some more. It have a little place close by.'

But Levi don't move to follow him. He stay standing next to the wall they was sitting on.

'You have somewhere more important to be?' The feelings just below the surface start to bubble in Darwin again.

But Levi shake his head and smile. 'I staying here, Emmanuel. Same place I always was.'

The dizziness back now, stronger. Darwin want to take the steps toward Levi but his legs stop working.

'You ask how I find you? Is you who find me. I figure the only reason I even up and about is because you come. My son here, so I here.'

'Up and about . . . ?' Darwin feel the knowledge knit together inside him. The asphalt at his feet seem to rise up to meet him, the night sky above crashing down. Of course. He feel he must have always known it, in his heart, in his bones. And all the anger that he was trying to push down, that was fighting to take him over, snuff out. Suddenly, he is a little boy again, no more than three, sitting on the front step waiting for his father to come home.

'It have so much I want to ask you. How? How this happening?'

Levi shrug. 'Any of it matter now?'

Darwin swallow hard. 'Nah. Not really.' If it feel like time slow down when he was talking to Levi, it seem to speed up again now, and along with it the weight of everything that happen to him since he came to Port Angeles.

'You have a long night ahead of you still,' Levi say.

They look at each other for a while and then Levi nod and Darwin turn and start walking toward the main road. He hear the sound of a car door closing, a engine starting as the last of the mourners pack up and make they way home, their respects paid.

He walk a little way, and something occur to him that fill

242

him up inside. He smile and turn around. Levi still standing by the wall.

'You know, you wrong about something,' Darwin call out.

'What's that?'

'Maybe police didn't care when you never come home, but she never stop wondering what happen. It didn't have a officer in the Southern Division that didn't know her name or yours. Even when she decide that you had a next family and you just leave us and she cuss you and hate you, she still wonder. How you think I know your name?' He too far away to see his father face, or maybe his face not really there anymore, maybe he was never there at all, but whatever he was Darwin know he smile and feel a kind of relief. Even when you dead, being hated better than being forgotten. 'And if I don't walk out from here, I know who would come looking for me.'

31

Yejide

Dark colours, sturdy clothes, a small Ziploc baggie of Mr Homer dried herbs wrap in cheesecloth, travel sewing kit, pocketknife, trench knife, wallet, phone, passport. Cash. Seema mother, Laurence, always say that the money in the bank is for taxes but a woman must always have something hide away in case she need to run. She rifle through the bills and stick them to the false bottom of a rucksack, and she pin a small leather pouch with a few thick gold bangles, rings – things easy to sell – on the inside of a light denim jacket. She look at her mother locket and Granny Catherine pipe, feel a pang of sorrow and leave them amidst the other heirlooms. It don't seem right to take them with her, not now.

Whatever Mr Homer give her to drink long worn off. Her head pounding, her stomach churning, and it feel like every single dead in Fidelis, across Port Angeles, all over the island, pissed as hell and want her to know it. She not sure if Darwin serious about this boat but she have enough money for options. Anywhere have to be better than this, this feeling of cold fingers grasping at her body whenever she forget to guard against it. And it getting worse. She don't know how Petronella had been able to stand it.

She need to get Emmanuel out. Whatever going on in that cemetery, she need to get him away from it. The fear on his face eating away at her insides – the black eye, the split lip, the bruised cheekbones, the foreman sightless gaze.

'Really, Jide?'

Yejide stop dead. Seema standing at the threshold, still in the white dress she wore to the funeral, two cups of steaming tea in her hands, her eyes blazing. In all the rush, Yejide forget to lock the door.

'You running away now?'

All the adrenaline that been building in Yejide disappear in a rush. She feel like a child caught doing something despicable. She can't look Seema in the eye.

'You wasn't even going to tell Peter?'

She turn back around, keep shoving things in the rucksack, not bothering to fold them. Having something to do with her hands make her feel less helpless. Brazening it out to Seema make her feel less terrible.

'He upstairs. In case you care. Gone to bed. I make some tea for him and it make him a little drowsy. Mr Homer say he will stay with him.'

Peter. Yejide swallow hard.

'Is a good thing Homer still here. He know how Peter feeling.'

'Well, good for him.' The words come out Yejide mouth before she finish think them. 'He don't need me then.'

'When you was going to say something?' Seema voice change from reprimand to deep hurt. 'Something been up with you since the moment Ms Pet die. But I expect that. Is only since last night I sure. When I see you and him pull up to the house.'

Yejide stop packing. She can't bring herself to face her. 'I didn't know you were up.'

'I was up.'

Yejide fiddle with the pouch in the lining of her jacket.

'And then the burial. The way your eyes on him. Is like

you eh even care that your mother in the ground once he was above it.'

Yejide whirl around. 'That's not true.'

'That man is the only person I see you look in the eye for days. You even look at me anymore? Every time you near I wonder what change between us, and I know they have, but I don't want to know it. Don't want to hear you tell me. But I guess that not a problem since you not talking to me anyway. Since you leaving.'

'Seema, I can barely look at anybody. My eyes. Is like . . . being blind all your life and not realizing what was always there and now you can't unsee it. You can't go back.'

'You talking about your inheritance or you talking about him?'

'Seema . . .' Her head hammering, fingers ripping at her insides. She need to get out of here.

'It was just us for so long.' Seema voice get quiet and she look to the big front window. 'Remember the place in the forest? Just us together away from all this?'

'We were children.'

'Look, I know you had your lovers, your flings, but you never bring that up the hill, to this house. Morne Marie is home for us. And you just bring him here in the dead of night with your mother burying the next day and you never even say anything. To anyone. To me.'

'We going to get into a fight today? Of all days? Because I don't have it in me. I really don't. I need my friend right now. I need my sister.'

'Yejide, I am not your sister!' The words come out of Seema like a roar. It make them both pause, silent. Yejide don't know what to say. She right, of course she right.

Seema slump down on the battered chair like she spent all

her rage. She start to say something else but catch herself and instead gesture at the clothes on the bed. 'So, you going and run away on some joyride? Like if you don't have no responsibilities? Like if none of this important?'

Yejide walk away from her, scanning the room, the things on the bed. 'I promise I'll let you know where I am.'

'Let me know where you are?' Seema leap right up and follow her. 'Why you talking like some silly girl? Like if you are not what you are?'

'I didn't ask for any of this!'

'Oh please! I am so fucking tired of hearing what you ask for and what you didn't ask for. Oh, your mother don't like you, oh you don't know your father. You had Granny Catherine! You had Peter! And you had me!'

Seema face red and swollen, like she had these words storing up for years. It never occur to Yejide that Seema was collecting grievances in boxes of her own.

Yejide feel the tears welling up. 'That is a lot of words just to say you jealous that I find somebody. You really think that little of me? We not the same, Seema. We pretend that we were but we not! You don't see what I see. Something in this place, in Fidelis all wrong and I have to get away from it and I have to get Emmanuel away from it too. Before it drown us both. You understand?'

'Wait. I don't even believe this. All this is because your little boyfriend having a problem with his job? Well, fix it!'

'That is not how it works, Seema. Some things you can't just fix!'

'You try? You even try to learn what you could do? You letting your rift with Ms Pet take you for a fool. She make her choice about how to handle this thing. We watch her do the bare minimum, watch her neglect you and not teach you because she couldn't figure out how to have a life she wanted. You don't have to be like that too.'

'How you know what she wanted?'

'You think everybody in this house blind? You think I blind? I see things. Maybe some things you don't even see, for all you are. If you had just take the time to talk to me, instead of running around with your head up your ass . . .' Seema almost incoherent now with rage. 'Your mother dead. What she want or how she feel about you don't matter! What matter is the line, the power in the line. What matter is your ancestors who build this house and my ancestors who throw their lot in with Maman because they believe in that woman, what she could do; she knew and her mother and her mother before that knew that someone have to make the sacrifice, somebody have to hold the line. And you don't get to turn away from that because your mother didn't love you enough.'

Seema run out of steam, her breath ragged. She and Yejide both on their feet, facing each other like two prizefighters, tears running down their faces, tea long forgotten, the clothes tumble off the bed.

'Yejide. I vex with you. I eh go lie, I am. But I not talking about that. You really think it have anywhere you could run that this would not be a part of you?'

Yejide hold Seema stare as long as she can then she look away. They stand in silence for a while, Yejide not looking at Seema, but feeling Seema eyes on her. Then she feel a cool wind on her face. She glance up but the window closed. The wind start rushing through her, and his voice coming from far off, saying her name loud like it could jump out of her own throat.

'Seema—' She reach out blind.

'What happen, Jide?' Seema voice suddenly sharp, fearful,

but Yejide can barely hear it anymore. The line that connect her to Fidelis pull taut – black gate, a battered white car, headlights, ragged breath, and pain and blood and the volume on everything turned up in surround sound. The cold wind blow harder, she feel it moving round the house and the air get heavy with rain. A storm rising up over the hills and she feel a darkening around her spirit. The storm coming from her or for her? She search her pocket for the keys. She not taking to her bed. Fidelis alive and in tumult and everything in her say that he is there.

'I have to go.'

'Let me come with you.'

'Seema, let me go!'

And she run. Down the steps, out the front door and into the night, and the storm come with her.

32

Darwin

The city outside soften and the quiet fill him up. The only sound is the crunch of his boots on the asphalt streets, the heavy chain clinking as he wind it round. He try not to wince at the thunk of the padlock as he click it into place, locking him in until dawn. He trusting Yejide to come through. Is only when them boys jump him that he realize he drop the keys to Fidelis in her room. They coulda beat him all night and still not find them. Tomorrow is another day, they will get a next set from the corporation – but not tonight. Tonight, she was the only person who could enter Fidelis. Tonight, they will know that is he who lock them out.

Next he go to the admin building. Let himself in, head upstairs and pull out the backpack he stash behind the filing cabinets that morning. He plan to settle in, catch some sleep in Shirley battered old chair, but now that he here, it feel a kinda way to be in this office without her, to sit in her chair. Is like he could feel her eyes on him, hear her voice asking, 'What you gone and get yourself into now, Darwin?' He still remember the first day he stand here waiting for her to give him the paperwork for Mrs Julius grave, the first day he look out and see the whole of Fidelis from a height. A lifetime ago.

The clock on the wall say hours before dawn. By the time the sun rise in the morning he and Yejide would be leaving Port Angeles, a new life ahead of them. He should feel hopeful, excited, but his brain churning. This whole place, everything that happen to him since the first time he walk through that big black gate. And Levi! He really just had a conversation with Levi? He try to process it all and suddenly the room feel too small, the walls more like a cage than a hiding place. He thought it was smart to stay where nobody can't see him, but now he feel like he back himself into a corner with nowhere to run. Maybe it better to be outside, stay awake, keep moving. Maybe that would make him feel more steady. He pick up the rucksack and make his way back downstairs. From the time the night air hit his face is like his feet start to move on auto-pilot, carrying him back to the St Bernard mausoleum.

He remember Yejide standing before her mother grave, her face tight and anxious. 'Pack light,' he tell her and close her hand firm around the keys. 'Meet me here at dawn.' It sounded like a good idea at the time. Is still a good idea. But he look around at the deepening darkness and he can't squash the feeling that he missing something.

He set down just outside the plot and pull his rucksack off, reach inside. The wooden handle feel solid and heavy, the metal edge sharp. He test it against his finger, and let it take a tiny trickle of blood. Years of odd jobs, construction, work-ing the land – he know how to handle a blade, how to feed it. He push the bag up against the low iron fence, turn and rest back down against it. The night deepen, settle on him like a blanket. He didn't think he would be able to hear frogs sing here, so far inside the city.

He wake to the distant clatter of a chain falling on concrete. Up ahead, headlights cut the pitch-darkness. It too early. How long he been asleep? He hear the creak of the gate being pulled open, a car engine rumble and the tyres crunching on the asphalt, rolling slow. He scramble up.

Darwin stomach knot. He lock the gate. He know he lock it. And the only keys supposed to be in Morne Marie with Yejide. The knots tighten. Errol lie to him. Of course he did. The old foreman have a key. How else they been getting in all those nights before? How could Darwin be so stupid? His head swimming, thoughts scrambled. He eh see anything clearly since the day he walk in this place.

He keep low and crawl to the end of the street, trying to see all the way down to the gate. The sputtering security light by the admin building give him a glimpse. They definitely there, park up just inside, he hear the car doors opening. Errol and McIntosh for sure. Jamesy, Cardo, maybe Mikey. Darwin wonder if he should make a run for it. Maybe skirt around the edge, slip out the gates while they deeper in the cemetery? Or try to head back to the Virgin Mary plinth and use it to scale the wall? But them old stones so smooth, no purchase at all, and it higher outside than in. To jump from the top risk breaking a hand or a foot or worse.

Darwin watch them go to the trunk, open it and take something out, come back to the front of the car. Then he hear Errol call out.

'You decide to play man with me here tonight, Darwin? Locking gate in my yard?'

A torch beam flick on, then another and another, sweeping the concrete in front of the darkened group. 'Pick your choose. Get some sense and come out now. Or we come and find you.'

Errol head turn to the men beside him, talking and gesturing, words Darwin too far away to hear. Then he turn back toward the main road and start walking into Fidelis. The others follow, spreading out from the gate through the streets of the graveyard.

Darwin heart pound in his chest, breathing get shallow. Errol eh stupid. First place he look will be the St Bernard mausoleum. He can't stay anywhere near here. Forget the rucksack. He feel for the blade, say a prayer and, careful as he can, he start to move.

Crouching low, ducking between headstones and statues, he head west for the Carmelite quarter. He don't think he can make it all the way back to the grotto, way south of the cemetery, but he not too far from the Carmelites here and he have a good start on the others. And it isolated and cut off from everything else. He almost sure they wouldn't think of there yet; could buy him some time.

He catch a movement out the corner of his eye, a figure stalking slow, the beam of a torch swivelling left and right, looking, looking. He freeze, slip into the nearest cover, a tall monument with two broad columns at the entrance. Rusted gate. No lock. Inside it smell like shit and piss and old wood. He hold his breath. Hear the footsteps move past. For all the years they working here, he feel in his heart that none of them know the place like him. He visualize the whole cemetery like a map in his head. How long they go search? He try to read the sky, figure out how long he sleep for. If he can just get out of the way, maybe he could outlast the dark.

He slide out of the filthy hiding place, drop to his knees and crawl, moving through low shrubs, crumbled rock and hard-packed dirt graves. His hands, his body, his face closer to the dead than he ever been. The time of year work for him and against him. Almost no tall weeds or brush left, no easy cover. But the ground soft and clear to move over. He raise up careful-careful and look across the gravestones. Couple of torch beams flickering far away to the south-eastern corner. He can't see where the others gone.

Darwin sit back on his haunches, try to calm himself. How far they could reach? He look around but no sign of other torchlights, no sound of boots crunching on the roads or rustling through undergrowth. He probably halfway to the Carmelite quarter. He think he can make it. If he could stay quiet and move fast, he just might. It start to rain, a little drizzle, and his heart leap. Please. Rain. He pray for the weather to turn. Anything to buy him a little more cover. Anything to mean they might stop hunting him tonight. Give up, go home. Just go home in your bed. He think about Mr Julius. His kind, proud, stubborn face, waiting by Emily grave. That old man never get to go home.

Think about Yejide. Holding her hand, driving through the mountains, the last rays of sun streaming into the car. The way her face set and serious when she look out at the sea. He think about the blue light before dawn in her room, the long road on the sea to a new life. So nearly there.

He think about Petronella, and all the women lying underneath the St Bernard plot. He hope to Jah is only them in there.

And then he think about the man in the blue tarp. The stranger he never meet, face he never see, name he never know. Think of all the others that he don't even know about, the dead who people still looking for, the mothers who light candles hoping their sons come home, the fathers who sit on the back step and cry for daughters they never stop looking for, the lovers who go in the station every week to ask the police, 'Anything? Any news?' knowing the answer go be no.

Suddenly McIntosh voice. 'It don't have to go like this, boy. No call for it. None at all.' Close. Too close. Darwin crouch low, his torso scraping dirt. He don't even dare breathe.

He try to trace McIntosh voice but the sound moving

round, like he pacing, searching. He speak soft, almost croon-
ing. 'You upset about the other night. The man we bury. You
know who that was? Neither me, and I don't care. I care
about my wife. I care about my two children home. People
don't end up dead just so, Darwin. Man must get take out
for a reason. You would feel better if we tell you the man is
a killer? That he gun down a woman husband in front his
children and get what coming to him? Believe that if it make
you feel better. The dead done dead, Darwin. Someone have
to bury them.'

Darwin barely breathing. He listen hard, trying to track
the direction of McIntosh voice. It further away now and he
can't make out the words as the wind carry the sound, the
rain swallow it up. He have to make a move. A few yards forward, tread careful as he can, and press up behind one of the
mausoleums that line the main road ahead. Check for torchlight, double-check, flit across the street to the next row of
plots. Keep going like that, avoiding the parts with only headstones, moving through the dense landscape of monuments
like a maze. The rain really coming down now and Darwin
cold, the dread and the weather soaking through him. He
reach a next tomb, look up and the sky turn a flat silver, unnat-
urally bright. He so tired. He should move again. But he can't
hear any of them. Where Cardo and Jamesy? Wait, just wait,
just wait a little longer.

'I know you here, boy.' He jump. Errol voice loud like if
he have a bullhorn in his throat. He could hear the foreman
crooked smile. 'McIntosh and them feel sorry for you. They
think you soft. But I know you're no different than the rest of
us. You wasn't studying bout what happen to your friend Mr
Julius when the police roll up in here asking questions. You
was studying to save your own ass. Now you decide to grow

a conscience? Hide up here with yuh two skinny foot and the keys I give you, playing hero like you name Batman?'

Errol chuckle. 'Not conscience hold you nah. Is woman make yuh balls drop, Darwin?' His voice get smooth, like a father talking to a child who testing his limits. 'I tell you about this already. Feel I eh see you and she watching each other whole day? Don't let pussy make you stupid.'

'He not here, boss. We wasting time.' Jamesy voice holler over the rain and he sound more pissed than Darwin ever hear it.

'He here if I say he here. Keep looking.'

The wind bend and swell and fill the cemetery. 'Boss. The weather bad. We eh go find him in this. We know where he living. Is not like he have anywhere else to go.' Jamesy voice still pissed but something else too now – he scared.

'Is rain. You fraid fucking rain?' Errol snarl.

The wind howl like it answer back and a clattering echo out from the far edge of the cemetery: the galvanize roof of the admin building juddering in the gale. Darwin look down where he stand and his boots squelch in mud, the noise absorbed by the storm. He hear a splashing, far off, like heavy feet running, running away, and a deafening crack as a tree branch rip off from its trunk.

'Sweeper, this eh no rain. Is a tornado or hurricane or something.' McIntosh voice ragged, wobbling.

Darwin almost smile. He know this storm now and he eh afraid of it this time. He whisper her name and he swear he feel the wind wrap round him like a caress.

'Allyuh fucking coward! What kinda man—' Errol call out, but the sound deaden and drown by the rain.

Darwin bruises aching and his limbs pulled down with their own weight but the storm give him hope. He remember the little boy who face was bruised then just like it is now, who lip was split, who take all the back roads home because he don't want anybody to see him, because he frighten they would find him again. When he reach the back step of his house and his mother see him, she stop shelling peas and put the basket to one side. He walk toward her and stand in between her knees, his tears falling fast on the chipped concrete steps.

'Lemme see, Emmanuel,' and her fingers tip his chin up, her eyes scanning the ripped pocket on his school uniform, the tam that she crochet with her own two hands roll up in his hands – dirty and stretch out.

'What they say this time?'

He shrug and shake his head. He feel shy suddenly. After making a beeline for his mother he don't want her to see him crying. And besides, better she had ask what they didn't say.

'You want me to come and talk to your teacher?'

He shake his head fast, no way. He know how they look at her when she come in the school with her head tie and her long skirt. Good enough to make everybody children school uniform but not good enough for the secretary in the principal office or the teachers who say her son rude and can't behave. The adults was same as the children, just bigger and with words and glances instead of fists.

'Alright. Cry. Go ahead cry. Let me know when you done.'

They stay in silence for a while. He could hear the sound of children heading home on the main road outside, could hear them laughing and joking with each other. He scrunch up his face and squeeze the last of the tears back then he look up at Janaya.

'Right. Come. I going to tell you something.' She set down the peas and pull him to her and wipe the last of his tears. 'Them children in your school. They just like you. No, listen

257

to me good. They look at you and see something different but they the same like you. All of us poor here. All of us does catch water by a standpipe. All of us does make something out of the nothing to put food on the table, trying our best to make something good and live good. So, them is not your enemy. You hear me?'

He nod uncertainly. He still taste the blood on his lip. How somebody who do this to him could not be his enemy?

'When people suffering, when they struggling, they does need somebody to push down, somebody to make themselves feel better. You pray for them and hope they find their way.

'But,' she pause and stare deep in his eyes and he see the flames ignite in the brown pools there, 'because them is not your enemy that don't mean they could take you for fool. Tell me. Samson. How he slew the Philistines?'

Emmanuel sniff and touch his tongue to the split lip again.

'How Samson slew the Philistines?' Her voice raise a little bit louder.

'Jawbone,' he whisper.

'What?'

'Jawbone.' He put some force in his voice.

'Yes. And David. Small. Like you. David had any armour?'

'No, Mummy.'

'Army rolling with him?'

'No, Mummy.'

'What he had? When Goliath come out and they say he too big that no one can't beat him. What David had?'

'Slingshot.'

'Slingshot. What that tell you?'

He shrug. 'It don't matter that I small or I don't have much things. I could still win.'

'No, my lion.' She reach over and run her hands through

his locks. And the look in her eyes both sad and fierce. 'It mean that when a army form up against you, you don't have to fight the whole set of them. Just find the biggest one, the one the rest fear the most. And aim good.'

The sky face swell up and churning. Darwin draw the blade from his waist and the streak of his own blood still on the edge sing. He step out from behind the tomb onto the path, stand tall and see Errol up ahead of him, near the main road, already ankle-deep in water. The swirl of leaves and bits of branches make Darwin pinch his eyes to slits, and the rising wind make it hard to hear, unbalance him.

'Sweeper!' he call out over the flood.

The old man wheel round. 'Stupid boy.'

Darwin make his way to the foreman. 'We could walk outta here tonight, Errol. We could just end this. I don't have no fight with you.'

'You don't have no fight with me?' Errol voice incredulous. 'Boy, me and you is not size; we not equals. You know how long I running this hustle? The things I see, the things I fix, the things I take care of would make you shit yuh drawers.' Errol voice start to get louder now and ring out in the night as he advance. This eh no silky-smooth salesman. This is a warlord.

'Half this country couldn't sleep at night because of some of the people we help disappear. You even know the kinda people we working for? Think you could just walk in here and grow some kinda conscience for stupidness? For a woman who eh going to remember your name tomorrow? For people who done dead already?'

Errol give a final lurch forward but Darwin ready with the blade, feel it connect with the flesh of the old man shoulder. He feel a rush of triumph and pull back to run but Errol on him like a landslide, the torch pelting blows to his head like the weight of a coffin smashing into him, and then he on his knees, the blade drop from his hand somewhere in the darkness. Errol boot connect to Darwin chin and he feel something crack.

Then the old man weight bearing down on him, so much stronger than he look, hands forcing his head down toward the rising water. 'You was just as coward as them fellas. You happy to benefit once you don't have to see how the money earning. Once you don't have to get your hands dirty. You going and dead here tonight, boy.'

Darwin feel his body slowing down. Every breath hard, every muscle heavy. But lightning crack once, twice, bright up the whole sky, and through the rushing water he see his blade. Too far to reach but there, so close, and he can tell Errol eh seen it yet. He take one big breath and let his body go limp. Errol push him under the churning floodwater, push him right to where his knife waiting. He grip it tight and twist his arm around, crash into Errol side. Thick thud like the blade split wet earth, he feel the sound though his head still submerged and the old man cry out, his body slacken, roll off him and blood everywhere. Darwin gasp up to the air, panting and staggering to get up, shaking. He kneel in the flood and his body tremble like it will never stop.

Errol eyes flutter open, the milky one enflamed and bloodshot, and Darwin almost relieved to see he alive, he eh make a murderer of him yet. Then he feel fire in his side, and he collapse next to the foreman on the ground, the old man mouth slack with pain but laughter gurgling from his throat, his hand gripping a knife cover in blood.

33

Yejide

Yejide speed down the hill, driving blind. Way too fast for the wet winding roads down from Morne Marie. One wrong move and the jeep could go careening off the bend and into the valley below. She try to focus on what she doing – hands, steering wheel, feet, gas, brakes – but is like her body splitting open and pulling in all directions at once. Something pushing her to turn back, to head back up the hill, but something stronger pulling her to Fidelis. *Find us, find us.* The voices screaming now, the ones she hear the night her mother die, the ones she hear again when she bury; she can't hear herself think for them and she know what they saying, she finally understand.

Outside look like a hurricane, the trees whip up into a frenzy. In her rear-view mirror the night is a swirling mass of debris and she know it is she in that storm, she in that rain. Her rage is the rage of the unclaimed dead, the unremembered dead, the unmourned dead. She hear her tyres screech on the asphalt as she take a hairpin bend, the road level out as she reach the highway and kick the jeep into gear. Cars stop on the shoulder, too low to drive through the floodwater. She speed past them, splashing water in sheets as high as the window, willing every single traffic light she pass to turn green.

By the time she reach Port Angeles, the city is a river. Drains full and brown water spouting out onto the roads, plastic bottles and polystyrene cartons floating down the streets.

Even the street lights can't cope with the storm – they flicker and die and Yejide guided only by the cord pulling her to Fidelis, to Emmanuel.

As she turn the corner to St Brigitte Avenue she hear a high-pitched noise and it bring slicing pain, like nails embedded in her skin. A clap of energy like sound made flesh, like flesh made grief, like grief made desperate, long-held rage, almost make her crash the jeep into the cemetery wall. And somewhere in the midst of it, she hear him say her name again, so faint, like a shadow or a farewell.

The gate wide open, clattering in the wind. She cross the threshold and run down the main road fast as the water let her, into the heart of the soundstorm. Up ahead, in the middle of the path, a dark mound in the rising water. Is not him is not him is not him. She can't remember the last time she pray but her mouth start to whisper, mumble long-forgotten noises that sound like hymns, like poems, the centuries-old stringing together of what in the end just mean *please* as she fly through the singing storm.

Two figures slumped on the ground, one over the other, dirty red water, blood and dirt swirling around them. Is Emmanuel but he alive, just about. She run her hands over his body, trace her fingers over his face, his mouth. Bloody and battered, lip split, forehead, eye. He blink awake at her touch.

She try to keep her voice steely and clear, keep the panic from her tone. 'Can you move?'

He struggle to sit up, gesture to the other figure. 'Errol. He was going to—'

'The foreman? What he doing here?'

'They come for me. The storm make the others run, but Errol . . . I was just trying to get out of here . . .'

Yejide bend low to the old man, close her eyes. She can feel the life still moving in him.

'He okay. Still breathing. You eh kill anyone today, Emmanuel.' She know her smile wobbly and hope he can't see. The dead shrieking, louder, louder. 'Here, help me get him to the car.'

He shake his head. 'I can't. I don't think I can walk.' He cough, breath ragged, double over and drop forward, down on his elbows.

She make herself look at his chest properly – so much blood. And the red-brown water of the graves and the dead leaves and flower petals rising up her calves and she don't give a damn whether Errol live or die. She have to get Emmanuel out. She look around and see a wide tomb, raised above the rushing water. She grip his arms and coax him to his feet, stagger with him to the side of the road. He stop short and she almost drop him. His whole body stiffen, and he start to stare around frantic, muttering, his eyes unfocused, squinting into the darkness as if he can see someone there. How much blood has he lost? She set him down, lie him back, try not to think about it.

She wade back to Errol and try to drag him through the water, but he heavy like sin. She cry out with fear and with rage. The panic start to bubble up in her again. How bad Emmanuel hurt? How much time he have? She should leave the old man to drown right here, just leave him and get Emmanuel to the jeep. And just when she resolve to abandon the foreman, she look up to see another man walk out of the dark.

Yejide do a double take and nearly drop Errol. Is Emmanuel. Different, yes, but the same. Dreadlocks flying in the wind as if he too is part of the storm. He just stand there silent, the body of Errol between them. And then, one by one, other figures come.

A few at first – dazed, disoriented. Some faint, others near-solid, as if they only just walk out of their old lives. Young women, too young, their faces contorted with betrayal; men with set expressions, determined, waiting; children of all ages clutching battered toys, a teddy bear, an old doll with one arm, a tiny schoolbag, a game console, a plastic ball. As each one materialize from the dark it feel like someone pluck a guitar string, each dead with its own tune, its own vibration. And they keep coming and coming, scores of them, hundreds, and their rage pour out with them.

She stand to greet them and they flow over her like flood-water, like a burning house, like earth moving down the hill after days of rain, too heavy to hold its shape anymore. And she feel herself reach out, wide-wide, covering the whole cemetery, even further. The rain pouring down on her head and the floodwaters rising up her legs and she hold them all in her arms: *I see you. I see the wrong they do you. I drink your pain till it fill me up, drink your sorrow till it fill me up, drink your joy till it fill me up, drink your death till it fill me up. I taste your flesh, yes you were flesh, I see it yes, I know. I know you have loved, yes I know, I know you have killed, yes I know. I know you were here, yes I know, and you, and you, and you were here. Nothing mark your grave but the earth have ways to mark those who come back to her. You are not forgotten, no you are not forgotten, no you are not forgotten, no you are not forgotten . . .*

And the storm reach fever pitch and the sky wail and the earth move. And the faces of the young women, twisted and bruised with anguish, grow calm and soft and they look like girls again. And the fathers, who looked ready to destroy an entire city, exhale. And the children, with their toys and their dreams and their too-few memories, grow thin and gauzy like mist and melt into the air, indecipherable from the rain. And the old men take to their graves again like they have an armchair waiting, and their favourite pipe, and a newspaper with only good news in it – gas prices low, the budget balance and backpay coming. And the youthmen who somebody decide live long enough already start to kick ball in between the headstones, stoop down and make pallet boats from sticks and race them in the fast-running water. The pressure ease and ease and everything hum quiet.

But the air have a waiting in it. The dead pause. The same thing in all their eyes – man, woman and child. They speak with one voice: 'Give us the man.'

Yejide heart stop. She look back at Emmanuel, where he lie lifeless on the tomb, and she shake her head, no. 'You cannot have him. I name him mine. He is for the living.' Terror hold her and the determination in her voice raw.

But the dead laugh and it sound like something tearing. And the man with Emmanuel face step forward from the crowd and speak aloud. 'Not the gatekeeper. The other one. Give us the sweeper.'

She know she can't stop it. She don't even want to. They move like a single entity and as they reach Errol he wake up, choke, bawl out in fear. His screams rend the night until the dead take them from him like a harrowing swarm drowning the rain. She turn away.

The sound fade surprisingly fast, and she sense them leaving, like the tide going out. The last of the rain wash over her, and as she turn her face up to the sky she see the first edge of pink in the blue. The air soft and clear and all the living and all the dead settle themselves like an old lady in a rocker on her front porch settling her skirts.

34

Darwin

The time in Morne Marie pass slow. The first few days and nights like one long streak of pain. Fever that make anything that touch his skin feel like fire, cold sweats that make his teeth chatter, faces he don't know looking down on him. Sometimes the faces look like Errol or McIntosh. Sometimes they look like a sea of rotting bodies swarming in the sky like bees. Them times only Yejide hands on his forehead like cool water could get him to sleep again.

He never know that healing could be sweet like this. That an aching body coming back to life, muscles reknitting themselves, bones setting, skin healing, could feel like peace. In no time at all, this mountain, this house, feel like home. When the place Errol stab him heal, he and Yejide would just lie in bed and stare at it. A ugly deep fish-mouth pucker on his skin, a reminder. Most times she fall asleep first and it take a while for him to get used to her being there when first light roll over the hills and come through the window. Sometimes she already awake, standing and watching him. Sometimes she don't realize when he wake, and he like that best, so he can just watch her looking out into the soft morning.

He also getting used to waking up and seeing her sitting in bed staring into space, her eyes blank like she somewhere else. Even though he eh go back to Fidelis he always know when a new soul need help figuring out how to rest. Sometimes when he wake and the bed empty next to him, he find her wandering the halls or standing stock-still like she talking to somebody who was there a minute ago but gone now. Other times she don't need him to find her at all – Agatha there, or Angie, sometimes even Seema. But when she come back is he who pull the covers over her and make the tea she need like how Peter show him. He starting to learn that to love this woman is to know that she half in this world and half in the next, that she belong to the people of this house as much as she belong to him, that anytime she could just up and leave and he would have the rest of his life to wish for the absence that he resented before.

'Unless you lucky enough to die before her,' Mr Homer say. 'I think Deborah man went before.'

'Babygirl husband too,' Peter remind him.

'Yes, yes, true.'

'Nearly happen to me.' The two men quiet down next to him. Feel like the whole garden pause and sigh at the thought. His mind drift back to the last things he see before he pass out in Fidelis, the last time he set eyes on the other gravediggers. 'I would be dead now for sure if she didn't come.'

'Don't sell yourself short, Darwin,' Peter tell him. 'You do more than most would have. You stand up and defend the dead when you lock that gate, and they know it. You have a good heart, son. Strong.'

He never meet men like this before – calm and settled, no knife-edge when they reasoning with each other – and he fall into step with them like he know them all his life. Peter don't smile as much as he used to yet, Yejide tell him, as his grief still fresh, but Mr Homer does keep an eye on him without making it obvious. And now they keeping an eye on Darwin too.

They sit on the gallery as the sun setting. Darwin arm still in the sling so Mr Homer roll for him and they smoke a while in silence. He can't believe that the first time he come here was only a few weeks ago – the pitch-darkness, the only light coming from the front porch, holding on to Yejide hand and trying to follow her footsteps, studying snake and all kinda ting that might be in the bush. Now he sitting easy on the same gallery her mother used to sit on and watching the same sunset.

'What you think happen to him, your boss?' Peter ask.

'If she wasn't there too I woulda say I lose so much blood it had me seeing things. I think I know what happen to him and is not something I want to see ever again. But is not what happen then that bothering me.'

'What, then?'

'I really think Errol was planning to kill me. Nobody woulda know. No witnesses. Not even McIntosh an dem. From everything he say I sure of it.'

'But?'

'But it had a moment. The second time my knife sink in. I wanted to kill him too.'

'Hmm.' Mr Homer pass the spliff to Darwin. 'Darwin, you is a man. You human. And all ah we have a right to fight for we own life. What else you was going to do? Dead to be polite?'

'Is not that he wondering.' Peter speak gentle with eyes close. 'Is it, Darwin?'

'Is just – when the dead come. Jide tell me what happen – they take him away. I wondering – I worried – if is because I wish him dead. If it happen because I wanted them to do it.'

Mr Homer start to laugh. It ring out in the evening air. 'I sorry, son, I not laughing at you, really. Lemme lay that question to rest one time. You go be with us for a long time so best you know this now. We don't have no power here. There neither. The power belong to the women. The dead don't listen to us. The dead listen to them. And they listen to themselves.

From what you tell me, that man been running this hustle long time and Petronella didn't give not even two damns. Sorry, Peter, no offence.' He glance over.

'None taken.'

'So, if that is what troubling you, son, you could let that one go.'

Darwin nod and pass the spliff to Peter. He feel a little better.

'What about your old man? How you feel these days about your father?'

'Sometimes I not sure I see him at all. The doctor say I had a concussion – could cause hallucinations. Maybe I just wanted it to be true.'

The evening falling all around them and he can hear the clink of cooking sounds coming through the window and the frogs and mosquitoes starting to sing. Mr Homer rise slowly, pick up the box of matches from the windowsill and look over at Darwin.

'Lemme ask you something.' He lean out to light the citronella flambeau at the bottom of the steps and the sweet sharp smell waft through the air. 'You spend your nights with a woman who does deal with the dead, even while she lying right there beside you. My woman was the same; Peter, same thing. You sitting here in a house that stand up longer than anything else round here, a house that build from blood and ash. And your stab wound healing good – no hospital – with just rest, tea, Seema good soup, Agatha novenas and my herbs. If you think it have no way your dead father could come to you,' Mr Homer old eyes dance in the firelight, 'you eh here long enough.'

35

Yejide

Emmanuel like to say Yejide save him. Make for a good story. But she know he save her too. Maybe that is the deal: she, her mother, all her mothers before that give up everything in service of the dead, but they get something back – an anchor. Somebody rooted and kind and alive, to tether them to here, so they don't forget that a spirit was a body once, so they don't forget how it feel to not know the day or the hour, so they feel the precious cost and the weight of dying without warning.

He is sentimental and she find she has grown less so, almost overnight, but is one of the things she love about him. So when he say what he had done, what he need to do still, she don't question it.

'You want to drive?' She throw the car keys to him and he catch them. She know he can't drive but she enjoy the joke between them.

'I like watching you take the corners like a crazy woman.' He smile, throw them back to her and they head down the hill.

She sneak a glance at him. His hair grow so fast without the razor touching it every day, and she reach out, bury her fingers in the new thicket of it, feel the way it start to twist and knit together again. That slow, radiant smile creep across his face and he lean into her hand and close his eyes.

The skies blue in the late afternoon and the breeze sweet. She still can't get over how the world don't look no different. They drive from the hills of Morne Marie, to the Lengua

Valley, past Canawi Lands and down the highway, and everywhere life continue as normal.

They take a different route to Fidelis, through Bellemere, and Yejide feel a softness in her chest for this place that was his first home here. They pass a man watering his hedges with a garden hose; an old abandoned couch sitting out on the pavement stained with watermarks; piles of tree branches and garbage bags still waiting for the bush truck to pass; and a thin purple three-storey house on a crossroads untouched by the storms. Something about it look familiar to her, like she see it before in a history book or a photograph. Somehow it make her think of Seema. She look at it in the rear-view mirror for a long time before they turn the corner and it disappear.

They drive through the big black gate to find Fidelis quiet.

'This way,' he point and she continue past the main building, along the road and down through the narrow lanes until they reach the spot. They gather the bouquets – pink gingers, yellow tiger lilies and white anthuriums they cut from the garden in the hills – and she follow him to a grave with a shiny new headstone, where the first green weeds start to poke up from the red-brown dirt.

EMILY JULIUS

BELOVED WIFE

1925–2018

She look at his face. His eyes shiny like they want to bubble over. 'You happy with it?' she ask.

'They do a good job.' He and Shirley had been on the phone back and forth, getting the proper dates. Shirley. Gem of a woman – never ask why.

Yejide squeeze his hand. 'He would be glad you doing this.'

Emmanuel shrug. 'He would be glad to do it himself.'

'You want me to try and find him?'

Emmanuel shake his head. 'Nah, this one I sure about. He say he wasn't leaving Emily. This is where they woulda find him, sitting right here. Nowhere else he would be.'

She squeeze his hand once more and step back, turn away to give him a little space to mourn a man who love his wife, abandon his son, and die still missing him. And for Darwin to mourn the version of himself that left him there. People does be made up of all kinda jagged parts and none of them don't fit together.

Fidelis had no right to look this beautiful, this unburdened. There was not a worker in sight, yet all the headstones and marble angels look new-scrubbed and the concrete grave borders still fresh white from All Souls'.

He come up behind her, two remaining bouquets in his hands, and kiss the back of her neck. 'Next.'

They take the long way around instead of cutting back to the main road. 'I never meet your mother. I should pay respects.'

'Since when Rastaman doing funeral and paying respects to grave?' She poke him.

He smile, but it have a seriousness in it. 'Life still. Just a different kind.'

He have a way of being so earnest, so human, that it stun her sometimes.

The family plaque have a new name now – Petronella Mavis St Bernard. She don't know what to say to her mother. She find herself wondering over the last few weeks whether she would see her in the house still, like she used to see Geraldine, but Petronella wanted freedom too much to stay. Up to her she would never have been a part of this family, part of this legacy. Just die a normal death, leave the hills behind and disperse into the air, not stick around to be a link in anybody chain. She wonder if her mother always felt so, or if that only came later, when Yejide was born.

The rain already flatten the grave mound and she reach down and touch the earth. She feel him watching her and she know the question in his eyes before she even look at him. 'Nah. No regrets.' She lay down the flowers and straighten up.

They walk all the way to the end of the cemetery, to a small plot on the perimeter, near a grotto built to the Virgin. She never ask why he choose here. Was hard enough to find a vacant plot in a cemetery as old as Fidelis but he had a way that make people want to make things happen for him, so Shirley make it happen. And she let Emmanuel know she expect to see him again when he ready.

'You don't worry about the regional corporation and the paperwork and all that, Darwin. I will sort it. Errol and dem? I eh see them. The corporation send some new fellas here. You go hadda train them properly when you come back. I handling everything. Ent I tell you don't let them boys trick you that is them does run things inside of here?'

It make Yejide smile to hear that. She like Shirley more and more.

The headstone small, inscription simple and the plot empty. Darwin say he don't want to know exactly where Errol had leave his father body. It was enough to have a place that say that he had lived. Anybody passing by this quiet, sunny corner of Fidelis would know that Carlton Levi Springer was missed, and in life and death he was Ever Faithful. Darwin place the last bouquet on his father grave and above the traffic sounds outside she hear a flock of parrots overhead – green, red and yellow – squawking, wings flapping their way across the sky. She will her beloved alive, alive, alive.

36

Emmanuel

He carry the letter with him for months before he finally decide to send it. He imagine it going from hand to hand, from cashier to postal worker, to driver, to the district post office to Enid hands to Janaya yard, up her front step and onto her kitchen table. If he lucky, it reach her and she don't burn it or throw it away when she see it from him. And if Jah is good – and he always good – she would make a cup of tea, sit on her front step when the breeze blow cool, open the envelope and read:

Greetings Ma,
I hope when you read this letter that your cupboard full and your hands not paining and your spirit ease and you happy.

I was thinking, you remember when I was small, and we used to go by the spring? You would make a little food, roast some nuts or some channa and pack some juice you squeeze from the sour orange tree in the back, and sometimes Enid would make some sugar cake for me to go with even though you say that sugar wasn't ital and you wasn't eating any. We start early before the sun get hot and walk out the main road then cut through the big estate, pass the reservoir and the old man garden, the one who used to leggo his dogs on us when he see us coming? And we would run and run and laugh because we know he don't feed them dogs enough to run fast like us.

Remember when the green get thicker and we hear the river singing before we even see it? And we take our shoes off and walk in the riverbed when it was low and on the mossy bank when it was high until we reach the cold, clear water pouring out of the black rock. And you let down your hair and it fall to your ankles and you rub the cool green jelly from the ratchet on your locks and then you put some on mine and then we let the spring water beat out whatever wickedness the world rest on us. We laugh and sing and eat and sun we self like two iguana and then bathe again before we head back. And we never had to share the spring with anybody because is we alone used to be up so early.

I does think about it sometimes.

I know how you feel about me being in the city and working in Fidelis. I know you think that I am not the man that you raise me to be. But is things like going to the spring with you and feeling the water of life beating me on my head and my back, and picking mango, and drinking tea in the evening and hearing your Singer sewing machine clack-clacking all hours and listening to you tell me about His Majesty, about Samson and David and Daniel in the lion den that make me who I am. I am still that man.

But something else make me who I am too, and that is feeling that my father just go away and leave us one day and never come back. I think it kinda make you the woman you are too. And that is why I want to write you, Ma. Because you should know that near the south wall of Fidelis Cemetery is a gravestone with the name Carlton Levi Springer, who leave this world and fly away to Zion in July 1998 – not long after he reach the city. That is all I know, but it change things for me to know it, and I hope it change something for you to know it too.

He never leave us, Ma. And I never leave you.

Your son,

Emmanuel

ACKNOWLEDGEMENTS

None of this without the ancestors – those so distant that I know them only as quiet guiding whispers in the dark; those who are so close it is as if they have never left. None of this without my living family who raised me with stories, music and taught me the power of lineage. I thank them, honour them and give them this book, one of many offerings I have promised.

Thank you to my teachers and colleagues at the University of East Anglia, especially Naomi Wood, Giles Foden, Jean McNeil and my MA Creative Writing cohort of 2018 who were such attentive and valuable readers.

Heartfelt and eternal gratitude to the Wainwrights for their incredible generosity, Bocas Lit Fest – especially Marina Salandy Browne and Nicholas Laughlin – for lighting a fire and keeping it lit, and to every person who said yes when I asked for help.

Thank you to Shivanee Ramlochan and Hadassah Williams, who know why.

Thank you to my dream team –Tracy Bohan, Hermione Thompson and Margo Shickmanter. Thank you also to Amy Black, Jackie Ko, Simon Prosser, Hannah Chukwu and everyone at Hamish Hamilton, Doubleday Books, Bond Street Books and Penguin who believed in this story.

Thank you to the city of Norwich for excellent streets, pubs, coffee shops and kitchen tables, and excellent people, especially Nathan, Katie, Sam, Jen, Mia, Wenys, Alison, Jeremy and Tessa who made a new city feel like a home away from home. Thank you to Ade, for your unwavering love and support and for knowing when to wake me up with coffee and when to let me sleep. This train doesn't run without you.

Finally, thank you to Lapeyrouse and to Port of Spain for being deep and wide, an eternal city of a million stories.

'Ayanna Lloyd Banwo is a rising literary star.
Read this book for its magic and its realism too, for
its deft weaving together of lives'
Monique Roffey

'Haunting – a novel of exquisite detail that opens up the
liminal space between folklore and the world we inhabit'
Avni Doshi

'A breathtaking novel from an irresistible new voice'
Tessa McWatt

'Banwo's spirited, finely wrought prose draws you in and
doesn't let go. *When We Were Birds* marks a distinctive,
bold and truthful new voice in literature. Long may she fly'
Courttia Newland

'Magical and intricate – a book that will haunt
you long after you finish reading it'
Shakirah Bourne

'Stunning. A work of real power and beauty, a
story of magic and love, the living and the dead
in Trinidad, this novel had me spellbound'
Zoe Somerville

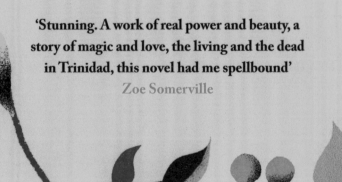